THE CLEANER

BRANDI
WELLS

A NOVEL

THE

CLEANER

HANOVER
SQUARE
PRESS

HANOVER
SQUARE
PRESS™

Recycling programs
for this product may
not exist in your area.

ISBN-13: 978-1-335-01810-6

The Cleaner

Copyright © 2024 by Brandi Wells

First published in 2023 in Great Britain by Wildfire, an imprint of Headline Publishing UK.
This edition published in 2024.

Hanover Square Press
22 Adelaide St. West, 41st Floor
Toronto, Ontario M5H 4E3, Canada
HanoverSqPress.com
BookClubbish.com

Printed in U.S.A.

for Susan Bowie Doss

EVERY DAY, SOME rogue shitter leaves a streak of feces on the back of the toilet seat, right where his ass crack would be. He picks a different toilet each time, like we're playing a game of cat and mouse. Sometimes, before I look, I imagine that this time he's shuffled forward and missed the seat, or that he's constipated so there's no shit at all, but it's always there. Imagine seeing that first thing in the morning. Imagine the kind of tone that would set for your day. Trying to write emails and finish presentations and smile in the hallway, but thinking *ass crack, ass crack, ass crack.*

Tonight, I go to the top floor, because L. will check the others first and, in the meantime, I'll have some peace. She spends all night following me around, as though without her supervision I might damage the building or commit petty theft. Like, oops, I meant to clean the floors, but I've accidentally stolen a sensitive file on sweaters and also spray-painted lopsided boobs across the lobby wall. But I guess she has nothing else to do, no threat to manage in a building like this.

I work from the elevator toward the back of the room, enjoying the wet flapping sound of the mop smacking the floor. I like doing this with no one else around—not having to do it quietly or neatly. Just doing it well.

At the back, I rest at Sad Intern's desk. It's stuck in a corner. All the other desks are pushed together in twos or fours, with dividers between them to create the facade of privacy, but hers is against the wall, an afterthought. She's been here almost two months and the top of her desk remains neat, but the drawers are full of information. What started as a bottle of probiotics, some B12 and a book on how to master your feelings has completely taken over her desk. There's zit cream and pimple patches and bobby pins full of broken-off hair.

Almost every day, I clean granola or cracker crumbs out of the top drawer where she's secretly eaten, hunched over and hiding her food. She doesn't want to leave her desk and miss anything. An intern has to maintain a kind of vigilance, waiting for something important to happen, for her chance to be important too. She lives not just *at* her desk, but in it. Her top drawer, which ought to be full of paper clips and notepads, is instead full of capsules and powders, all geared toward self-improvement. Get rid of stress! Strengthen your hair! Increase your sex appeal! That one has a picture of a tiger on the front and includes "real animal pheromones." And pushed way in the back are two different kinds of diet pills, one bottle covered in cartoon flames and the other with the word "miracle" in large print. I consider leaving them on top of her desk in full view, but she seems so helpless that I can't bring myself to do it. I dig into another drawer and find a tampon, not even in its plastic wrapper or applicator, but loose, and three new books, all about feelings and what to do with them, who's having them, and how to produce the ones you want.

She's awfully sad, I think. *Sad Intern.* Her first week here, I found the feelings book in her desk, under a photocopied welcome packet full of pointlessly underlined phrases, huge blocks of text highlighted in greens and pinks, and hearts and stars she'd drawn in the margins. The packet was mostly instructions for how to work the copier and forward phone calls, but you'd think she'd been given something precious, detailing the company's deepest editorial secrets.

Her supplements have multiplied over the last few weeks. The sex dust is her newest. It's shimmery, probably in an attempt to make it seem less sad. Young women have been trying to look less depressed by coating themselves in glitter for decades.

I decide to throw away one of her self-help books—the one with a man on the cover, pointing accusingly at the reader. She'll think she misplaced it. I try to get rid of these things gradually and steadily. If I don't, they'll spread to the rest of the office, a contagion. Other people will start taking supplements. Women will think they have to manage their feelings. Someone will bring in a bunch of crystals and sage. The whole place will begin to shimmer and reek. That kind of atmosphere is not conducive to productivity.

I clean the offices and bathrooms and lobby five nights a week, but my actual job is to take care of everyone. They need so much help.

I idly wonder if Sad Intern and Mr. Buff might get along.

His desk is pushed out into the middle of the floor like everyone else's, but the only thing to hint at a personal life are a few travel-sized containers of different protein powders in his bottom drawer. It feels extra pathetic to bring them to work, and then somehow sadder that they're his only possessions. I never even have to clean his desk. He wipes it down every day. Something about this is pathetic too—a man who erases himself.

I consider mixing his protein powder with Sad Intern's sex dust, so they each have a portion of the other. I imagine holding the two of them up like dolls and making them kiss. Two lonely people sitting in the same room, never knowing the other exists because they're each so preoccupied with maintaining their own appearances. But as I'm rifling through his desk, I find a half-full pack of cigarettes. I don't know if it's a new habit or something he's been hiding from me. Maybe this is why he's been so conspicuously cleaning his desk. But if he keeps smoking, Sad Intern is never going to like him. She's probably already smelled the smoke on him, in the elevator, their breakroom, or just walking by his desk.

I empty the pack and carefully line up the cigarettes, to be sure they don't roll off the desk and get away from me. I spray them with cleaning spray, rotating them a couple times to be sure I've saturated them all. Enjoy smoking these, Mr. Trying to be Buff, Trying to be Cool, Trying to be Sick to Death. Here's a little new poison to go with the old. I tuck them back into the pack and put them where I found them. If I didn't leave everything so clean, you'd never know I was here.

I'm standing up from his desk when I see L. making her rounds, holding a Maglite even though all the lights are on.

It's bright enough that I can see her black "Security" shirt has gone dingy gray from too many washings with the wrong detergent or at the wrong setting. The fabric is starting to pill up and go nubby. No one would see her and feel intimidated. I'm bigger than she is, probably because I do more work. Maybe she uses the flashlight to kill the roaches on the first floor. I've put in complaints about them several times, but if pest control's coming at all, their chemicals don't do anything. In fact, I think the roaches appreciate the challenge. They get revved up and multiply. But when my supervisor went and looked for the roaches in broad daylight, they were nowhere to be found. As though they'd just be lounging around in the afternoon, sunning themselves. She left me a note anyway, telling me to "make sure to clean the area," like I was responsible for them. Like I pack them up and bring them to work with me every night. She thinks of me and all she can picture is garbage and distress.

"I see you're working hard," L. says, like her hourly stroll around the building is extremely arduous. She doesn't look like she's prepared to do any sort of work. Her hair is pulled back loosely, but spilling out, almost an afterthought. She's cuffed the sleeves of her shirt and has it half-tucked, hanging out on the side. I can tell she thinks this makes her look younger and hipper, but she's only a little younger than me, and her socks don't even match.

I give her my best eat-shit smile.

"You know if you start at the back of the office and mop toward the elevator, you won't have to walk over what you've already done," she says.

"I wasn't walking over it," I say, glancing at her clunky, supposedly no-slip work shoes. Somehow, she's found the most obnoxious ones she could buy. They're so large that they become the main thing about her. Mine are slim little things, hardly noticeable. And you know what? I've never once fallen. While she talks, I luxuriously picture her sliding and falling down the stairs, which she never takes. Feet twisted, elbows bruised, everything a beautiful tangle. At the end of her fall, I'd be at the bottom to tell her where I got my shoes. "They're not even that expensive," I'd say.

"You'd get it done faster if you mopped toward the elevator, though," she says.

"I get it done in plenty of time," I say. "But thank you."

I like sitting at the back of the office, waiting for the floor to dry. It's part of my process. When I walk back to the elevator to do the next floor, I can inspect my work. If I missed a spot or it's drying funny, I can go over it again. It's called quality control.

"I heard they were going to install cameras," she says. "To watch people and see what they're doing."

"Then they won't need you," I say.

"They'll mount them over the desks," she says. "They don't care about us. They're watching everyone else."

But I'm up now, rolling my cart toward the elevator, floor be damned.

"You see the mess in the lobby?" she calls after me.

I'm getting farther away, so I pretend I don't hear her. Of course I saw the mess. But I'm surprised she even noticed it, because the mess was way at the back of the room, where I hardly ever see her walk. When she's not chasing me, she spends most of her time rifling through breakrooms or lounging on her stool in the lobby, which she gets to have because she's pretending to have a bad knee. All night, she's groaning and popping pills, talking about how she was a star athlete back in high school, which is probably at least a decade ago. She's lost any muscle definition she had since then, gaunt through lack of exertion. But her knee is fine. I've seen her dancing to music on her phone, moving hips that she doesn't have, or jogging to go meet someone who's brought her nightly lunch. There's nothing wrong with her knee except for a lack of motivation.

"See you on the next floor," she calls after me.

Whatever floor I do next is the one she'll patrol.

In the elevator, there are crumbs and a full cheese puff in the corner. I already cleaned inside here, and I wonder if she made the mess on purpose to try to put me in my place. She probably stole the cheese puffs from a breakroom. Somebody ought to be guarding *her*.

I go back to the lobby, partially to clean the mess and partially because I know L. will look for me on all the other floors before she finds me here. And then once she's back on her stool, I'll have at least an hour to clean in peace before she musters the energy to patrol again.

The breakroom we share with day-shift maintenance is disgusting, but I refuse to be the only one who cleans it. L. leaves food molding in the mini fridge until I throw it away. She's never taken the trash out—I'm not sure she even knows where the dumpsters are. And she won't claim several dirty sweatshirts and a hat that she left strewn across the table, even though they're very clearly hers and smell like her too.

If it was up to her, she'd have me come over after work

and clean her kitchen and bathroom, watching to be sure I got all the hard-to-reach places. Recently she brought in a little plant with green, heart-shaped leaves, "to warm the place up." I dig into the soil and carefully bury a layer of salt, making sure to cover it completely and smooth the dirt back over. When she waters it, the salt will dehydrate the plant. It'll slowly shrivel and brown without her knowing why. She can take it out into the sunlight, water it more or less, and give it a special fertilizer, but she won't be able to stop its death. The only thing she can do is repot it, but I'd salt that one too. I have a lot of salt.

A WEEK LATER, I find a single cigarette in Mr. Buff's desk. Maybe it fell out of the pack. Maybe it's new. I give it the ol' spritz to freshen it and put it back where I found it. I don't know if he threw the rest of the pack away or smoked them, oblivious to the extra poison. His desk is otherwise unchanged, and I appreciate this consistency, his ability to be known.

In the next desk, Neck Massager is far less stable, still trying to find her own rhythms, her own set of preferences. Sometimes her desk is neat, but sometimes it's in ruins: crumbs and papers, a half-eaten apple resting in the open air. She never eats the same kind of snack. It's hard candy one day and unsalted cashews the next. For a week straight, there were greasy wrappers and salt packets in her trash. Then banana peels. Several bananas each day. So much potassium. She must have been eating nothing but bananas. Shitting bananas. Then, suddenly, no more bananas. Anybody would have gotten sick of them. So, it's hard to conjure an image of her beyond her one consistency: the battery-powered massager in the back of her bottom drawer.

But Mr. Buff, I know. His neatness and protein powder point to a specific kind of man. You wouldn't have to ask him what he was thinking. You'd already know that he wasn't. And now that I have the cigarette problem pretty much under control, he's almost ready for Sad Intern.

But I'm not sure she's ready for him. She's only become sadder this week. Her notes are increasingly full of doodles— more than just hearts and stars. Her latest is a small woman with clothes drooping off her body. The bottom half of her is almost liquified. Her mouth is a grim little line, and her eyes are the slightest pinpricks, as though a bright light just blinked on and she's meeting its gaze. In the intern's desk are new supplements: St. John's wort, valerian root, and creatine.

I get up to make sure—and yes, Mr. Buff also has creatine. I knew it sounded familiar. But his is just loose powder that he can scoop out. Hers is bright blue and in capsules shaped like bears. I think of switching them. What a mystery it would be for the two of them, how their creatine changed overnight. They'd sit dumbfounded at their desks, slowly looking around the room, trying to puzzle it out, until they saw one another.

You? she would mouth.

"You?" he would say back, tilting his head for emphasis.

They'd laugh over the unsolved mystery and switch back, but after this they'd have a point of connection. They'd get coffee or go for a drink. It'd turn into dinner, more drinks, a late-night walk home. He'd stand at the entrance to her building. "Want to come in?" she'd ask, smiling, looking away, and then back at him.

That'd be it. She wouldn't be sad anymore. She'd be Mrs. Buff. Maybe he'd take a little of her sadness for himself, incorporate it into his workout routine, and burn through it. Or maybe she'd always be a little sad, but she'd learn to live with it. She'd wake in the night and feel quietly unhappy, listening for some small sound, some change, that might light things up again. It probably won't make any difference, but at least she's trying to deal with the problem of how she feels. She isn't just letting it consume her. She's sad, after all, not pathetic.

Before I can make the switch, creatine bears in one desk and powder in the other, I hear the elevator open. L. holds the door while I roll my cart over. I wait for her to get off when I get on, but she shakes her head. "I'll ride down with you," she says. As though I can't ride the elevator alone. Does she want to help me go to the bathroom? Show me how to use the soap dispenser and then dry my hands? And how can she be certain the top floor is secure without at least a casual stroll or little jaunt? If she's trusting me to take care of that, what's she even here for? Shouldn't I be paid to do both our jobs?

"Someone's been taking my reports," she says.

There's animal hair all across the front of her shirt, like she rolled in it. I try not to inhale too deeply, worried I'll be able to smell it.

"I normally file them away every few weeks," she says. "But they've been disappearing."

She gets off on the third floor with me, but sits at a desk near the elevator while I start bagging up garbage. My work is recreational for her—she's just here for the show.

"Why would anyone want your old reports?" I say. Next, she'll tell me someone wants her old candy-bar wrappers or sweatshirts. If anything, I'm glad someone's helping me manage her clutter. She probably left them sitting out, maybe on her stool, and someone kindly threw them away. She ought to leave them a thank you note, and maybe enclose a portion of her wages, since they're doing her job for her.

"I'm not sure it's malicious," she says. "Maybe they're just taking them to read, and they throw them away afterward. That's why I asked you."

"If I've been reading your reports?" I ask. "I would never." Imagine how bored I'd have to be to do something like that. I lean over and spray the inside of one of the trash cans where the bag has leaked. Someone had a very liquidy lunch.

"If you've seen them in the trash," she says, pushing her chair back so she can prop her feet on the desk she's sitting at. She rubs her knee, and I'm not even sure it's the same knee she said was hurt last week or last month. It's one of those changeable, contagious things. No wonder she can't get rid of it.

I look around. If there were cameras mounted over the desks, surely this would be an infraction. She's probably forgotten she ever believed that would happen. She made it up after she saw something similar in a movie. She's always trying to make her life more interesting. She's always trying to be important.

"I don't dig through the trash," I say, pulling a few cans out of the trash to put in the recycling downstairs.

"But you know what my reports look like," she says.

"I've never looked at your reports," I say.

"You've seen them," she says.

I finish wiping out the trash can, and then fit it with a new plastic liner. I wish people would be more delicate with their trash. Sometimes they toss out half-full drinks. I wonder if they live like this at home. No big surprise that we have roaches. Last year, we had to shut down for a week, because there were bedbugs on some of the breakroom furniture. The same people who throw away these drinks and soups would never notice that the underside of their mattress is crawling with musty, sweet-smelling bugs that bite them and drink their blood while they're sleeping. They come into work and sit in the breakroom, talking loudly to their friends, so that anyone whose desk is nearby can hardly concentrate. Then they leave these creatures behind and the bugs multiply.

Bedbugs mate by traumatic insemination. The male bedbug stabs the female's abdomen with his reproductive organ and leaves his sperm in the wound. It's vicious and disgusting and it works. I felt nervous to go into my apartment after that. I threw away my clothes and bought new ones. Streamlined my whole wardrobe—no reason to have anything that I wouldn't work in. I suggested in a note to my supervisor that we dust the floor with diatomaceous earth, a white powder that kills any insects that touch it. The stuff is completely harmless to people, but she responded in an all-caps note saying, "WE COULDN'T LEAVE ANYTHING LIKE THAT ON THE FLOOR IN A PLACE OF BUSINESS." It didn't matter what it was for or how well it would work.

L. pulls a folded piece of paper out of her pocket and waves it in my face. "Like this," she says. It's one of her reports, a sample. Of course, she knew I would have no idea what her reports look like. "If you could keep an eye out for them,"

she says. As though I find her missing reports deeply important, and I'm going to crouch down and dig through every
single trash can in the building, looking for them.

"Maybe the rest are in your pocket," I say, gathering all
the trash together. "Or our breakroom. You could do a little
straightening up. Probably the easiest way to find them."

She ignores me. "Just so we know who's throwing them
away," she says.

"We?" I ask.

"Don't you want to know?" she says.

Maybe if I had to fill out little reports to prove I was working, I'd be really attached to them too. But I shrug and start
running the dust mop along the floor, getting as close to L. as
I can without actually hitting her. I do a few close passes and
I'm really looking forward to making contact, but she heads
back to the elevator before I can. Maybe she saw it coming,
or she's bored, unsatisfied with my general lack of interest.

I quiet the urge to chase her, and keep sliding the mop
dryly along the floor, catching bits of paper and hair, mostly
unobstructed, but I'm still picturing what it'd be like to make
at least a little contact. I wouldn't fully knock her over. I'd hit
hard enough to bruise and feel it reverberate in my hands, but
gently enough to say, "Oops, I'm sorry, my bad," and still be
believable. If you're quiet and nonreactive, anyone will believe that the worst thing you do is an accident.

L. HAS LEFT the front door propped open yet again, and our delivery person, M., waits in the lobby, slouching against glass windows that I've already cleaned. I can envision the smudges they'll leave behind after rubbing the dirty fabric of their shirt and khakis against the glass. It would have been better if they had just sat on the floor. No one ever notices all the maintenance that goes into the spaces they inhabit. I'm constantly cleaning dirty fingerprints from glass, light switch covers, and sometimes even the wall. No one thinks of themselves as dirty. They look directly at the mess they leave behind and don't see it. It doesn't belong to them.

Of course, now that there's something for L. to do, she's vanished. Security cameras would be a great investment, because then L. would have to do her job. She probably thinks she was going above and beyond by leaving the front door propped open, but what's the point of even having a lock if

she constantly leaves the door open? I would ask to get M. a
key card so they could swipe in, but then M. would be my
responsibility. There'd be a record of me taking them on. So,
we do the dance with the clipboard: I sign, they shuffle pages,
and then they haul the delivery in on a big dolly. It probably
goes without saying, but this is not part of my job. L. should
have to tip me for doing it.

"What's that?" M. asks, nodding at the floor.

The rat droppings are minuscule. No one else would have
noticed them, not even L., who's always ready to point out
work for me to do. But it feels like M.'s goading me, because
they have pet rats and love to talk about them. Their litter box,
their treats, the tricks they can do. They've shown me pictures
and even asked me to hold their phone to watch videos of the
rats running around their apartment. I took the phone and
held it out of politeness, but touching someone else's phone
feels akin to holding unwashed hands or letting someone lick
your fingers. I didn't know how to refuse, so I held the dirty
device and watched. My hand felt greasy afterward. I kept
thinking about the smudges on their phone screen, the oil and
sweat from their hands and the side of their face. M.'s rats have
names like children from the early 1900s, but I can't remember them now. Incredibly proper names that evoke images of
tiny savants, mathematical or musical prodigies.

"Smarter than most people," M. said. And I know that
if I say the wrong thing, it'll be twenty minutes of rat talk,
and I'll have to hold their phone again and watch video after
video, until I find a way to politely fade away.

When I took this job, I expected my nights to be solitary—
I looked forward to it—but I spend most of each shift dodg-

ing someone or other and avoiding conversation. And then I have plenty of company: the ghosts of all the office workers. They might go home at the end of every day, but they're still here at night. They leave crumbs and broken headphones and bitten-off fingernails. The building smells like them: bodies and stale perfume and salt and blood.

A few nights ago, I found a jar of cloudy, gray water that was labeled "Do Not Touch," and I absolutely did not touch it. I did not even clean the desk it was on. So, even if I can't see the people who work here, they're always present, reaching toward me, leaving offerings. I could never be lonely here.

M. smiles and looks at the droppings and then at me, as though I should stop what I'm doing and get on my hands and knees to look at them too, or maybe clean them up. It's hard not to feel like my privacy is being invaded, just by M.'s looking. I hate to feel looked at, am overwhelmed by the impoliteness of another person following me with their eyes. I would never do that to someone. But if I don't prod them along, M. will probably give the imagined rats names and start making a tiny obstacle course for them. A series of hurdles and a little tightrope with an arena. Ratcus du Soleil.

Somehow, L. always manages to vanish right before M. gets here so that I'm stuck with them. Then, as soon as M. is gone, L. will seep back into the room, following me around, asking about what M. said, what they did. She tells the same stories about M. over and over. Do I remember the time M. sat out on the front steps and ate their sandwich? As though a person doesn't deserve to eat. Does L. also feel annoyed that *I* eat, that *I* exist?

But even though she's fascinated by M., she keeps her dis-

tance. Maybe there's something about M.'s overall persona that
I can adapt to ward L. away. There's the relaxed way that M.
waits, acting like they have nothing but time. The swoop of
their hair, never pressed back with product, hanging in their
eyes—unless they're sweaty, and then it's slicked back, but in
a natural way, like they aren't even thinking about it. They're
so unbothered and I'm not sure how to feel that way. I can
only hope to look like I feel that way.

I watch while M. loads everything off the dolly and onto
the elevator, because the larger dolly won't fit. I don't say anything about how they're lifting or how their grip is all wrong,
because I don't want to prolong our interaction. Maybe I'll
make them a quick handout and give it to them next time, as
they're leaving. Then they won't strain their back. I see them
shudder as they bend and lift—and then they see me watching them, and they wink at me. Before I can say or do anything, the elevator door closes, and they're gone.

Talking to M. always leaves a weird feeling in my stomach,
like I'm gearing up to be sick. I go and sit in the bathroom and
slouch, pressing my cheek against the side of the stall, which I
know has been disinfected. I like knowing the bathrooms are
perfectly clean because I cleaned them. I flex my bare fingers,
and I can almost feel the clammy rubber gloves I wear to do
it. I can feel the sweat that collects inside the gloves so that
my skin starts to prune if I don't move fast enough.

This bathroom is probably cleaner than the one in my
apartment. I like to sit in the row of empty, unused stalls.
I'm comforted by the promised vacuousness of such a public-
seeming space—it's all mine. Sometimes I talk to myself,
using different voices, the way you might talk to a cat you

live alone with. It's just me and all these ghosts. "Hoo," I call out, to test the acoustics.

Afterward, I hide out in our breakroom to make sure I don't see M. again. I salt the plant some more, note its yellowing leaves, eat some dried fruit, and then, when enough time has passed, I work on the gray floors. I call them this because you can't really tell one person from another there. No one is lit up. No one stands out. The desks don't have the same kind of personality as the ones upstairs. It's all numbers or notes written in a shorthand that I would never try to understand. It wouldn't be worth my effort. These floors are all the same. Everything that isn't the top floor is a gray floor, a nothing floor. Even the private offices on the gray floors are sad and dull. The furniture is the same. The rugs are identical. I move through them in a kind of haze, thinking only of my people, my team, upstairs.

All the desks and people on these gray floors only exist as the foundation for the top floor, which is the brains of the operation, the face on the front of the company. Everything up there is sharper, brighter.

THE INTERN HAS a new bottle of pills tonight, labeled "Mood Magic." Both the bottle and the pills are dark purple, and she's well into them. She must have just brought them in from home. Something happened that made her want to alter her mood while in the office. Doing it at home just wasn't enough anymore. Someone stopped by her desk and said, "You should smile," but she thought she was smiling. She thought, *This is me happy. This is me doing my best.* But her best doesn't register for the people around her. And then maybe Mr. Buff is all wrong for her. He's been watching her, hovering near her desk, lingering a little too long to talk about their days. I should have seen this coming—that he would be overpowering and unpleasant, leaving no real room for her to contribute anything.

Maybe he can use a little magic. I take the laxatives from her desk and sit down at his. One by one, I empty the capsules into his protein powder. It's all the same color, and even though the volume has doubled by the time I finish, he won't notice. No one ever does. He'll keep mixing the powder with water, trying to get buffer. But he won't have time to hover over her desk anymore. Mr. Buff, Mr. Trying too Hard, Mr. Oh Shit. Of course, it's potentially a sacrifice for me, too, if things are urgent and get messy, but I'm willing to suffer for the greater good.

I give the bottle a gentle shake. I don't want to mix it perfectly—I'm hoping for a higher concentration of laxative at the top. I don't think he's a lost cause—he just needs a little help, like everyone else. He might still be a match for Sad Intern if he learns to reel it in and take up less space.

After I empty everyone's trash, I sit at Yarn Guy's desk, my current favorite. There are spools of yarn in his bottom drawer, gathered in colorful bundles. Recently, he's rolled a few of them into balls. I unzip a black felt bag, and inside are smaller bags of beads and sequins, tiny plastic cases of needles, sparkly glue and assorted stray beads and puffs of fabric. I run my hands over his collection of crafts with a kind of wonder. The surface of his desk is still covered with the normal work stuff—I don't think he's slacking off. In fact, it's the opposite. Forever absorbed into activity, he's someone who thrums with life. He'd never be found slumped over a stool in the lobby. He'd never fill his desk with supplements and self-care literature. He knows what's real.

Recently, he's started a larger project, a multicolored throw with a tight knit. It's mostly blues and greens, and I wonder if he's making it for himself. It's his color palette, for sure. I drape the throw across his desk to note how much progress he's made. No work on it since yesterday, but some days he's busier than others. It's the kind of thing he works on for a few hours one day and zero for the rest of the week, or he might get in twenty minutes every day for a month. His progress is steady. *He* has no problem with commitment.

I think about him while I clean the windowsills, a chore I don't do every day, but one that helps ground me. So much of my work is fleeting—I empty the trash, mop up the day's mess, and shift chairs and desks back into place. I do these tasks one day, and then have to do them again the next, and the next, on and on, forever. Every day, the building fills with people who undo my labor.

But some of my work revolves around the actual building's upkeep. The windowsills get scummy and have to be soaked and scrubbed. It's one of those things you only notice if you don't do it. Enough filth collects that it's all you can look at. If I didn't clean it, my supervisor would eventually leave a passive-aggressive note. She'd call it mold or mildew, even though it's just dirt—there's no arguing with her. But if it stays perfectly clean, it's invisible.

It's like how you don't really appreciate not being sick. You only think about not being sick while you're sick. You're throwing up and you long to be not throwing up. But once you're not throwing up, you're never like, *Ahhh this is great, I'm living the dream*. The sickness is over and you don't even appreciate it. This is how appearances work. Imagine how beautiful people might think you are if you don't shower for a few weeks and then, bam, you shower. You brush your hair. It's a way to trick people into thinking you're lovely. Later, they'll remember that you're lovely, even when you aren't.

So, I like to let the scum along the windows build up enough that the bright new cleanliness will be a visual shock. Once everyone notices how clean it is, they'll realize I exist. They'll be embarrassed they hadn't thought of me before.

My back's to the rest of the office, all the desks a couple of yards away, and I'm about a third of the way across the room, scrubbing along the windowsill, when the elevator doors open and close.

I don't need to turn around to know it's L. She always sounds like she might collapse, shuffling along in a slow, draggy rhythm. She doesn't worry about scuffing the floors, even if she can tell I've already cleaned them. I think she does it on purpose. I pointed it out once and she said it wasn't her, because no-slip shoes don't leave marks, but I watched her do it. She left two long marks and one short one. We argued about it, and I took the stairs to get away from her.

In the windows, I can see her pacing, winding through the desks, stopping to lean against one and then starting up again, but I keep myself fully absorbed in the task of scrubbing and rescrubbing the windowsills, tackling the difficult corners where grime collects. I like the sound it makes, the pitch and squeak of it, like a very small scream.

She doesn't get too far away, staying behind the row of desks closest to me, fidgeting with pens and staplers, biting her nails, stretching.

"Did you know the delivery person is writing a book?" she finally asks. She cracks open a drink that she'll probably dribble all the way back to the elevator. I'm not sure if she brought it with her or found it in someone's desk.

She makes a little sound, hoping to prompt a response, but I keep cleaning. It's nice that she had to deal with M. for once. More than a few times, we've missed a delivery or M. has had to stand outside in the cold, waiting to be noticed, because L. was wandering the building or asleep in our breakroom. I guess that's why she's been propping the door open. Her job requires so little, and yet she stays overwhelmed.

"An erotic one," she says. "Like BDSM."

This is just a way for L. to pry into my life. She wants to see how I'll react, if I'll be embarrassed or intrigued. I can't really imagine M. writing a book like this and then telling L. about it. I wonder if she's exaggerating. It's a romance novel, or just sexually playful, or maybe L. is making the whole thing up. Or L.'s the one writing it and wants to hear what I think before she says so. Or she just wants an opening to talk about her own sex life. She finds herself endlessly fascinating.

"Good for them," I say, trying to sound extremely blasé about it.

She shakes a bottle of pills before she downs a couple with her drink. She's being purposefully loud, hoping I'll ask about the pills, so she can talk more about her knee. She has the world's most mesmerizing knee. Soon there will be a podcast about it. Her knee will have its own Wikipedia page.

I work to tune her out, but she goes on and on about the kind of book she would write if she ever wrote one. A thriller, a mystery, something with intrigue and double crosses and a surprise love story. I'm sure she's picturing herself as the spy, the lover, the main character. But in a book, L. would probably die in the first scene, or she'd be someone on the periphery. The protagonist wouldn't even know her name. She'd be some background mumbler.

"You should quit and do that," I say.

"I could never," she says.

Of course she couldn't. She lucked into this nothing-job of following me around all night and eating snacks pilfered from breakrooms or from people's desks. Why would she ever leave? If she could move in full-time, she would.

I can see in the window that she's trying to meet my gaze, but I keep cleaning, working to scrub in a loud way, to get the glass to squeal as I drag the cloth over it.

"Did you ever find my reports?" she asks.

"What reports?" I say, trying to sound earnestly curious to demonstrate how little attention I've paid her.

"I think someone wanted to know what hours I'm here," she says, ignoring my question. "What hours I'm patrolling."

"What hours are those?" I ask.

She skids to a stop behind me and I know I'm going to have to go over the floor there.

"So they'd know when they could slip in and out," she says, as though I hadn't spoken.

"For what?" I say.

"Lots of things," she says. "It's a big building."

"You should patrol more, then," I say.

She stands there and I keep cleaning, moving farther away from her, but she drifts along behind me. There's nothing I can do to break the invisible tether between us. Even though we have sharply different jobs, she believes we are coworkers. I could believe this too—if I'd ever seen her doing any work.

"Did you know the company's losing money?" she asks.

"Where'd you hear that?"

"Around," she says.

I can't help myself and I turn to look at her. "Around where?" I say. "We aren't here at the same time as the office people. Who would you even hear things from?"

"I'm friendlier than you," she says. "People talk. I'm getting here as they're leaving. We chat."

"You listen in," I say.

She shrugs.

"I have work to do," I tell her, and I turn back around and go at the windows with renewed vigor, picturing Yarn Guy's hands, gently callused from his knitting or crocheting, with long, slightly crooked fingers. His hands would swallow my hands. His palms would be dry and cool, never clammy. I imagine his well-practiced grip and the sureness of it. In turn, he would appreciate the small coolness of my hand. L. keeps talking at me until she gets bored, and then she goes back to her stool and leaves me alone. When she gets bored of that, she'll find me again. Back and forth between me and the stool or me and our breakroom, all night. She has a clear trajectory.

Sometimes I feel like an appliance utilized to maintain the building, rebounding from one chore to another, propelled in this way until I manage to find the door and leave at the end of my shift. But I do more than mindlessly clean. I watch over everyone, help them manage their days. I shuffle important work to the top of their inboxes, leave snacks so their blood sugar won't drop, and help course-correct by weeding out the duds. I can easily spot someone who isn't a good fit here, someone who's going to waste the company's time and resources before moving along to something they think is bigger and better.

It's best to oust these people as quickly as possible. Every-

one else who works here is part of a team, a family. There's a
certain warmth on the fourth floor, a lived-in feeling. We're
a unit, and it's my job to run the household as efficiently as
possible.

Alone, I sit at Yarn Guy's desk again. It smells like vanilla,
and I don't want to clean it, because then it won't smell like
vanilla anymore. Already the smell from the window cleaner
is starting to overtake it. I make a note to look for vanilla-
scented cleaning products. Everything we keep in the office is
in an industrial size, nothing with any of the personal warmth
I think we'd all appreciate. Maybe if I buy the vanilla with
my own money and everyone gets used to it, I can convince
my supervisor it's a worthwhile expense for the company.

Maybe Yarn Guy will start to notice the vanilla scent twisting along hallways, bathrooms, and the elevator. He'll walk
slowly through the building, trying to smell it on someone,
but he won't be able to find the source. Then one day, I'll get
here very early, pass by his desk, and he'll smell me. That'll
be it. We'll start having breakfast together in the mornings
whenever I'm leaving and he's arriving. We'll sit outside in
the park. Maybe I'll do some of my cleaning in the daytime,
and he'll smile at me when I walk by, but we'll be coy about
it. Little looks, little smiles, little snapshots of glee strung
throughout the day. But his friends will know, will see the
way he smiles at me—or maybe he's told them and asked
them to keep things quiet. Since they know anyway, we'll
all socialize on the weekends, going to bars or house parties
or taking trips out of the city. They'll like me and want my
advice. I'll talk them out of bad dates or ill-conceived purchases. "Green looks better on you," I'll say, or, "The apart-

ment downtown will be so much more convenient." And they'll all nod at my sage advice.

Later, when they get home, they'll think how lucky Yarn Guy is to have me. If they could just find a woman like me. I'll tell them, "You have to pay better attention." Because how many years did I work in the same building as Yarn Guy before we managed to find each other? If I hadn't gone to work early that one time, we might have never met. Or maybe these men aren't appreciating their current lovers, who are working double-time to make their relationships seem effortless and fun. They only need to appreciate what they already have.

But Yarn Guy will appreciate me, and he'll start to work late into the evenings. Without saying a word, he'll help me clean up around the office. He'll start emptying everyone's trash before I get here. He'll chastise others for not cleaning their spills or for leaving paper towels on the bathroom floor. I'll tell him that he doesn't have to, that this is my job, but he'll assure me that he's only displaying common human courtesy.

"We all work here!" he'll say. "We have to take care of this place together!" I won't argue, even though I know that a building like this needs one decisive overseer. An office is made up of objects and people and activities, and it needs one person who makes sure the whole thing is running smoothly. I've been that person for years. Head of the household, heavyweight, hotshot, big daddy, a luminary: the pillar of the company. That's me.

It's just that he's so cute when he's worked up like this. I imagine him holding yarn in each of his hands, gesturing with it, without even thinking about how silly he looks, a grown man ornamented by springy poms of brightly colored yarn.

The knits and loops soften everything about him. When it's cold outside, we'll wear matching hats that he's knitted for us, with our initials on the fronts.

The woman at the desk next to his has spilled something sticky and orange and left it there. The proximity of this spill to the clean, dry yarn makes me nervous. I stoop over her desk and try to smell it, but I have to almost touch my cheek to it before I pick up the faintest hint of sweet chili and peanut. I spray the mess and work to scrub it away. There's a pen stuck in it, and I pull it free and clean that too. She probably won't even notice my extra labor and her fresh pen, but her day will be smoother because of it. She'll naturally work faster and harder. I think of throwing the pen away because it has bite marks on the end, but then all her pens have bite marks. She's an introvert, someone with anxiety, gnawing away at her pen—and probably her nails too.

I see it all the time. These are the people who need me the most.

Her password is on a sticky note attached to her monitor, so I log in, open her email, and pull up her calendar. No wonder she's stressed. Her schedule is packed with meetings and reminders, back-to-back and sometimes even overlapping. This is no way to live. I move a few meetings to later in the day, so she can sleep in or have a few mornings to herself. Maybe then she'll have the energy to clean her desk. I also clear out some of the reminders, more clutter than anything else. Then, for good measure, I clear all the events for Friday. She's lucky to have someone like me watching over her.

I close the calendar, clear my history, and leave a small bag of lavender potpourri in her top drawer. I found several of them in a breakroom on one of the gray floors. They're tied with shimmery ribbons in little blue bags. She'll be calmer now. She'll see that ribbon, how it shines in contrast to her mess, and think, *I can do better. I can get my shit together.* She won't leave a mess like this again. She'll be a good influence on everyone around her. *Good Influence.* She'll be neater and more organized. In an office like this, where everyone is packed together in such close proximity, people can't help but model the good or bad behavior of their neighbors.

On my way to the elevator, I see a neon green flyer advertising "K-BBQ First Fridays! Help Us Meet Our Goal and Pig Out to Celebrate!" Below that is a clip-art pig, smiling, happy to be a company-wide incentive.

I leave my cart by the elevator and go back to Good Influence's desk. I deposit two more bags of potpourri and also a small, prepackaged cookie I found in someone else's desk a few days ago. A little sugar never hurts.

I CRACK OPEN a drink and see there's a note from my supervisor taped to the front of my cart. There are a dozen ways to communicate with me that would be less insulting. Call me, text me, email, leave a note in a sealed envelope in the breakroom. Write my name on the front in kind, loopy letters. But she's taped it to my cart with the note facing outward so that anyone can read it.

"Please clean the lobby thoroughly. Be sure to get the corners. Spray extra cleaner if you need to."

I clean the lobby every night and the corners are perfection. But it's not like I can put some sort of sealant on an entire room that repels mess for twenty-four hours. She sees any kind of mess at any point during the day, and I'm to blame. Someone can spill something at 10 am, and it's my fault. Like I should have been there, following them and holding my hands out to catch their mess. There are paper towels on the floor in the bathroom after lunch? That's me. A coffee spill in the elevator? That's me too. My cleaning ought to be preventative. I could take a video every night to showcase my work, but I shouldn't have to do this. How many videos can my phone even hold?

Someone must have complained. There was some dirt tracked in, they had a client visit, and they felt sure that this small smear of dirt is why their meeting didn't go well. It couldn't possibly be their fault. It couldn't be that they were poorly prepared or generally unlikable, and the client decided to look elsewhere. No, they're very likable and it was certainly this aggressive clump of dirt that I strategically left to do them in. It's possible the client is the one who tracked the dirt in, but this doesn't matter to the person complaining. What matters is directing blame at someone and making sure that everyone else knows you're doing an excellent job.

On my way to the elevator, I'm surprised to see the door to the stairwell is propped open with a brick. It locks if you close it, so I wonder if some person without a key was in the building and needed to use the stairs. It could be something left from earlier in the day. But if some delivery person or assistant needed to do a quick scamper, why not use the elevator? And an assistant would have their own key anyway. Maybe some person snuck into the building and wanted to creep unnoticed along the stairs. But still, why not use the elevator? Who is this intruder, and what do they want?

The idea of them taints the space, and I'll work extra hard to scrub them away, because it would be easy for someone to mistake general bad vibes for an unclean walkway or a dirty bathroom. Even if they can't pinpoint the mess, they'll gesture vaguely at a room or the entire building. "See?" they'll say to their coworkers or manager, as though they've made a clear point, and someone needs to tell me to buckle down.

I consider walking up the stairs to see if the building's potential intruder is still here, hiding in the stairwell, but it's the beginning of my night and I'm not going to strain myself this early on. I think of cleaning the lobby and waiting them out, but that's a good way to get stuck with L. So, I leave the lobby for later, and take the elevator to the top floor.

There are more lights on than usual, and I wonder if L. has left them on again. I'm always following her around, turning lights off. I think she might be afraid of the dark and can't even bear to leave a dark room behind her, like whatever's there will creep and spread if everything isn't lit up. But also, she thinks whatever she's doing is the most important thing. Why wouldn't she cast a spotlight on herself? She treats the offices like they're hers, even the fourth floor, which is clearly my domain.

I don't think she even cared about this floor until she realized I did. But once she noticed I took longer here and then caught me sifting through a desk, she took an interest too. "How's your guy?" she asks about Yarn Guy or Mr. Buff, or even Sticky Doorknob, who I think I've traced to a desk near the breakroom, because the surface is all greasy fingerprints and splotches. I keep leaving him wet wipes to no avail. Maybe he thinks everyone's getting wet wipes. Everyone has unclean hands. He's just your average sticky guy.

But L. thinks I have a crush on anyone I pay attention to. I try to explain. "It's the most important floor. It's where they're doing the most work. Everything they do requires more attention, more care."

But she can't hear that. She puts the same amount of nothing-effort into everything, so when she sees anyone really try at something, it's noteworthy and she wants to pick at it.

I'm gearing up to rehearse the lecture I'll give L. later, about responsibility and conservation, because leaving all these lights on is a real drain, but there's a woman at Sad Intern's desk.

At first, I think she's the intruder. No one besides me and L. is ever here at this time. It's black outside, several hours before the delivery person could possibly arrive. Nothing but a few palm trees waving at the building. It's too late for even the late-night crowd to be on the streets.

But this woman is dressed for daytime: a shirt with buttons, hair upswept in a clip, and a manicure that I can see from across the room. A kind of gross pastel sheen. She's holding her face in her hands and crying gutturally, fully using her vocal cords, really digging into it. She believes that she's alone and giving birth to her sadness or passing it like a kidney stone. She whimpers between blustering, like the crying itself is hurting her. It's embarrassing, and I think about stepping back into the elevator, but inexplicably, I edge forward. Maybe it's because it's so strange to see someone else here, inhabiting my space, fully corporeal and not just present in traces and clues. But maybe it's because of where she's sitting and who that means she is.

The intern is more or less how I pictured her: young and sad and pretty.

She finally sees me and stops sobbing. Just abruptly cuts it off, and says, "What are you doing here?" Her face is wet, and she doesn't move to dry it, as though this would be admitting vulnerability. Instead, she glistens under the office lights and looks at me.

"What are *you* doing here?" I ask. Surely she's noticed it's dark outside and her day is long over.

She stands up, trying to evoke the image of a very pulled-together person. As though I hadn't seen and heard her crying seconds before, or as though I can't see how her makeup has run and her hair has begun to escape its clip. She has the look of a long, slow day, not broken up by enough tasks, no spikes of interest or busy stretches. Instead, she's lived every minute of it, painfully aware of herself and her time. This can be overwhelming. It's important to disassociate for certain parts of the workday. Otherwise, you might not make it.

She folds her arms across her shirt, which does nothing to disguise how wrinkled it is. Even her collar has an unnatural crease, causing one of the corners to flip up.

"What are you *doing* here?" she repeats.

I look down at myself. My black work shirt showcases the company's logo and I'm holding a half-full trash bag. There's a cart with cleaning products across the room that I wheeled in, and even if she didn't hear me, she can't think the cart appeared from nowhere, a nightly apparition of cleanliness. I probably smell like chemicals and polish. I hold my arms out as though to say, *Look at me.*

"I need to get back to work," she says, like I'm keeping her from it.

I grunt in the affirmative, but she keeps looking at me, and I wonder if she expects me to excuse myself and apologize for bothering her. I look over at my cart and then back at her.

She sits down and finally dabs her face with a tissue I didn't realize she was holding, already crumpled into a wet ball. It's basically a sponge.

"I guess I could take this home with me," she says, gesturing at the papers on her desk and speaking softly, less defensive now.

I nod, thinking about the pack of Kleenex a few desks away, in the top drawer. She clearly needs them, but it might look strange for me to walk over there, pull them out, and offer them to her.

"It doesn't really matter," she says. "Whether I'm home or here. We're always working, right?"

Maybe she wouldn't even notice where the Kleenex came from. Her eyes are glazed over and she's not fully looking at me. That pack of Kleenex has been in that desk, unopened, for months.

"I mean, I know *your* job is here," she says. "I'm not saying that I think you take this home with you."

"Work is work," I say.

She's worse off than I thought. Sadder, but with a confusing ennui, an awkward mishmash of feelings. From angry to monotone sadness in less than a minute. She's pretty from across the room but kind of repulsive up close. Something about the way she holds herself, an angular hunch. Her collarbone looks sharp and her knuckles shine. She's glossy, kind of wet, and not just from the tears. I would think she looked dirty and out of place if not for the nice clothes, the desk, her obvious comfort here. I wonder if her voice is hoarse from crying or if she always sounds this way.

She leans over her desk like she might embrace it. I'm already thinking of spraying it down.

"I mean, you don't stay up thinking, did I clean the bathrooms the right way, do you?" she asks.

I'm not sure what she's talking about. Her desk has been more cluttered lately, but I hadn't thought much of it. I just thought they were giving her more responsibility. Maybe she was gearing up to be more than an intern. I could imagine a promotion on her horizon. I should have paid more attention to the erratic snack foods, the energy drinks and coffee cups filling her trash. But in an office like this, all trash is communal. Her desk is along the walkway to the CEO's office and the copier room, and her trash could be anyone's. Because of this, when I'm thinking about an individual I try to stay grounded in their desk, their computer.

For instance, there was a person who used to vomit into different trash cans on this floor. Sometimes in the breakroom, but more often at random desks along the path from the elevator to one of the meeting rooms. Once even at the intern's desk, but before she worked here. I don't know if The Vomiter got fired because they ultimately couldn't handle the stress of the job, or if they got their anxiety and reflux under control. Maybe they've been vomiting in the bathroom and they're very neat about it now, so I have no way of knowing they still exist. It's nice when someone learns to manage their own problems.

The intern sighs, and for a second, I think she's annoyed that I haven't answered her, but she isn't really looking at me. Her eyes are glazed over and she's fully in her own head, thinking of her own problems, her own day. This place can be a big adjustment. Sometimes new hires don't make it, but I've been rooting for her. I know what it's like to work somewhere you don't fit. My last job was that way. But here, I fell into my work easily and quickly, as though I was made for it. She only needs to embrace her work and become a part of the building.

She still looks frazzled, so I give up my trash and sit at the desk across from her. I hope I haven't made myself unlikable by sitting at this particular desk. The guy who sits here always seems to be collecting scissors—at a minimum, he has three pairs. If I opened his drawers and counted right now, there'd probably be more. He's an easy person to understand. He needs a pair of scissors and instead of looking through his own things, he takes someone else's. He probably imagines that person stole his scissors. He spends all day feeling defensive about how people just take things from his desk. And the intern's been here long enough to fall victim to his accusations. He misplaces a few important documents, she catches his eye, and then he feels certain it was her. Why else would she be looking at him? And what's she waiting on? Can't she see he's very busy and needs these documents so he can finish his work?

I try to make myself look friendlier than him, to offset his residual presence. I smile and relax my shoulders, breathing slowly and evenly.

"What's wrong?" I ask her. I make a note to hide everyone's scissors sometime soon, just to see what'll happen. Fuck this guy. What does he even need scissors for?

"I'm just tired," she says.

I tilt my head at her.

"Work," she says. "All of it. It's this thing." She holds her hands out like she's showing me, but of course, there's noth-

ing there. Just two feet of empty space between her hands.
"I can just—" she says, turning her hands into claws, clench-
ing the air.

"What happened?" I ask. "What's the actual thing you're
upset about?" It's like when children are angry, but it's only
because they're tired and it's so difficult for them to articulate
their tiredness. Sometimes it's hard for adults too.

Her hands are still claws for a few seconds, but then they're
hands again. "Nothing!" she says, but she sits with it and then
sighs. "There's this pitch meeting. I want to go."

"You asked and they said no?"

"Not exactly," she says. She's playing with her hair, pulling strands loose, making the whole thing worse. I can see
why she would pull it back.

"Ask them," I say. "Tell them you have ideas."

She doesn't say anything.

"You have ideas?" I ask.

She shakes her head.

"You could ask to sit in," I say. "See how things work.
You're the intern, right? You're here to learn."

"How'd you know?"

"I clean your desk," I say, smiling.

She looks embarrassed, probably thinking of all the things
I've seen. The sex dust, the diet pills, the laxatives. This week's
addition is fasting supplements, white capsules with flecks of
green, reminiscent of mint. Maybe you're supposed to believe you're refreshed when you take them. The green evokes
the idea of health. But what she should really be embarrassed
about are all the books telling her how to feel.

"I should go," she says. "It's late."

"Early," I correct.

She nods, gathers her things, and leaves without looking back at me. The smell of coconut trails behind her, proof enough that she hasn't really been thinking of work. In her head, she's on the beach, living a structureless life with no responsibility. That's probably what she's used to. But that's no way to live, no way to be happy. Everyone needs a task, something to work toward. If you're not swimming, eventually you'll drown.

With enough disinfectant, the smell of beaches will go away. It's the least I can do for her.

I realize as she's getting on the elevator that I should have asked if she propped the stairwell door open—but then, why would she when she's clearly using the elevator?

I wait until she's gone, and then I sit at her desk. There's no reason I should be upset, but I feel like I've just been on a bad date. It's that unsettled feeling, and a desire to go back over everything that happened, everything we said, how we looked and sounded. She's taller than I'd thought, but not by much. Her skin is as smooth and clear as I'd imagined—with all the supplements, it's no wonder. Her tone was inconsistent, but she had just been crying. That's why she took so much prodding. That's why she seemed rude at first.

I rifle through her things and find new laxatives. She's probably not getting enough fiber. I leave some trail mix and granola from the breakroom in her top drawer and make a note to bring in some flaxseed. I appreciate that she leaves all these clues to help me fix her. When I scrub down her desk, I'm extra thorough. I get the insides of her drawers and the underside of her chair. I work to disinfect the messiness of her feelings, her tears. There's a smell to it—not salty like you'd think, but mildewy. Sadness leaves behind a dankness that settles in if you let it. You have to get at it first thing before it's ingrained in your life.

Before I head downstairs, I pop a couple of her Mood Magic pills. I know they're fake, but they're probably packed with caffeine or something akin to ephedrine. So many people think they're sad, but really they're tired. They think the day is divided into thirds: eight hours to sleep, eight hours for work, and eight hours for what you will. But if you really want to get ahead, you should divide it into halves: twelve hours for work and twelve hours for sleep. No one needs an entire eight hours for leisure. You'd just burn through your pay anyway. Better to save. Better to prepare for later.

A little Mood Magic wouldn't hurt anyone. It'd give them the get-up-and-go they've been needing.

In the breakroom, I down the last of the drink I bought at the beginning of my night. It's going flat, but not there yet. At least L. hasn't messed with it. I left it behind a jug of water, so she probably didn't see it. I think about watering her plant, but it's doing worse, browner than before, so I don't bother to help it along. Best to let it die on its own for a while. When L. doesn't pop in, I go out into the lobby, just in time to let M. inside.

"Been waiting long?" I ask.

They smile and say no, but they've probably been there for almost as long as I've been in the breakroom. They never seem irritated about anything, though. I'd love to see them really worked up, see what kind of thing or person they aren't willing to tolerate.

"They're going to set traps for the rodents," I say, though of course they're not.

"It's a big building," M. says. "Be hard to catch them that way."

"They'll get hungry eventually," I say.

"Plenty for them to eat in a building like this," they say, smiling.

"I leave it pretty much spotless," I say.

"I mean in the daytime," they say. "Hard to keep people from making a mess, leaving things out."

It's true. I can't keep any of the daytime people in line, not even with cleaning products left surreptitiously around. I am, after all, here to serve.

My stomach churns while M. tells me what their rats will and won't eat. It only gets worse the longer I stand here, listening to M. talk about rats. I don't know if it's the rat talk, something about M., or the Mood Magic, which is even less magical than I thought. No wonder the intern is having such a hard time. I make quick excuses and clamber onto the elevator to go up to the next floor's bathrooms—but, of course, L. is inside.

"I'll ride up with you," she says.

I don't say anything back. I stand very still and breathe shallowly.

When she goes to follow me off the elevator, I stop and turn to her. "I'm going to the bathroom," I say. "I'd love to go alone if that's okay with you." I walk away and don't look back.

While I'm on the toilet, I try to look up the exact pills the intern has, but I can't find them online. She's buying weird artisanal pills that could have come from anywhere, be made of anything. It's not the kind of thing that gets properly regulated. People could be paying to choke down dry bits of gravel or random ground-up plastic. Price it high enough and people will be even more excited about it.

I'll wait a week or two and then throw them away. She won't even notice. She'll probably already be on to something else in an attempt to feel alive, to glean the positive affirmation a person needs in order to keep going. There are an endless number of supplements or snacks or expensive skin-care products that she hopes might make her feel like an actual human being. She can't be sure unless she tries them all.

IN A TRASH can on the second floor, I find a stack of L.'s reports, and I have to laugh. On the back of one of them is a list of lunch orders, and then the rest are all notes: phone numbers and messages, a to-do list, some doodling.

For once, I feel excited to find her in the lobby. "You left them on someone's desk and they got used as scratch paper," I tell her.

"Just because they got repurposed later doesn't mean someone didn't take them," she says.

"You don't think it's more likely that you set them down to look at your phone, forgot about them, and someone took notes on the back?" I ask.

"No," she says, like I'm asking a stupid question.

"Look," I say, pointing at one of the reports. "Two meat pies. One fish-and-chips. It doesn't seem particularly nefarious."

But L. decides at this exact moment that she needs to pa-

trol. She has important work to do, after all. I watch the elevator go up to the second floor. Maybe she's going to look for
the rest of her reports and bust up the office's criminal lunch-
order underbelly.

Once I'm sure she's up there and I'm not going to call the
elevator back down with her in it, I hit the button. I get out
on the fourth floor, and it's blissfully L.-free. It's nice to be in
my own space, knowing that she won't interrupt for a while.

I sit at Good Influence's computer to go through her tabs,
see how she's doing. There's nothing immediately interesting. It's work stuff, some shopping, and a few how-to pages
troubleshooting problems with Excel. She has some brightly
colored sweaters and boots in her shopping cart, and I'm
tempted to click "buy," but she'd know exactly what time
the purchases were made. Her emails are mostly work-related
or spammish, but then I open one from a woman with the
same last name as her.

"Attaching some in-text comments but nothing big. I think
it looks great. Don't undersell yourself. You can do better."
Attached is her résumé, with a header in some ridiculous
loopy font.

Better than what? Better than here? Better than whatever
her job is? I'm shocked that she's trying to jump ship, and I
can't help but reflexively look around, worried that somehow,
someone will be reading over my shoulder. She certainly wasn't
discreet about this. Her password is right there, and her email
is logged in and open in one of her many tabs. I feel disappointed in her. If I'd known she was leaving, I wouldn't have
bothered investing time in her. I wouldn't have cared about

her or thought about how to make her a better, more productive employee.

I take the bags of potpourri I left her. She doesn't deserve any kind of comfort or calming energy. She doesn't deserve the luxurious breaks I created in her schedule. This is like being slapped in the face when you were reaching down to pull someone out of the water so they didn't drown.

This woman is no Good Influence.

Yarn Guy's password isn't on his monitor, but it is on a sticky note in his top drawer. I appreciate that he's been more cautious without making things unreasonably difficult for me. I go through his computer, but everything's respectable. He's not online-shopping at work. He's not sending his résumé to his sister for feedback. He's doing his job and knitting beautiful scarves. He did look at some sports stats earlier this week, but it's not an everyday thing. Probably someone else asked him a question about the game and he had to look it up because he's no jock. In fact, it was polite of him to even look. It shows he cares about his coworkers.

I look at a few other computers, ones with passwords in plain sight, and check their emails and minimized documents, but no one else seems to be working on their résumé. Maybe it's just this woman. Instead of Good Influence, she's *Résumé Woman*. She's the kind of person who's never satisfied with what she has. She always thinks she can do better without ever stopping to consider, "Do I even have anything appealing to offer?" I go back to her desk, open her résumé, and print a few copies. I leave them in a wide splay next to the copier.

On the wall, there's a flyer for "Meditation Mondays," held in the second conference room. "Relax as part of a team," it says. Imagine being encouraged to do nothing for a chunk of your workday. L. would love it. Then, on the door as I'm leaving, there's a new flyer for some kind of leadership committee. "Join us!" it says in a bubbly font above a drawing of people all standing under a single oversized light bulb. Before now, the people on the fourth floor didn't seem like such flyer people, but what with these and K-BBQ Fridays, it seems like someone's going all out.

While I'm mopping, I can't help but worry that the company is suffering in some way that I can't see. Maybe Résumé Woman is only a symptom of some larger problem, and all these flyers are very cute attempts at papering over the cracks. The company needs help, and instead of rallying all their employees together, they're hiding it. I wedge my cart between the open elevator doors so L. can't pop in on me unexpectedly. She'll never take the stairs, will never pant all the way up here, not with her intermittently bad knee.

But if there's some creeping illness affecting the company, I'm going to find it.

I sit on the floor in the copier room and dig through the papers in the recycling bin. I mostly skim: meetings rescheduled, a conference coming up, a complaint that the copier keeps getting jammed when it's set on collate, and an email about a dress-code violation: T.'s dress wasn't too short or tight, but it was kind of sheer and does B. think that's anything? Should they speak to her? Let him know. There's little difference between the complaint about the copier and the discussion of T.'s dress. It's all incidental mechanics to them. Is this one running right? Should they get a newer model? Can repairs be made? It's nice, sometimes, to be largely unseen.

Under that email, I find a few copies of a handout describing a new complimenting policy. "Compliment three people a week," it instructs. A bulleted list includes example compliments, which are extremely detailed and verbose. One of the examples is someone complimenting their manager on how they led a meeting, how well organized it was, and how inspired they felt afterward. I think about keeping a copy to show L., but she might expect me to compliment *her*, and what would I say? I like how long her hair's grown? I appreciate her general self-esteem, even though I'm not sure how she developed it?

I shuffle through financial reports, charts, and an annoying amount of blank paper. Why would they recycle perfectly clean blank paper? I sort it into a pile to put back into the copier, and then toss the actual recyclables into the bin. I've been at it for long enough that I'm sure L. is annoyed that she can't use the elevator, but not annoyed enough to drag herself up multiple flights of stairs to see why. I'm basically on autopilot, stacking and straightening all the blank paper, so I almost throw the memo back into the bin without reading it.

It's a bad copy, text starting to go grayscale and then completely vanishing. I can still make out "bridging the gap," and "cuts to in-house spending" and "only temporary until." I dig through the rest of the recycling, but there's nothing that matches, nothing else troubling.

When I unblock the elevator, I almost get the feeling that the elevator doors are relieved, like they've been doing a lot of work, holding themselves open all this time. I think it groans on the way down. Maybe someone needs to give it a closer inspection.

As usual, L.'s in the lobby, slouching on her stool. Her "Security" shirt is tied around her waist, and she's in a plain gray T-shirt that anybody could wear. You'd never know she worked here. To be fair, she's never done anything to indicate that she wants to look like she works at all. She's sectioning her hair off and twisting it into a braid that wraps around one side of her head. She didn't even notice the elevator wasn't operating.

"I was thinking about what you said the other night," I tell her, leaning against the wall and not the front glass, which is clean except for some smudges along one side of L., where she's clearly touched the glass with her hands or arms. I'll have to reclean it after she's gone.

She raises her eyebrows but keeps braiding.

"About how we're losing money?" I add.

"We're not losing money," she says. "The company is."

I work to not roll my eyes. "Don't you think there's some trickle-down?" I say. "That we're affected by things overall?"

"Maybe *I* am," she says, snapping a small band onto the end of her braid and then tucking it back into her hair. "I can picture them not being able to afford a security guard. If things get rough, they'll let me go." She sits up. "But they're always going to need someone to clean. If it was a hundred or fifty or ten people, you'd still be here, cleaning. It could be down to two employees, and it'd be you and the CEO. Can you picture him cleaning anything?"

I've seen his desk. I've scrubbed coffee off his mouse more than once, and I've wrapped a half-eaten bánh mì and put it in the fridge, even though I know he's never going to remember his leftovers. There will always be a new lunch. He'll start the day with a clean desk, a clean office.

It's boring to say men don't clean up after themselves, but anecdotally, it's largely true. Recently, a woman who sits near the elevator left her husband. She wrote to her friend that her husband cleaned their toilet with his hands. No brush or scrubber. Just a paper towel and some spray. He didn't even put on gloves. He just reached his hands into the toilet and wiped the inside of the bowl.

Even now, I cringe, imagining his fingers pressing through the thin paper towel against the cool, damp bowl. Did he wash his hands afterward? Probably not. Because he'd just been cleaning, he felt clean. Of course, it was more upsetting for her than me. Because he would use those same fingers to touch her. "It's too terrible to think about," she told her friend. I found it gripping and read the email several times. In response, the friend said she never liked him anyway—he was tall and often talked about it, like it was something he believed other people found interesting. She didn't even react to the story about the toilet bowl, and honestly, having seen the state of the bathrooms here, I'm not really shocked to hear about Toilet Woman's husband, either.

But I want to tell L. that I do more than clean, that I'm more like the head of a large household. I plan and facilitate and rectify any number of missteps taken in the daytime. But instead of saying any of this, I ask, "What more did you hear about the money? About what's going on?"

"You didn't seem very interested before," she says.

"I was working."

"Well, I'm working now," she says, jutting out her chin but

still slouching on her stool. I think of ways to slowly destabilize the stool over time. I could sand the bottom of one of the legs, so it gradually becomes more and more unsteady. I could grease the floor beneath it. Maybe there's a screw to loosen, a bolt to remove. I can turn it over and look when she's not here.

I'm ready to give up and go back upstairs when a car pulls up out front, music blasting, stopping at a slant, halfway off the street and onto the sidewalk. A guy pops out, white paper bag in hand, and casually walks up to our building, like he isn't parked inappropriately, like there's nothing disorderly about anything he's doing.

L. smiles and goes out to meet him. They stand very close together, and she touches his arm while they talk. Maybe the reason she spends all her time sitting here on this stool is because she's waiting for him. I start to back away, but I can't help myself. I stay and watch them. I've only conceived of her inside the building, working or generally avoiding work. But never outside, never with other people, not like this. She belongs to the office and the building like me, so it's unsettling to see her stray. She rocks from one side to the other like she does when she talks to anyone or does anything. She can't have a conversation and stand still. With all her pent-up energy, I'm amazed that she wants to sit hunched over a stool all night. She ought to be up, doing things, burning through some of this useless energy.

While I'm watching, they both turn to look at me a couple of times, laughing, and I freeze. L. and I make eye contact. If I shirk away, they'll think I'm embarrassed to be watching them, that there's something wrong with my simply looking. As though they aren't in an extremely public place. Standing outside with the mountains looming behind her, L. must imagine she's been given some kind of romantic backdrop. She must think the way she feels is special. When they start to embrace, I go.

In the breakroom, I give L.'s plant a jostle and one of the leaves falls off, a yellow and brown heart, crumbling and dry when I pick it up. I can't imagine what about me might be funny, what a person like L. could possibly ridicule. I hadn't really thought of it before—who she is outside of the office. I wonder for a second if she's happy, if there are things about her life that she'd change. But I think of them laughing again and I harden. Maybe I'm reading into things. They were only looking at me because I was looking at them. Everything was normal. I was normal.

L. brings her lunch into the breakroom, but I don't look at her. Just the plant, more than half dead now.

"That wasn't my boyfriend," she says.

"I didn't say he was." Women are always embarrassed of the men they're dating.

She sits on the other side of her dying plant, though she doesn't mention it or even look at it. I don't know if she's even noticed it's in distress. I could probably set it on fire, and she wouldn't comment. Maybe she'd ask me to put out the fire and clean up the mess. She must be watering it though, for the salt to have made it down to the roots. In a way, I haven't really done anything wrong. She's the one killing her plant. All I did was add a little something to the soil.

She pulls out what I think is chicken shawarma and takes a big bite. The smell fills the room, and almost immediately she splatters tahini on the table.

"Have you been propping the stairwell door open in the lobby?" I ask, but she shakes her head and keeps eating.

I make myself look as bored as possible, letting my eyes glaze over while I count backward from a hundred. I know she'll talk if she thinks I don't care. She's desperate for the attention.

"You eat yet?" she finally asks, but she doesn't wait for an answer. "I heard people might start coming in on the weekend," she says.

"That sounds expensive," I say. "We must be doing okay, to pay everyone for all those extra hours."

She laughs. "They wouldn't pay anything extra," she says. "They're all on salary."

"We aren't on salary," I say. And I wonder if we'll get overtime for the extra days. I wouldn't mind being here more. Think of all the extra things I could accomplish.

"I'm not talking about us." L. gets up to pilfer through the fridge, sliding things around and crouching to make sure she doesn't miss anything, and then she sits back down with a half-empty bottle of some sort of red juice. At least it's not mine. I poured vinegar into a few of my drinks earlier this month. She never said anything, but I could tell she'd tried one of them, because since then they've stopped disappearing. None of the office people use our breakroom but maintenance men and various techs use it during the day, so she's probably stealing from them, helping herself to anything they leave overnight. They must think it's the both of us, stealing their things.

I keep waiting for a note from the supervisor chastising me for eating food that isn't mine. I've rehearsed the very stern call I would make in response. I wouldn't even call her. I'd call HR. I have their number saved in my phone just for this. I'm not going to let anybody get me before I get them. I'd tell HR how I never touched anyone's food, and how she never even asked, how I was just accused. Then I'd tell them about the roaches, the rats, the conditions things are left in. I should be paid hazard pay for some of this, but I've been just kindly doing the work. Now here I am, accused of theft, accused of this intimate violation—taking someone else's meal or drink. Do they think I'm paid so little that I cannot feed myself? If so, why not pay me more? And what are they going to do to make this right?

Then I would wait in silence. I'd let it stretch out, make them be the one to say something. My supervisor would be chastised, maybe fired. I'd be issued an apology. I'd like it to be handwritten and taped to my cart, though.

"They'll stretch everyone really thin," she says. "To see how much they can get from them. Then they'll start cutting people."

I shake my head. "Things seem good upstairs." I think of all the flyers, the optimism of their bright colors and curly fonts.

"You'll see," she says. "Things are going to get tougher. They're putting the squeeze on."

"Maybe," I say. I hesitate a few seconds but decide to go ahead. "I meant to tell you that I found something. Part of a document."

She looks at me but keeps eating. I can smell the char on her meat, and I look away because she's chewing with her mouth open.

"It was just on the floor," I say. "It mentioned some cuts to spending, but it's a bad copy and I couldn't read the whole thing."

"Let me read it," she says, as though maybe I couldn't read it because I'm illiterate. Or like it's no problem for her to read invisible words that aren't even on the page. She'll just intuit them. Easy.

"I said it was a bad copy," I tell her again.

"Do you still have it?" she asks.

"Of course not," I say.

It's in my pocket, folded into a tiny square.

"You should find the original," she says, as though I hadn't already thought of this, as though I don't know how copies work and this is my first time ever seeing one, in spite of working in this office almost a year longer than her.

L. operates on a very basic level and assumes everyone else does as well. Once, when I had a complicated inner ear problem, she asked if I had tried holding my nose and blowing, the extremely well-known solution that even children understand and also the first result for any internet search about ear problems. I had already been to the doctor, who prescribed two different medications, but sure, I haven't tried holding my stupid nose and blowing.

It's hard to talk to her sometimes. Not just because she's stupid but because her own stupidity confuses her, and she thinks it's everyone else who's dumb. Anytime she doesn't understand something or it's too complex for her, she thinks the problem is someone else. "It's definitely you!" I want to scream, but instead I practice looking very calm and nonreactive when she frustrates me. I work in an office that does Monday Meditation, after all. That sort of energy goes a long way.

So, I take my cart back upstairs. While I finish cleaning the gray floors, I think about what this money trouble might mean for the company and the intern. She'll never get her life on track if she loses this job. She'll spiral even further. She's not a naturally substantial person, but she's trying to be, with all these supplements and creams and books. If she relaxed, it might be easier. She doesn't have to build this desirable-seeming personality. The fakeness of it is actually off-putting, but she can't see that. She keeps putting on makeup even though she hasn't showered, hasn't washed her clothes. She shakes them out and puts them on again. These wrinkles aren't noticeable at all, she thinks. She's a woman who's been practicing the right way to smile in front of the mirror for so long that she's forgotten what her natural smile even looks like. If she were to catch a glimpse of herself, unaware, she'd be shocked.

But if there's a problem with the company at large, it won't just hurt her. It'll hurt everyone. Yarn Guy and Mr. Buff and even Scissors Guy and Résumé Woman. Even me.

I won't let this happen.

But I don't know how to assess the realness of any money trouble the company is having. Everyone's still here, working and reasonably happy. Everything looks the same. It's not as though a problem with the budget would suddenly change the quality of the desks or office furniture. It'd be more subtle than that.

I look through everyone's desks, searching for the original copy. You'd assume everything would be emails and shared online workspaces and video calls, but there's a shocking amount of paper strewn through the office. It's just that none of it is interesting. I wonder what makes certain things worth printing out. Is it something they all do by reflex, or is it an insecurity? If a person prints and stacks piles of work on their desk, then everyone can see how valuable they are. So much work! So impressive!

But after my search, all I have is a paper cut, and when I go downstairs to get a Band-Aid I see L. talking to M. in the lobby. They both look happy, laughing, like they're having a great conversation. It feels like I'm seeing something I wasn't meant to see. L. stands so close to M. that they might accidentally touch her. If they did, she wouldn't mind. She'd act like M. was the one instigating things and not her, jutting her little chest out as far as she can. She's fidgeting and bouncing from leg to leg, knee injury be damned. If you asked her right now, she'd say her knees are great, twisting her words on the end to emphasize the innuendo.

When she laughs, too loudly, I make a beeline for our breakroom. It's too embarrassing to watch. They're not even coworkers. It should have been a quick delivery with hardly a "Have a nice day," before M. was on to better things. Unlike L., M. has an actual job to do. People are waiting on them.

I throw all of L.'s sweatshirts and her hat into the trash. She keeps saying they aren't hers, so she can't be upset. I'm just straightening up. You're welcome. I also empty some chunky red soup into the trash and toss the plastic container in too. I know it's hers, but it's been in the fridge long enough for the soup to sour and grow a fine layer of mold. People are precious about their presumed belongings—Scissors Guy is a great example—but of course, a mess doesn't belong to anyone. It exists extemporaneously and it's my job to eradicate it. If anything, everyone thinks it belongs to *me*. But the room smells terrible now, so I head back upstairs. Unlike L., I have work to do.

THE NEXT DAY, L. doesn't even say hello or mention me throwing anything away. She just launches straight into things.

"They're going to hire another security guard," she says. "For the day shift. I might switch over." She winds her gum around her obviously unclean finger, and then sticks her finger into her mouth to scrape the gum off with her teeth. She probably chews gum in the bathroom too, with her mouth open, that little wad absorbing all the germs in the air.

"Why would they need anyone in the daytime?" I ask. "With all those people around?" I put my lunch in the fridge and try not to look at her or think about her gum, her teeth, her mouth, all so unclean.

"People want that feeling of safety," she says. "It's about consistency." As though she provides any kind of consistency, napping and wandering the building, more ghost than guard.

"They have the budget for that?" I ask.

"Some costs are unavoidable," she says. "You invest up front so people feel safer, work harder. And if someone's cutting corners, you catch them. It's a big money-saver, actually. They just want to get things back on track."

"You don't know what anybody wants. Who would you even talk to about it?" I ask. "Except M. And what would M. know about what happens here?"

"You like M.," she says.

"I don't dislike them," I say. She's projecting, trying to goad me into asking about her and M., but I won't do it.

"And besides, lots of people were talking about it," she says. "You should be nicer or get here a little earlier, like I do."

No matter what L. writes on her time sheet, I almost always get here before she does. I grit my teeth, still too awake to absorb her lecture. If it was later on in my shift, I could maybe take it. I could float away to somewhere else and listen to her buzz around me, waiting to see if she offered any valuable information. She'd be like anything else: the hum of the overhead lights, the rush of the pipes in the walls, the sound of the heat or air-conditioning kicking on, depending on the season. Just the creaks and groans I'm used to. But I'm not yet into the groove of the night, so I stop her.

"I have to get to work," I say, pivoting away.

"Our breakroom looks pretty good," she says. "Maybe you can wipe down the counters too."

I go to the storage closet, trying to walk loudly enough to drown out anything else she might say. There's a note from someone on the fourth floor, complaining about the "fakey vanilla smell" and asking me to use something else. L. hasn't seen it, because if she had, she would have been thrilled to

point it out. There's no greeting or signature. It's simply affixed to the door. And they've not included an actual question mark in their question, though they've phrased it "Can
you." I've been using the vanilla for a while, so it's strange to
complain about it now. I wonder if Yarn Guy has noticed it
yet. Maybe I'll clean his desk and the space around him with
the vanilla but go back to my usual for everything else. I hate
to think about the smells mixing. I wouldn't want the vanilla
to become too muddled.

And imagine leaving a note to complain about the way
someone cleans up after you. Maybe they want to come and
show me how to mop or empty their trash cans. I fold the
note and stick it in my cart.

I think about cleaning the grout between the tiles, a thing
that doesn't have to be done frequently, but makes me feel very
Zen whenever I do it. There's an evenness to the work, a pattern that I'm sucked into. I go from line to line, tile to tile.
The clean floor blooms out from a corner, everything shining
and brightening as I go. But I'd like to start the project away
from L., so I'd have a while to get into the rhythm of it before
I have to listen to her prattle on or ask endless questions. Am
I stripping the finish off the tiles? That'll make them easier
to scratch or break. Don't I know that? And do I know that
slouching will cause irreparable damage? I ought to be more
cognizant of my spine and how it lines up with my neck. As
though she doesn't spend nearly her entire shift slouching te-
diously on her stool in the lobby, visible to the street as only
a hunch.

I hit all the buttons in the elevator so that if L. follows me
to the lobby, she won't immediately know what floor I'm on.

Then I get off on the top floor and I go from desk to desk, comparing handwriting to the note left on the storage closet door. It was written childishly, in all capital letters, so it's hard to compare them as precisely as I'd like. I find two or three desks that seem possible, but I can't be sure—and then I see that Résumé Woman's desk is cleared out. I wonder if she found something better, or if they let her go because they know she's ungrateful, disloyal. Her desk has already been carefully wiped down, so it shines. Someone took note of her bad vibes and made sure to scrub them away. It's a good desk, near the windows, and I wonder if someone will take her spot, or if they'll hire her replacement before anyone can move in. The turnover isn't generally that fast here, but good desks don't stay empty forever.

I move over to Mr. Buff's desk. He's farther from the windows, but because of his angle, the view is actually better. I look carefully and the handwriting isn't his, but I hadn't suspected it was. He's not the type. There are no cigarettes tonight, and no sign that he's connected with the intern. I wonder if he's playing her hot and cold: he's too much and then not enough. Is he pouting after my reprimand? Or maybe he's generally unattractive and the cigarettes hadn't mattered at all. Maybe he's older.

If he and the intern knew how much desperation they had in common, or if they could look at one another without judging this quality that they hate in themselves, they'd see a perfect match: someone who understood them, truly. Instead, they're set up to judge one another, to sense weakness and strike. It's hard to know them both and watch them live this way.

So much of the office is like that: people who hate themselves and their jobs, but then direct those feelings toward everyone else. It's why I'd rather work alone, at night. There's no one to compete with, no one to think I'm coming for their job, no one to stand over my shoulder and tell me that I'm not doing something right, that I missed a spot, and also, I should be working faster, don't I know that?

I enter Mr. Buff's password and log in to his computer, but then get up and tilt his desk, angling it toward hers so they might look up from their work and see one another during the day. It's a slight adjustment—nothing that puts the room off-kilter. I admire the view and look through Mr. Buff's computer, but there's nothing interesting. I'd be shocked if there was.

On a whim, I look up the CEO. He's easy to find and looks like any other man. I visit his LinkedIn page but it's boring. It lists this job and one like it, and another and another. His education is stacked beneath that. School is the most boring thing you can learn about a person, like hearing that they enjoy trivia night. It's strange to me that anyone would take glee in answering questions or taking tests. What if we just told them they were very smart? Would that be enough to end trivia nights?

I search his name "and wife" but nothing comes up. He gets his own picture, his own news article, but who is she? I know he's married because I've seen her photo on his desk. There's also a picture of a dog there, a breed I've never seen before, not common in this area. It's big and goofy and looking to the side of the camera. This dog might be their only progeny. Put a tie on him and make him the shortest, cutest nepotism hire. Animals are straightforward in their demands. They won't leave notes complaining about the "fakey vanilla smell," whatever that means.

I hear the elevator open, so I close the window, turn off Mr. Buff's monitor, and stand up.

"I'm doing the floors," I say, and shepherd L. back to the elevator, back toward her stool. There are probably cars she could be watching drive by. Maybe an ambulance, if she's lucky. Maybe a sense of purpose or achievement. If she logs enough hours and waits patiently, someone will leave her a note telling her she's good. She'll tuck it into her pocket and walk around all shift, maybe all week, thinking, *I am pretty good, aren't I?*

"I heard about this new cleaning spray," she says, as the door is closing. "It's made with vinegar." She says something else, but thankfully the doors are closed now, and she's heading back downstairs where she belongs.

In the breakroom I find they've switched to generic coffee. I don't know how expensive the other kind was, but it'd been the same one since I started working here. The granola bars are also a cheaper brand and seem largely untouched. A few months ago, they changed the brand of industrial cleaner I use, and I hadn't thought much of it, but maybe the new one is cheaper. These kind of low-level budget cuts aren't that noticeable, but they might be a window into more. What's next? Maybe an inventory of what I use to clean? Will they ask me to count trash bags and measure out ounces of cleaner?

I wonder what else we're cheaping out on that I can't see, and I study the room. There's a new flyer above the counter to the left of the microwave. "Remember to cast your vote for who will cater our employee appreciation lunch!" Under the text, there's a clip art of some balloons and then, strangely, a goofy smiling dog with long ears and a little bow tie. I don't see any way to cast a vote of my own. They aren't thinking of me.

On my way back to Mr. Buff's desk, I see a crocheted coaster on the desk of a woman who I would have said was otherwise unremarkable. Maybe she was Soda Woman in my head before this moment, because she drinks several cans a day, but I'm not sure I've actively thought of her at all. But now I can see she's Coaster Woman—and, of course, this coaster is one that Yarn Guy made. I can tell by the stitching, the colors. There's a blocky orange cat face in the middle of a patchy green background.

The yarn's already frayed from use. I'd never care so poorly for something he made, but she's been utterly cavalier with it. Who does she think she is? Maybe it was a platonic gift. He drew her name from a hat. Her grandmother died and he's just that kind of guy. Or maybe she stole it. Maybe she wanted a coaster and just took it from his desk. I look through her things to see if it's part of a set, but this cat is a solo artist.

I do find nail clippers, something only a depraved person would have in their desk at work. Imagine cutting your nails in the middle of the workday. That little *click, click, click* while people are trying to write emails. An errant nail could shoot halfway across the room. It could hit someone in the eye or fall into a drink. I'll have to be extra vigilant around her desk, looking carefully for her snipped-off nails caught in the fabric of someone's chair or resting on the edge of their keyboard.

I squint. If Yarn Guy knew what kind of person she was, he wouldn't have bothered with her.

I take the coaster and slide it back into his desk, in the bottom drawer, beneath several spools of yarn and some funny-shaped scissors. She doesn't deserve it and probably won't even notice it's gone. I fluff everything back up, give it a quick pat, and close the drawer.

I've been thinking of learning to crochet or knit, or at least learning the difference between the two. And then, when I'm almost as good as him, I can leave him a gift, my own handmade coasters, or a scarf. I'll write a note to go with it. "Noticed we're both knitters or crocheters or whatever. We should have tea!"

I'll draw a picture of some yarn and the needles I used. Then I'll leave my phone number. It'll be very casual, cute. We'll talk yarn and crafts, and maybe that'll bleed into helpful gossip. Does he know, for example, that the guy three desks over and two desks back watches gifs of porn on his work computer? Porn Guy's back is to a wall and maybe no one walks that way, so he's not worried about anyone seeing. He and another person in the office, though I'm not sure who, exchange these gifs all day, like a running commentary of how they're feeling or what they're thinking. What does a three-way kiss signal? How about a detached cartoon ass? It's hard to say, but this is one small thing I can tell Yarn Guy about the people who sit around him. And once I help him get ahead, I'll be irreplaceable. He won't think of Coaster Woman at all, not even if it's her birthday or she's gravely ill.

A WEEK PASSES and I find the intern at her desk again, not crying this time, but clearly overwhelmed. Her hair falls around her shoulders, unbrushed, and I wonder why she doesn't use a handful of bobby pins to at least pull it out of her face. Maybe she's so exhausted that she's forgotten them. After she leaves, I can set one out, so she'll remember them next time.

"Evening," I say.

In response, she combs a hand through her hair but otherwise ignores me. I clean the desks around her, lifting papers and folders to wipe beneath them but being careful not to look like I'm reading them. I don't want to give the impression that I'm snooping. In my peripheral vision, I can see that every few seconds her hand is in her hair again, a nervous tic. Then her hand snags and she works to pull it through, to split the tangle or knot collected there. It would be better if she waited until she was in the shower and conditioned it to try to work the tangles out. She's going to have so much unnecessary breakage with these dry tangles. It's only going to make her look more frazzled later. It works this way sometimes—your own nervous energy is the thing that cracks you apart.

I hum while I clean, a popular lullaby, but I keep it uptempo, so she won't recognize it. Eventually it works, because she's calmer, and she looks at me and smiles. "You want a drink?" she asks.

"I have to work," I say, but in a friendly tone. Not dismissive or judgmental.

She shakes her head and pulls two beers out of her bottom desk drawer. She's never had alcohol in her desk before, and I worry about what this means, but I sit, catching myself before the desk chair gives me a little spin. I try to remember the last time I went through her desk, drawer by drawer, and cataloged everything. The night after I saw her last, there was a jar of spicy mustard, half eaten, and I took it and put it in the fridge. Even closed up tightly, that smell was still going to make its way out of the jar. Her desk, her papers, her clothes, her hair—it was all going to smell like spicy mustard. I know this isn't the impression she wants to make, not with all her preening and scented lotions.

But I haven't looked beyond her supplements since I found the mustard. I've been busy with other people. She could have been drinking at work for days. I need to be more watchful. I could get her some energy drinks. I could mix something into her powders or supplements. Maybe some crushed-up caffeine pills.

Several months ago, a man on this floor threw all his caffeine pills away. It was three bottles and I assume he'd bought them in bulk, a smart shopper. They didn't seem any more harmful than a cup of coffee, so I took them. Two of the bottles weren't even opened. A few days later, he wrote an email about it. His girlfriend had found a bottle at home and, holding them up, she asked, "What are you, a truck driver?" as though staying awake is occupation-specific. All kinds of people need to be alert. Imagine thinking you have any say over how someone else lives or works.

I've tried the pills a few times but generally don't need them—I have plenty of get-up-and-go. Maybe the intern could use the help.

She gestures toward me with one of the beers and gives it a jostle.

"No, thanks," I say.

She shrugs and softly puts the can back into her desk, opening the other one.

I'll check later to see how many there are, and if there's a bag or a receipt. It's important to know the scale of the issue.

"Have you sat in on one of those meetings?" I ask.

"Meetings?" she says, like we've never talked about them before or I'm using a term she's unfamiliar with.

"Your pitch meetings," I say.

"I did," she says, clasping her hands and leaning back from her work. She has rings on every other finger and wears a man's watch, blocky and swallowing her wrist. I squint and maybe there's a bruise from it, but I can't be sure. She clearly wants to look small, enjoys this caricature of herself, and needs people to think, *How does she manage to accomplish anything, as tiny as she is?*

"How'd it go?" I ask.

She downs nearly half her beer. "A little stressful," she says. "But I think I have some ideas." She motions at the notepad she's holding. It's never in her desk and must be something she takes home with her. I'm eager to page through it and help her figure out how to proceed. I reach for it, but she settles back in her chair, almost imperceptibly, but it's enough. I won't give the impression of chasing her. Instead, I make my face very gentle, adopting a maternal expression. My own mother was never the supportive presence I wanted. It's easy now, not talking to her, not suffering through a phone call or uncomfortable visit. I once worried I might feel sad on holidays, but instead I feel a kind of lightness. Even ignoring her calls feels like a respite.

"Are you okay?" the intern asks.

Perhaps I wasn't making the right face, after all.

"I was wondering what your ideas were?" I ask.

"It's stupid," she says.

"I'm sure it's not," I say, trying again to soften my face. I think of the woman from the real estate commercial that I like. She's holding coffee and her purse and her keys all in one hand and gesturing with the other, welcoming people into a building. She's happy to be doing it all, not overwhelmed in the least. There's no amount of things she could carry that would make her drop one or stop smiling.

"I was thinking about a new fundraising event," the intern says. "A gala, something very luxe."

I want to ask her about the company's money problems. Has she seen the new, cheap coffee? And if we've switched to generic snacks, we probably don't have the money to fund a gala. But this might be too direct. She needs a gentler hand.

"Don't they do a party already?" I ask.

"People like parties," she says.

I nod. "How about a walkathon? I don't think we've ever done one before."

She frowns, but it'll be far cheaper. And Mr. Buff would probably work on it with her. He could be the walkathon's spokesperson. He'd flex his arms and lead warm-up and cool-down stretches for everyone in the office. It'd be community building. He'd start a daily plank—everyone would flatten themselves a few inches above the floor for thirty or sixty seconds, right before lunch. I could do it at home. It'd feel nice to be part of the group.

Then I think of Yarn Guy in athletic shorts and a slim-fitted running shirt, something that showcases his body without being ostentatious. He'd never want to be the center of attention like Mr. Buff, but people are still drawn to him. He has a quiet charisma and asks questions that make other people feel really seen. Like me, he can zero in on what's happening in someone's life. He'll naturally know things about their families and relationships and how they see themselves in the world, because he's such an active listener. He'd be a good platonic friend for the intern, someone to be there for her, and she'd really benefit from his grounding presence. There wouldn't be any flirtation, because she's far younger than him. She's probably the youngest person here, and I worry again about how old Mr. Buff might be. The bareness of his desk initially made me think he was young too. He simply hadn't had enough time to acquire a personality other than his fitness disorder.

But Yarn Guy will look out for the intern, won't let her involve herself in an age-inappropriate dalliance. He'll gently steer her away, without her even noticing she's being steered. She'll start to think of us as her work-parents.

"I think walkathons are more of a charity thing," she finally says. "Like for cancer."

"I don't think they have to be," I say.

"I don't think anyone here has cancer," she says.

"No one has to have cancer." I scoot my chair toward her.

"I should probably head out," she says. She half crushes her can, drops it into her trash, and then looks up at me like she's embarrassed to have created a mess in front of the person who has to clean it. I just shake my head. It's like when people don't want to eat meat when it's still shaped like the animal it used to be. Fish is fine unless it has eyes and fins, and you can imagine a name for it. Pork is okay, but not a whole pig, because you can imagine it playing and taking naps. You could walk it on a leash, put it in a sweater. Like most people, she's fine with someone cleaning up after her, but she doesn't want to think about the actual person who does it, what they see, what intimacies they're granted.

"The walkathon could be like a party," I say. "There'd be food and drinks afterward. The company logo on T-shirts. You could design them." I've seen her doodles. I know she could do it. And this would finally get her noticed. "Oh, the intern," someone would say. "You should see the logo she designed. A real up-and-comer. We're lucky to have her." They'd remember her when they needed someone for a similar project. Her name would come to mind when they talked about hiring and promotions.

"I'm not sure that's the right aesthetic," she says. I can see her collarbone and picture the curve of her spine. She's not an athlete, could never be a runner. There's no meat to her. I've embarrassed her by suggesting something like this.

"Maybe we could do a bonfire," I say. "People love bonfires."

She looks confused. "We couldn't set anything on fire," she says. "Not in the dry season."

She slides her notepad into her bag and heads toward the elevator, her walk kind of prim, which feels unsettling. There's something grating about that prissiness in the context of the empty offices and the smell of cleaning solution. When I go home, I smell like it. Even after I shower, I smell like I've been cleaning. I've adapted to it. It's not like it's a bad smell. No one smells cleaner and gets grossed out. If anything, my smell is reassuring. It's just, who is she being prissy for at this hour?

"There doesn't have to be a bonfire," I call after her. "It's just a suggestion."

She smiles and gets on the elevator without saying anything else. I wonder if this is what she's like in meetings. So closed off, unwilling to have a discussion. She's going to have to learn to collaborate. She's the bottom rung of the ladder and should be enthusiastic about other people's ideas, finding ways to bolster them and make herself a part of the team. The walkathon was my opening gambit, a suggestion. It wasn't my one and only idea. If she'd stuck around, she would have seen that. It can be overwhelming to work on something like this if you're new to it, though. Hard to launch yourself into an ongoing conversation without feeling like you're interrupting or appearing to ride someone's coattails. But I'm

happy to have her piggyback. At least she's on the right track
with fundraising.

I want to ask her how we're losing money. She should be
paying attention to that kind of thing. What's changed in
the last few months or year? Work still piles up and moves
from desk to desk. Sometimes the same work goes back and
forth between two desks, but it's clear that something is happening. There are angry red marks or frantic notes jotted in
margins. I can tell which people like working together and
which people don't. Everyone stays busy.

I think about making M. that list of useful tips for lifting
and transporting packages, and I go to sit at the CEO's desk,
because where else should I work? Why not set myself up for
success? His office is objectively nicer than anywhere else in
the building. His desk is huge, made of a burgundy wood with
a nice polish on it that I'm responsible for even though they
warned me he would be fussy about having his things touched.

I sprawl out and rock back in what is probably the most
comfortable chair I've ever sat in, with cushioned arm grips
and support for my lower back. It's more comfortable than any
piece of furniture in my apartment, most of which was thrifted
or found on the curb and lugged back on foot, or sticking
out of the back of a helpful neighbor's car. The energy in this
room is entirely different from the rest of the office. There's
the sound of rushing water from a little rock-pool fountain he
keeps on a small table by the door. His bookcase is half-full
of knickknacks but not a single book. There's a Kleenex box
and a statue of a lizard and a red vase with dry brown stalks
in it. This sparseness gives his office the appearance of cleanliness, even if I haven't wiped it down or dusted in weeks.

On his desk, his wife and dog look at me, waiting. I never noticed before, but the picture of his dog is slightly bigger than the picture of his wife. I have to admit, it's a nice-looking dog, smiling at me the way animals do. I feel very friendly toward it, and even find myself warming to the idea of the CEO. A man with a dog like this might not be so bad. If he tilted the picture of his dog outward instead of toward himself, people might see the dog and feel open and friendly toward the CEO as well. They probably wouldn't even realize why they felt that way. It'd just happen—a general softening. I tilt the photo so he can still see it but anyone coming into his office can too.

I move his mouse and I'm prompted to enter a password, but he doesn't have it written down in any of the typical places. What could he need to hide that's on his work computer? Who would want to snoop through his things? I start to type in a guess, but I'm nervous about being locked out if it's incorrect. Now that I know he's hiding something, I don't want him to have time to cover his tracks.

But surely, I have at least one try. I tentatively type "password" and hit "enter," but the little window shakes at me and the computer grunt-beeps the sound that means "no, that isn't right." I feel fully chastised, but also invigorated, taunted. I will not be fucked around with by a man without a single book and a statue of a goddamn lizard. I'll try again tomorrow. I can risk one try a night. That couldn't possibly be enough to lock me out.

I sit at his desk for a while longer and imagine what it would be like if this was my desk, my dog, my wife. She's almost imperceptibly slumped, like she's overwhelmed or disappointed. What about her life is such a disappointment? She's younger than me and more polished, but we're not so different—both underappreciated and largely unseen, moving behind the scenes, ingrained in a place that doesn't know us.

I'd like to meet her. I could figure out what kinds of places she goes for coffee or groceries or a walk and I could insert myself into those spaces. It wouldn't be hard to find his home address, and then her name. It's all in a file somewhere, one that HR has. But he probably doesn't live nearby. He must live outside the city, somewhere more peaceful, and commute in. His dog looks like he's in a backyard and not a park. This kind of space would be nearly impossible to come by in the city.

I can't picture myself using precious daytime hours, usually allotted to sleep, to ride a bus out to their suburban neighborhood. I certainly don't want to pay for a car. But maybe there's a way to lure her into the city, to the office. A certain kind of event, like a walkathon, would require the presence of a wife, even though I hate to imagine that kind of unpaid labor for her. No one even knows she's a person, except me.

Her ears look like they aren't pierced, which is so interesting, because I don't know another adult woman besides myself without pierced ears. Mine were pierced briefly as a kid, but one got knocked out and I just took the other out and let the holes grow back in. But she probably never had them done. Didn't want them, so she didn't get them. It's nice to have something like that in your life.

I go and stand at his window, looking out over the city. Does he appreciate this view? His desk is positioned so his back is to the window, so it's hard to imagine he cares about it. In the daytime, if he turns and looks, he can probably see a stretch of green park and a fountain, children running loops around it, shouting in a friendly way. At night it's dark, a mass of gray. If I didn't know the area so well, I wouldn't even know there was a park out there.

I turn off the CEO's lights and leave his door cracked, as usual, then head back into the fray. The singular jar of "Do Not Touch" cloudy water has become two jars, though only the first is labeled. I hold up the new jar to examine it in the light, but can't discern anything more about it. It's grayish water with a bit of sediment at the bottom. Are they growing something? Is this some kind of fermentation process? People are comfortable doing the strangest things at work, as though they aren't in public here.

Before I leave, I open a tab and search for "walkathon" on four different computers, spread across the office. I erase my history, so they won't know what time the tab was opened. It'll just be there, among their existing tabs. They'll think they forgot why they looked this up, but the idea will be in the air. Maybe the intern will hear someone mention it and she'll think, *A walkathon wasn't such a bad idea after all*, and she'll do some research too, look up stats and prices and athletic gear. Then whenever she presents her idea, the office will be primed to hear it. I won't even let her thank me. "It's nothing," I'll tell her, holding up my hand to silence her.

But she'll listen to me next time, because she'll know that I know what I'm talking about.

THE STAIRWELL DOOR in the lobby is propped open again. I've tried hiding their brick, and even throwing it away, but today the door is propped open using an empty trash can. I walk up one flight of stairs and back down, but nothing is amiss. Maybe it smells a bit like cigarettes, but that doesn't explain the door. I stick the empty trash can on my cart and see M., so I wait for them in the lobby. The longer they have to wait to be let in, the more talkative they are. If they stand outside long enough, it'll be at least twenty minutes of rat talk or book talk or whatever new thing it is that they've made into their personality.

I think of them again, standing and laughing with L., both so comfortable with one another, like they're old friends and not the vaguest of work acquaintances. But where is L. now that M. needs her?

I hit the button for the front door, and it lurches open.

"Smaller orders lately," M. says, settling the dolly back into an upright position with a clank. "Everything okay?"

"Not that much smaller," I say, but M.'s right. They didn't even have to use the large pallet. Tonight's order of three boxes fits neatly on a two-wheeled dolly. But I think everything upstairs seems like business as usual. People are making the same messes they always make. I wonder if the people on each floor who process deliveries have noticed any shrinkage.

"Seems fine to me," I say.

"Maybe it's the season," M. says. "Just time for things to slow down."

But there's never been a noticeable difference season-to-season before. There's a brief slowdown around the holidays, but it's just a few days or a week. Maybe this is the same: a small gap between busy stretches.

"What can you do?" I say, shrugging, keeping my voice light and easy.

"Maybe you could clean houses on the side," M. says, though I've said nothing to indicate that I need any other kind of employment. I bend down to retie my shoelaces, which have somehow grown loose. If I wanted a different job, I'd have one. I've waited tables, answered phones, bagged groceries, and once, for a week and a half, I was a dental assistant. The dentist wanted to try training an assistant rather than hiring one out of school, and I came by, looking for work, at exactly the right time. But the job had been overwhelming: I couldn't remember the names of the tools and wasn't ever sure I was using the ultrasonic cleaner correctly. "The autoclave," as they called it. The whole process made me nervous, and there was no one checking behind me to be sure I'd done it right.

I imagined patients swapping bacteria and diseases. Maybe a high-risk patient would get some kind of infection. I didn't want to be responsible for this level of harm. And then, when I wasn't using the autoclave, I wasn't sure what to do with myself. I stood awkwardly in the hallway, waiting for someone to call me into a room. I asked the front desk if I could help them with filing and they looked at me strangely but let me file away the last week's patient folders. I felt valuable, knowing I was fulfilling a task in exactly the right way. But when the dentist finally fired me, I was relieved. He was so gentle about it, and paid me for three additional weeks, which felt like such a boon at the time, when I was newly on my own and struggling.

So now that I've found a place where the rules all make sense and I know how to perform every facet of my job, why would I want to do something else? I love that I can tell if I've done my job by simply looking around. The floors gleam, the windows are streak-free, and you'd be pressed to find a sticky surface. I have a real effect on the people here. I shape their day, their work, the way they think and act. Not many of them could pinpoint me as the impetus for their choices, but that doesn't change anything. It doesn't change me. A person is lucky to stumble into the place where they belong. They don't go looking elsewhere at the first sign of trouble. Instead, they stay on, bail water out of the boat and help patch the holes.

I finish with my laces and stand up. "Clean houses?" I ask M. "Why would I need to do that?"

They shake their head and look so chastised that I almost feel bad. Because aren't they like me? We're the kind of skilled labor that everyone needs but no one really sees. L. can't even bother to let them in, so a few times a week, M. is stuck standing outside, waiting for someone to let them do their job. It's probably like this all the way down the street. Otherwise, why would they bother waiting?

"I like your shoes," I say. Even under the bright lobby lights, I can tell that M.'s high-top sneakers must glow in the dark.

M. smiles and glances down. There's a mole on their neck that I can't stop looking at. It's only a little raised, and if you weren't looking closely enough, you might call it a freckle, but I can tell it's not. Then M. looks up and sees me seeing them. For a moment, I feel caught and can't look away. I would give anything for L. to burst in, for her frenzied movement and loudness to crack the moment open. But she doesn't come, and instead the moment goes on forever. Or maybe not forever, but something just shy of forever, stretching out inside a few moments in the middle of one night. We stare at each other, and I feel like they can hear me breathing. I try to inhale quietly, slowly, but my breath is still ragged. And then, so gradually that I'm not sure at first that it's really happening, M. rolls the dolly onto the elevator, smiling and looking over their shoulder at me. The door closes so slowly that I wonder if it's broken.

I sit on L.'s stool to catch my breath. I can kind of see why she likes it, being raised up higher and positioned right at the front of the room. I look outside and there's no one in either direction, and then I see headlights cresting closer and closer, and a car becomes fully visible in the night, a slick red thing, and then its taillights, getting farther away until there's nothing. I wait a few seconds and there's another pair of headlights. The really early-morning people are starting to kick into gear.

I can see how someone might pass the night this way. How thrilling it must be to see an ambulance or a police car amid so much nothing. A heavy blackness, and then sirens and flashing lights. It might feel like a personal accomplishment, like you willed it into being. L.'s adrenaline would kick up and she'd feel like she was finally working. *Look what I did*, she'd think. The rush from it would make her feel essential, important. Maybe she'd come upstairs and find me and tell me a little something about how to do my job, hitching her thumbs in her belt loops and really sauntering around. It doesn't take much for her. Kill a bug, sign for a delivery, and then she feels endlessly necessary. Her few minutes of labor will devour my whole night's worth of effort. *Anyone can clean*, she thinks.

I LEAVE A homemade flaxseed cookie for the intern. She's eaten the last three I've left, so I know she likes them. She's probably intuited that they're from me and she trusts me, knows I want the best for her. She hasn't had to mess with the laxatives for a while either, so the cookies are doing the trick. People her age don't think enough about fiber. So many trendy diets geared toward starvation, but nothing circling around real wellness. Sure, she's skinny, but does she feel alive? Does she feel like she can keep climbing out of bed every day and enduring the general malaise of life? Some flax fixed her right up.

I remove one of her supplements too, one of the more woo-woo sounding ones with a list of confusing ingredients and no clear purpose. The bottle simply reads "Feel Good Alchemy." I toss it into my trash to take out to the dumpster. I'd rather she keep drinking at work than ingest random powders and supplements trying to "feel good." What even makes people think they're supposed to feel good? Who told them that? Life is made up of lots of small- and medium-sized pain, if you're lucky.

Tonight, the door to the stairwell is propped open on this floor. I still don't understand why they're doing it, who needs to come and go this way, and to what end. It's annoying that L. doesn't seem to notice what might be an actual breach in security.

The elevator dings and there she is. I sigh. It must be hard for her, having so little to do. But imagine being bored at work and then finding someone who's very busy and making your boredom their problem. She watches me empty trash cans and wipe down desks while she tells me about the show she's watching. It's about a woman who's trying to get her boss to notice her. She just wants to do well at her job, but he can only see how attractive she is. It's like her work is invisible. L. describes the show like it's a comedy, but I've seen it— everyone has—and I would not have described it as funny. But when she asks if I've watched it, I shrug. I don't want to give her the satisfaction.

While I'm cleaning the floor near the stairwell, I remove the brick propping the door open, so it snaps shut. I'm not sure where they found another brick, if they're retrieving the ones I discard or if they have some endless supply of old bricks. I don't know what to do with it, so I put it on my cart to throw away, again.

"What's that for?" L. asks, gesturing at the brick, as though this isn't an ongoing issue I've already brought up.

I shake my head. "Maybe some late-night tryst," I say, and

she watches me stoop over and scrub a nearby black mark off the floor.

"Would you bring a date here?" she asks, even though I've seen the same guy bring her lunch a dozen times. "Besides, I would have seen someone coming or going," she adds, as though she's particularly good at her job.

"You fall asleep in our breakroom a couple of nights a week," I say.

"I'm just resting," she says.

"Well, why do you think it was propped open, then?" I ask.

"Someone's stealing something," she says. "Early in the night, before either of us is here."

"Why would they need to prop the stairwell doors open?" I ask. "Wouldn't it be easier to bring whatever they stole down on the elevator?"

"How should I know?" she asks. "Do I look like a criminal?" Then she heads off to do her highly rigorous and extremely necessary patrol of each floor's breakroom.

After she's gone, I sit at the CEO's desk and look at his wife. I try to imagine her voice, softer than mine but somehow more authoritative. I'd love to see what she looks like talking or moving in real life, but she remains stationary on his desk. Maybe in different lighting, she's less attractive, more approachable. In real life, she might not look that sad, either. It's just that she hates having her picture taken. I smile back at her, my own performatively sad smile.

I've tried a different word every night for a week, but his password isn't easy or obvious—not yet. Last night, I even looked up his wife's name in his HR file, which was scant and less detailed than anyone else's, but her name wasn't his password. Tonight, I try her name backward and think about trying a second word, but I can't bring myself to risk being locked out and clueing him in to my search. Instead, I scrounge through his desk. He must have his password jotted down somewhere, or there's got to be some clue that will lead me to it.

I normally don't do much with his desk, besides a very careful wipe down and surface polish, and even that feels risky. Early on, I was warned not to move anything, not to throw anything away. "His work is very important," the hiring manager who I've never seen again told me. She talked to me but never saw me, didn't seem to register my eyes on her or my general expression. If anything, her voice was near-reverent, as though I should be honored to be cleaning his desk. His work was important and by extension, so was she. I have no idea what her job was, outside of instructing me on mine. I would love to go through her desk and belongings. I really regret that I can't remember her name. She must have said it, but I was so inundated by other information that it didn't stick. I can remember a glass charm she had around her neck and the way it reflected light. I thought, *How dangerous if someone's driving or operating machinery. She could kill them.* But in an office, it must not matter so much.

Tonight, in spite of her instructions, I brazenly dig through the folders and papers stacked atop his desk, looking for something with asterisks or a note declaring, "PASSWORD." But so far all I can find are random names, simple arithmetic, phone numbers, and dollar amounts. Nothing feels significant enough to be a password, and there's certainly nothing he'd miss if I moved it to another spot or threw it out.

There are stacks of these scribblings, aged by coffee stains, water marks, and bits of food crusted into the paper. No one thinks about how dirty paperwork can be, but it's sickening. My first three or four months here, I was always getting sick, some cold, some bug. I touched so many things that other people had touched. You might think bathrooms or trash would be the most disgusting part of the job, but it's actually the thought of touching all these papers that have been so thoroughly touched before. People picking their nose and then carrying stacks of papers. People not washing their hands after they use the bathroom and clutching countless handouts. The whole place is like a preschool—germs smeared over everything, knocking you down until you build up an immunity. I try not to think of it now.

Most people's work areas are neater than the CEO's. The size and sparseness of his office might trick you into thinking he's clean. His oversized desk works to minimize it. The empty shelves in the room play into it. But it's still a disgusting amount of scraps and paper. I find little torn-off bits that he's rolled into a fine point and then used to clean under his nails. He leaves them thoughtlessly on his desk, the floor. Everyone else is probably worried about what other people think of them, but he's not. He's so much better than everyone that it would never occur to him that they had thoughts at all.

Maybe the huge window behind him makes his office seem clean, nice. Unlike the windows out on the rest of the floor, which face a different direction, this window goes from floor to ceiling. His office must get such good light. Maybe that's why he sits in front of the window, where he can't see the view. In order to look at him, people have to gaze out at the buildings and skyline too. And if they see both him and this idyllic view enough times, they start to equate the two.

His drawers are a disordered jumble: stray pens and half scraps of paper, pieces folded up as though to hide their contents, but it's only more scribbling, nothing anyone would need to hide.

I almost miss it, but in the back corner of the second drawer, I find a phone.

It's just a black flip phone, obviously cheap. Nothing a CEO would use. If it were nicer, I'd think it was an old phone, discarded or forgotten, but this could never have been his everyday phone. This is small and cheap on purpose.

I get up and walk out of his office to be sure I'm alone, and then I go back in and sit on the floor beside his desk. I open the phone. Unlike his computer, there's no password required. He never imagined anyone would find it. I look at his texts first, and there are dozens. It's amazing that this cheap phone has room for all these messages. None of them are from anyone with a saved name, but I see one person texting fairly frequently and open their most recent text. It's a picture of a topless woman in her bathroom with one arm curled around the top of her head. Her breasts point slightly outward, but the strange thing about the picture is her smile. It's a full-on, tooth-showing pageant-girl grin. It's well practiced, as though she's beaming at a panel of judges and not the CEO. She's not even thinking about her shirt, wherever it is.

They've made plans to meet up several times. She texts in full sentences with punctuation, but he's turned schoolboy on her and responds in fragments with the sort of textspeak I'd expect from a teen: "u xcited?" and "cant wait 2 c u."

Enough scrolling, and I see his dick. It seems short but thick and bent. Nothing anyone could pick out of a lineup but he's proud of it. He's sent her three pictures that look identical to me, all close-ups with no kind of context, nothing to give a real sense of scale, which is why I assume it's short. But he must think each picture is really different. He must think he's really showcasing his dick's enormous range.

I'm laughing, imagining the dick going to auditions, carrying around its headshots in a little briefcase and folder, when L. interrupts.

"Having a good time?" she asks.

I look up at her, then at the desk drawers, all open, and back down at the dicks in my hand. No way to hide now.

I hold up the phone, show her one dick, two dicks, three dicks.

"Holy shit," she says, and we go through the phone message by message, reading them aloud to one another. L. drops her voice low and reads his responses in a pseudo-sexy voice, all throaty and whispery. "Got my dick so hard," L. says, drawing out the word "hard" for an extra few beats. She runs a hand through her hair like she's trying to look sexy and then she bites her bottom lip. I cover my face and laugh so much it starts to hurt. "If he's as hard as he's telling all these women, I think he has a medical condition," she says, turning the phone to scroll through the messages in one quick swipe, showcasing how many there are. It's all the same: plans to meet up and exchanges of nudes. A disembodied dick from him, but from the women it's full bodies, faces, a few close-ups of ass or pussy, but always a smile. Like, here's my gaping asshole and I'm thrilled about it, thrilled about your dick, see my teeth?

"None of them look anything like his wife," L. says, glancing up at her picture on his desk.

It feels inappropriate to talk about his wife in the presence of these pictures and texts. It's like L. has found a way to disrobe her from afar or put her hands on her. It's nearly assault. L. is right that none of these women look like her. I wonder what she'd look like with these kinds of forced toothy smiles. I try to imagine her face warped in this way, but I can't do it. Maybe when they aren't posing for these pictures, they all look as sad as her. Maybe this is how he makes every woman feel. In his phone, all the women are glammed up and sparkling, thick and sexual, almost spilling out of the device. How do they even fit in there?

He should have hidden the phone better. Now that I've seen the contents, it's surprising that I didn't somehow sense it before, dripping and lascivious. The phone itself feels warm in my hand, and it's hard to imagine feeling safe having something like this in one of my drawers. Maybe it's a turn-on for him. He feels dangerous, knowing that if someone opened this drawer and pulled out his phone, there it'd all be. But more likely, he doesn't think it's possible that he could ever experience consequences for anything he does. He is, after all, the CEO, and that means something.

"Who are they?" L. asks.

"There's no app or anything on the phone," I say. "They're just women."

"He must meet them online," she says.

I nod up at his computer. "I don't know what his password is."

"Stupid," she says.

"They're all so young," I say.

"Aren't they always?" she says.

I think of the intern, probably the same age, sitting outside his office, in the nearest corner, desperate and eager for any kind of validation. She sits out there with her sex dust and diets, finding new ways to punish herself until she's finally good enough.

"Did you ever cheat?" I ask.

"Not exactly," she says. "But sometimes I'm well into a new relationship before the old one is all the way over. Just a little bleed-through. It can't be helped."

A circular way of saying yes.

After L. goes back downstairs, I shift the Sad Intern's desk a few inches away from the CEO's office. She's still pretty much in the corner. The move isn't noticeable, doesn't make a difference yet, but if I move her desk a tiny bit each night, eventually she won't be anywhere near him. She won't even notice it happening, but after a month or two, I will have pushed her to safety, halfway across the office, with so many people between them as buffers. A person can adjust to anything if you do it slowly enough. Like being boiled alive, but in a good way. Like being held.

I SEE M. and L. smiling and talking in the lobby again. They both see me this time, but neither of them smiles at me or motions me over, so I keep going, roll my cart onto the elevator and head upstairs. Let them have each other. I have an entire floor.

There's a new knitted coaster on Coaster Woman's desk. This one is a splotchy pattern of reds and oranges, no cat in sight. It's in better shape than the last one, so maybe she appreciates Yarn Guy's efforts more this time—or maybe she hasn't had her way with it yet. I think of her mindlessly picking at the other one while she's on the phone, frizzing the yarn, ruining the cat's little whiskers and all Yarn Guy's careful work. I have to put the coaster down, so I won't damage it myself, thinking of the entitled way she moves through the world. I sit at her desk and straighten her sticky notes, so they aren't pointing this way and that, a confusing overlap of angles that, if intentional, point to a kind of madness. Who could work in these conditions? And who is she that Yarn Guy should make her a second coaster? What does she have going for her?

I dig through her desk, and it's mostly work stuff: semi-transparent delivery forms, notepads full of names and numbers, and a few jumbo paper clips that she's almost completely straightened into little silver rods. She has a lot of nervous energy, maybe a kind of dissatisfaction with herself. No wonder she's damaging things around her. It's easy to take that anxiety and direct it outward. Certainly, Yarn Guy deserves better.

In the very back of her top drawer, I find a piece of hard candy, unwrapped and stuck to the inside of the drawer. I try to pry it off with one of the unbent paper clips and then with a pen, but it's really stuck, and I'm worried I'm going to noticeably damage the cheap plywood the drawer is made from. I give it one more try, and accidentally touch the candy with the side of my hand—it's still sticky. I wipe the side of my palm on her chair, rubbing away the stickiness, and then spray disinfectant on my hand and wipe that on her chair too. She probably doesn't wash her hands after she goes to the bathroom. She doesn't care what she touches or ruins. Here's a woman who doesn't care about anyone.

I go to the breakroom, open the fridge and stare for a few minutes, and then grab the mayo. It's in a squirt bottle, over half full. Even the condensation on the outside of the bottle feels gross, sickly. I know this moisture is only water, but I can't help imagining that the mayo has thinned and is somehow seeping out of the bottle. I sit at her desk and in the back of every drawer, I squirt a glop of mayonnaise.

The bottle makes a sickening noise, and even though no

one else is here and no one could possibly hear me, I feel embarrassed. I use an envelope to smear the mayo, so it won't
be noticeable. Then I wipe the envelope nearly clean on the
underside of her chair. If she does figure out where the smell
is coming from, she won't be able to pinpoint the time of the
crime, would never guess it was me. Maybe she won't even
notice it, so careless and self-absorbed. Other people will,
though, and they'll keep their distance.

The jars of gray water have become clearer, and I wonder
if that was the goal. Leave something alone for long enough
and it'll brighten and clean itself? I pick them both up and
shake them until the water is murky gray again. Even though
I know there are no cameras, no security system, L.'s gotten into my head, and I look around to be sure. I wouldn't
want to work somewhere people monitored me via video. If
I wanted that kind of oversight, I'd work at a larger place, or
during the day, but here, the night is coolly my own.

I glance out at the cityscape and instead of stars, I see buildings dotted with little squares of light, even at this hour. All
that reflective glass is lovely, crafting an artificial night sky
that dips low enough for everyone to see. I couldn't bear the
constraints of the daytime, people working side by side at
the same task, an unspoken marathon stretching out ahead of
them. They sprint and fall back, sprint and fall back, none of
them really going anywhere, racing around the same incon-
venient loop of their workday. No time to appreciate anything or even enjoy their work.

I make sure to leave another flaxseed cookie for the intern, to keep her regular. It's hard to get anything done if you
aren't. I also have a vanilla candle for Yarn Guy. Ultimately,

I decide to leave it in his bottom drawer, under all his yarn. A gift from the heart. I don't need any kind of reciprocation, but the coaster I took from Coaster Woman is still there, and I think he'd want me to have it. A little piece of him, a piece of the office, nestled in my apartment. So, I stick it on my cart, beneath some trash bags.

I've taken enough over the last few years to make my apartment into a mini office. I have a small corkboard and a matching dry-erase board hanging over my bed. I left the text on the dry-erase board, a few columns of numbers and a figure at the bottom circled in fading red marker. But I keep the corkboard fresh. I pin various handouts and notices to it that I find on the fourth floor. Company Growth! Exciting Opportunities! Mostly it's things from desks or the copier room. I have a few sticky notes from Yarn Guy's desk, reminders to himself about meetings and a phone number that turned out to be for a nearby restaurant. His handwriting is small, slanted and intimate. I also have a few pairs of scissors that I can't help but laugh at, a three-hole punch I've never used, some pens, and then a few more personal items: a brassy key with an antique look, a birthday card, and a mug with a three-dimensional face. The nose protrudes and it has eyelashes and even a little concave mouth. I also recently took Neck Massager's device, because who would she complain to about that, and it's really been helping me work the cricks out.

Then, in the drawer of my nightstand, I have a photograph of the woman who used to be my favorite. It's her and her mother, I think, outside somewhere. Their heads are inclined toward one another, and they smile softly. Imagine someone feeling that way about you. She was so earnest in everything she did. All of her notes were written in longhand. I liked her immediately, but when I first started working here, she was really struggling. I hated to see anybody really try at something and just miss the mark. She wasn't unmotivated—just ill-prepared for the job. Her desk was disorganized, and she missed deadlines, even meetings. I spent months helping her get on track, straightening things, jotting down small notes in her handwriting to prompt ideas she could take credit for. It took me hours to learn to mimic her handwriting, but now it's easy. I could still do it if I needed to. But in the end, I helped too much. She was promoted and then promoted again, fully out of our office. After she moved, I considered trying to move too, but in the end I stayed. I mourned her and learned to help people in smaller ways, to pace myself.

Now, I dole out punishments with rewards, circle my flock, keep them in line. It's important not just to help them get ahead but to endear them to the office, the floor as a whole, and to me. I've seen what can happen when people don't care about their jobs, when they just let themselves go. The whole thing crumbles. And maybe the intern has been markedly difficult, but I love a project.

I've been reading one of her self-help books. It claims to be about self-actualization, but seems to be mostly about standing up for yourself and not accepting the smallest and least of everything. She's folded the corners of a few pages that she clearly thinks are important. One of these pages includes a list of ways you might interject into a conversation: "That reminds me of _____," or "I agree that _____ is a great idea and we should also _____," and on and on. Templates for how to talk. Somehow, she's reached her twenties, and she doesn't yet know how to be a person in the world, how to make herself heard. She's marked another page that has a list of affirmations, very basic stuff: "You deserve happiness," and "You are worthy."

I made up a few of my own and tried them on her, not all in one night, but scattered across a few weeks, though I haven't really received the positive reaction I was looking for. "I really appreciate your focus on work," I told her. She looked down at herself and then at me, waiting for me to say something else, but I only smiled at her. I also tried keeping it very short. "You look smart," I said, but she looked confused by that too.

"What do you mean?" she asked.

"Oh, I've got to get something to remove this stain," I said, pointing a toe at the rug, which wasn't stained, as far as I could see. She always seems to shirk at any mention of my work.

She can't watch me do it. Any task too noticeable unsettles her and she leaves. As though rugs normally vacuum themselves and the floors are self-mopping. She'll tolerate dusting and sometimes my emptying the trash, but she can't easily speak to me while I do it. Her reactions are slow, pained. Even if what I'm doing is very quiet, she acts as though she can't hear over it. She can really only look me in the eye and talk if I sit at one of the desks. Maybe she's pretending I'm just another office worker. Maybe I remind her of one of her coworkers.

I sit at her desk after reading through her affirmations, try-ing to think of how to help her. In her top drawer, there's a new bottle of dry shampoo. I think she hasn't been showering regularly. She's in such a rush that she doesn't have time to get wet, doesn't even have time to primp at home, so instead does it in the bathroom on this floor, where anyone might walk in and see her. Such expensive clothing and products, and she can't even be bothered to properly bathe.

I go to the breakroom to see if I can find her a small treat, something to ignite her day, give her a little oomph, and I find a lamp that wasn't in here before. I could put it on my nightstand at home. There's overhead lighting at the office, so they don't really need a lamp. It's ridiculous to have one and they'll never miss it. Imagine asking someone what happened to the useless lamp in the well-lit room where people reheat their leftovers.

No one ever reports anything I take. If they notice and care at all, they suspect one another, and quietly harbor that resentment until it becomes large and well-defined enough to act on. In these cases, I think I've provided a nice outlet for entirely necessary expressions of dissatisfaction. Too often people swallow these kinds of things and never speak out.

Two men with adjacent desks near the elevator hate everything about one another: their appearances, voices, smells, how they move, the kind of work they produce. They've both talked about it in emails to other coworkers and in notes scribbled at their desks. But in emails to one another, they're very cheery. You'd think they were brothers, or at least good friends: Cheery #1 and Cheery #2. I tried messing with them to get them to blow up and have it out. I took every pen from Cheery #1's desk and moved them to Cheery #2's. I left Cheery #2's trash, with his name on it, balled up in Cheery #1's chair. But they only got aggressively more cheerful. It made me uncomfortable, so eventually I gave up on them. Not everyone can be saved. I don't even like to clean their desks anymore.

Back on the intern's desk, I find a folder full of handwritten notes. There are dates, menu items, themes, and venue ideas, all listed out and then drawn into a chart. It's her plans for the gala. There's also a printed email from the CEO. "You'll have to take care of sponsors, fundraising. Let me know what you come up with and I'll get you the information to hold the funds. If you could bring in a few new accounts, that wouldn't hurt." Then he's signed off as "C.," which is both his initial and his title, CEO. Did she think printing this email, hardly an enthusiastic endorsement, would lend a sense of credibility to both her and the gala?

There are no financial notes in the folder, so I wonder if she's even thought about that side of things. Maybe she's disappointed to have to raise the money, rather than simply being given a budget. But I tried to warn her. There's already a party every year. I can hear the higher-ups saying, "How many parties do these people need?" Then they'd discuss the intern. "Maybe she's not a good fit here. Probably best to start phasing her out. What's an intern really do anyway? Whose idea was it to hire an intern?" Everyone will look at one another. If it was one of their ideas, they'll never admit it. They'll never say anything to set themselves apart from one another. It's best to be the same all the time. *But in an innovative way,* they each think, smiling to themselves about how valuable they are. How special.

But maybe if she comes up with the money herself, turns the whole event into a profitable affair, they'll see how useful she can be. She could bring in more than a couple of new accounts—really throw herself into the work. I give her desk extra attention tonight and let her keep all her supplements. She's going to need the kind of metaphorical safety blanket they provide if her job is truly in danger. She's going to need me too.

I think about her gala all the way down to the lobby, wondering if she'll hold it in the office or somewhere nearby. Maybe it'll go on late enough that I'll see everyone, all dressed up, drunk and easy to talk to. With my collared black shirt, I'll blend right in, camouflaged among their formality. It'll be nice to see their faces, hear their voices.

The next night, I'm still thinking about it when I let M. into the lobby and generously ask them how their book is going.

They manage to blush while maintaining eye contact. "Still working on it," they say. "I like having something to focus on, something I'm doing all on my own."

They must not get that from work. I'm fortunate that what I care about aligns with what I'm doing. Not everyone can be so lucky, I know.

THE INTERN SITS in a conference room with documents spread so far across the table that she'd have to get up and take a few steps in order to see them all. It doesn't seem like a very efficient system. She's slouched over her work, one hand on the side of her head, propping herself up. Her expression is grave, concentrated. She obviously thinks her work is of the utmost importance. There are three different beverages next to her—tea, coffee, and an almost-empty aloe juice. Condensation rings bloom out far enough to dampen some of her work, and I wonder if she's even noticed the damage.

She must have heard me approach or seen me in her peripheral vision, but she doesn't acknowledge me. Finally, I clear my throat. "What are you working on?" I ask.

She glances up and then back down at the table. "Gala," she says.

"Did you get sponsors?" I ask. "Or some new accounts?"

She looks up at me, tilting her head, and I realize we haven't talked about any of that. I only read it in her notes.

"Is that how it works?" I rush ahead. "That's normally how it works," I add, trying to sound confident.

She shakes her head at me, apparently convinced. "I'm just working on plans. I figured, if the party's enticing enough, people will want to work on it with me. If enough people care about it, then they'll have to fund it."

No one's going to want to work on a project that doesn't advance them career-wise. No one is going to go home and brag about how they helped plan a pointless gala.

"If you get a new client or two, that'd probably make you look appealing," I say, sitting down at the other end of the long table. "People want to work with someone who's already successful."

She doesn't say anything, but she stares at an empty space on the table, probably thinking about how she would even do that.

To give her some time to think things through, I get up and empty the conference room trash can.

"Do you want me to take any of these?" I ask, gesturing at her mélange of beverages.

She just shakes her head, so I leave the room to throw out the trash, and return with a new liner for the trash can. While I'm fitting it in and knotting the side so it won't sag, I study her. This manicure is new, but her shirt looks wrinkled from more than one day of wear. It's clearly nice—the fit of it, the material, even the buttons are beautiful. But she wears it cheaply. I think of my outfit by comparison. I'm in a black shirt and khaki pants, but they're clean and starched. There's some fade to the material and maybe a few places where the fabric is beginning to pill, but this is only because I'm so fastidious about running them through the wash.

"Normally, junior people work with a senior person to make connections," she says. "I should be working with existing clients, getting experience."

"Are you not?" I ask.

"Not really," she says. "People act like I'm trying to take something from them. It's just not the culture here."

"I keep seeing flyers about mixers," I say.

"I have so much to do," she says. "I can't leave right after work and meet people for drinks. You can't imagine how bad that would look. No, I have to stay and work. If I go out and drink, it looks like I have loads of free time, nothing to do."

I nod. Of course, if she looks too available, they'll think she doesn't do anything. And if they think she's not doing anything, why would anyone want to be paired with her?

"What if you looked up old accounts?" I say. "People who used to work with us last year or five years ago, and now don't. See if you can reignite something?"

She starts stacking her papers, something she does whenever she wants to signal she's done talking to me.

"I could help you," I say.

"You can take these cups," she says, though she hasn't taken a sip from any of them since I got here, and certainly not since she refused my earlier offer to take them away.

I smile graciously, but leave her—and her cups. I'll get them after she goes home. She ought to appreciate that I'm busy and giving my time to her out of a sense of generosity. I don't need her. She needs me. I make myself extremely busy while she leaves for the night, and neither of us says good-bye to the other.

L. comes in later while I'm rearranging the things on my cart. "What happened to people working on the weekends?" I ask.

"I heard there's some pushback about it," she says, sitting down. "People want to have their weekends to themselves. Spend time with their families."

"Lots of people work on weekends," I say. I had looked forward to coming in more, having extra time to really dive into things.

L. trails behind me while I clean the fourth floor, telling me about her upcoming weekend trip. I let her tire herself out going through all the details, all the possibilities. I'm crouching under a desk, pretending to work at a stain on a rug, when she finally decides to retreat downstairs.

Once I hear the elevator doors close, I feel more at ease, and I go to the CEO's office. He has a new plant in the corner by his desk, a little two-armed cactus that comes up to my waist. It's better than the dead stalks across the room. Certainly prettier. I wonder if it was a gift. But I leave it be and go through his phone like I do every night. It's always in his desk. I worried at first that he might take it with him, but he never does.

There are new exchanges every couple of days: dicks or plans to meet up or compliments both to and from him. He uses the same dick pictures again and again, and I wonder how old they are. Does his dick even look like that anymore? But the women tell him they like his dick, they like spending time with him. He's all, "babygirl" this and "babygirl" that. I hadn't thought he was the kind of man who'd say "babygirl," but this is one of those unknowable things. Unless you go through someone's texts, you can't really know how they talk to the people they're fucking.

I type "babygirl" into his computer and it finally unlocks. It feels dreamlike, almost too easy. It wasn't even a real person's name. It wasn't something specific about one of the women. Instead, it's the nickname he uses for all of them, more about him than them. It's a tic, a mannerism. No one has ever called me this. When I was younger, a man I was seeing called me "dear," and I ended things shortly after. It felt infantilizing. I was no one's child, not even my own mother's, really. But no one calls me anything now. They haven't for years. I don't even get catcalled anymore. If a man on the street yells at me, he's asking for money, which I take as a compliment. I look like I might have some money. It could be worse.

I think of going back downstairs to get L., but decide this first perusal of the CEO's computer will be just for me, something I've earned through ingenuity and hard work. L. would probably ruin it. But it's frustrating, because all I can find is general work stuff. Why would anyone be so secretive about all this? It's financial statements and emails about meetings and boring updates on projects. I'm not even sure what some of it says. I check his browsing history, but he's been very tidy, probably doing anything scandalous in an incognito browser. I look through his spam and trash, but there's nothing. I open folder after folder, and my eyes start to glaze over.

I probably wouldn't even recognize a red flag if I saw one. I don't understand what his job is, what any of this is. What does a CEO do? What do the letters even stand for? I click and scroll and click and scroll, and I'm about to give up when I find a very old email confirmation of another account set up a few years ago. Bingo.

I wipe my history, so he won't see all my searching, and then I go incognito too. I'm creeping along behind him, and I'm

almost nervous that he might turn around and catch me. This
new email is already logged in and everything, no password or
verification needed. He must feel very secure behind his bril-
liant password, "babygirl." No need for further protections. If
you know this one thing about him, you know everything.
And it's all here: verifications for hookup sites, email notifica-
tions of messages, and a few emails directly from women he's
seeing. I'm overwhelmed by it, unsure what to do with it all.

I visit three dating sites I see linked: "Naughty Young
Women," "One Night Stan" and "K1nk," but all of them require passwords and aren't logged in. He's been more careful
here, at least. I try "babygirl" for each of them, but it doesn't
work. I feel frustrated to have made all this progress only to
hit more walls.

I click back to his secondary email account and open the
most recent one that appears to be from a real person and
not a bot. "Can't stop thinking about you," it begins, and
then it's more of the same, like one long text typed out as an
email, mostly descriptions of her body. There's nothing that
would set her apart—her body could be any body. He must
see all these women this way, and then probably the people
who work here too. One person is the same as another. They
can be replaced or shuffled around. He probably thinks Yarn
Guy, Mr. Buff, Porn Guy, and Cheery #2 are all the same
guy. They might as well be from a gray floor. Maybe all the
floors are the same to him. There's him, in this little office
with a view, and then there's everyone else who works here.

He hasn't responded to her email, and I wonder if he texted
her instead. Is there something about this woman throwing
herself at him that isn't good enough? Or is this all he wants

from her: these descriptions of her body and how eager she is? He reads it and goes home to his quietly sad wife. Why are women made to feel like they need to be good enough, like all the men in their lives are arbiters of what's right and best for them? And then his own beautiful wife wasn't enough for him?

But I know well enough that these kinds of indiscretions are a sign of worse to come. I've seen it before. He'll be messy and then messier. People will start to care less about their work. Hours will be cut short. Balls will be dropped. Everyone will dread coming to work. They'll be unpleasant to one another. They'll call in sick, look for new jobs, really phone it in. Eventually, they'll run out of people to criticize, and someone will show up to the night shift to examine my work, complain about how I do it, criticize *me* personally. You have to put a stop to something like this before it gains traction. You have to excise the tumor.

I'd like to figure out how to read financial statements. Right now, it's a mass of numbers, but give me time. I'm quick and attentive and I certainly have the access. Already, I understand all the people who work here, and that has to count for something. I just need a foothold, a little help.

I straighten his office and then finish cleaning, breezing right through desks I normally spend more time at. Intern's fine. Mr. Buff is fine. Yarn Guy, fine. They're all fine, fine, fine. Then I do the gray floors, all very quickly, to make up for the time I spent in the CEO's office. No one will complain. No one wants to admit to being dirty or producing garbage. They probably don't even notice when I take it away. Things would have to be pretty bad for most people to complain because they generally expect to be at least a little miserable at work.

I'm almost done when L. comes looking for me.

"I heard downsizing will start soon," she says. Something about her tone makes me feel defensive, like she's saying I'm responsible for the downsizing. Like it's my idea.

"You're always hearing something," I say.

"I'm always listening," she says.

There's no one she could have talked to since I last saw her. Is she texting with someone from the day shift? All night she's on her phone, watching videos and playing some game with colorful dots. Or maybe there's some daytime straggler I don't know about? Or has she gotten friendly with someone in the building next door?

"Everyone seems pretty busy," I say. "Who could they even let go?"

She shrugs and nods her head toward the rest of the floor, but if anyone's in danger of being let go, it's her. She has one EarPod in so she's only half-listening to me and she scuffs the floor I've already cleaned. There's no reason to point it out. She won't care, won't see the marks, will probably claim I did it myself. Imagine creating extra work for myself so I can complain about her hideous but apparently unimpeachable shoes.

I empty the last of the trash and almost tell her that I finally got into the CEO's computer, so I can talk to someone about it, but what would I say? I didn't find anything new. Somehow, she'd twist everything, make it all worse. L. doesn't know any more than I do, but she's so confident about all her nothing.

THE INTERN'S BEEN here late every night this week. She's fully thrown herself into finding money for her gala, though when I ask her about it, all she'll say is, "It's really happening." I look through her notes and emails later, and I can see it is happening, just very slowly. The money comes in dribs and drabs, with a few larger donations that I suspect come from friends who feel sorry for her. But it's enough to keep her working and keep her mood up.

In her presence, I've had to slow my research on the CEO's computer to almost a standstill. It's hard to juggle how glad I am to see her with how annoyed I am to not make any progress. I think about sitting down at his desk while she's here and going at it, because maybe she wouldn't even notice, but I'm not ready to risk her seeing me do it. In quiet moments, I've been reading about the financial system we use, but compared to what I normally do, it's dull work. So I hover around her, asking questions about the company and how things work, trying to ground myself enough that his computer's contents will make more sense. If she can learn it, so can I.

All week, I've been bringing her baked goods: oatmeal cookies one night and lemon squares the next. It's tiring to spend what should be my leisure hours at the grocery store and then baking in my small, stuffy apartment, but I think these gestures have been paying off. And my lemon squares are pretty good. So much lemon flavor from only one lemon. The trick is to use the zest. She eats three of those and asks for the recipe. She tells me how her mother hates any dessert with citrus, but it's actually her favorite thing. I listen carefully to all her preferences because I know what it's like not to be heard.

"Have you had yuzu mochi?" she asks, and when I say no, she writes down the name of a shop that makes it. I think she's starting to see me as a colleague and friend. Maybe I won't even have to understand all the files and documents. I'll be able to sit her down at his desk and let her rip. We'll be a team. I'll show her all the dicks in his phone. That's the kind of thing women bond over.

But tonight, she's extra frazzled, papers spread across her desk and on the floor in sloppy piles. I wonder why she's not in the conference room. Maybe she's feeling a little less self-important tonight.

"Gala going okay?" I ask, and she nods without looking at me.

I brought her homemade toffee in a plastic bag on my cart, but I don't want to give it to her while she's being dismissive. I won't reward that kind of energy. Instead, I empty all the trash cans and wipe down the desks around her. She's moved her desk back toward the CEO's office, and I haven't been able to correct it because she's always here. In fact, I only made about a foot of progress before she noticed and pushed it back. I feel even more worried that she's intentionally trying to be close to him.

"When will you throw it?" I ask. "While it's still warm?"

"He said I have to nail everything down in order to access the funds," she says.

"A walkathon would be a great way to raise money," I suggest.

"This isn't a charity event," she says.

"I think—" I start to say.

"I really need to finish this," she says, looking at her computer.

I rearrange my cart so the toffee isn't visible. I crush a piece of it in my fist, through the plastic, but it's hard to break this way. It's such sturdy stuff. I clean the desks around her, looping farther and farther away, while she clicks and reads and types and then shuffles through the file on her desk. I leave her and do the bathrooms, humming along to the sound the fluorescent lights make. When I first started working here, the sound was all-encompassing—I thought about it all the time—but I got used to it without even noticing. One day, I just realized it didn't grate at me anymore. In fact, the lights in my apartment make a different sound, an almost indiscernible squeak, and when I'm home, I miss the smooth, solid sound the lights in the office make.

While I clean the sinks, I think of the intern. It would have been better if she was willing to talk through the fundraising with me. She's the kind of person who really thrives as a member of a team. She needs energy and input from someone else. She needs to bounce ideas off other people, revise, and then go at it again. But they've made her feel like it's some shortcoming of hers if she can't do everything by herself. I'm not sure what to say to correct this bad training. I hope she's still new enough that she can unlearn it. And I hope she appreciates the space I'm giving her. I need to think of a way to offer help that won't put her further on the defensive. If she keeps going this way, so sensitive and stressed, she won't make it here.

When I come out of the bathroom, her desk is empty, though all the lights are still on. I look around to be sure, checking the breakroom and copier room, but she's gone for the night, so I sit down at her desk with her toffee. I guess she was tired, it was late, and she didn't want to bother me. I pop a shard of toffee into my mouth—I really nailed this bitch. It was my third try. The first was the wrong color and the second never solidified. You had to chew it and chew it and it never got any easier. But after how distant the intern seemed, I decide not to leave her the toffee.

Instead, I toss it onto Scissors Guy's desk, right in front of his keyboard. Maybe it'll make him nicer to everyone around him. Or he'll think someone's messing with him. He always believes himself the brunt of practical jokes—or worse, people are stealing his scissors just to rile him up. Why should this be any different? Why would anyone be kind to him now?

I page through recent projects the intern's taken notes for—that's mostly what she does, takes notes for other people's work. These are the kinds of clients she should be finding. This is where her energy should be. I make a list of all the clients, their needs, what sort of businesses they run. Then, after a few quick Google searches, I find similar clients who don't work with our company. This would have been easy for her to do—she probably could have made a more thorough list. But I've had to do it myself because she was unwilling to listen, unable to heed my helpful advice. I compile everyone's contact information, title the document "potential clients," print it, and then leave it on her desk.

Pleased with my work, I survey the office and wonder again what's in the gray water jars. Is it something vaguely noxious or harmful? Would it hurt L.'s little plant any faster? I don't know if she's watering it enough to kill it. Her lack of care is the only thing keeping it alive.

I could take one down, dump it out onto her plant, and bring it back up at the end of the night. I like the thought of mixing the fourth floor with my breakroom this way. But I guess I'm not paying attention to what I'm doing, because I knock the other jar over and it spills across the desk, dribbling onto the floor. I decide to leave it. It says "Do Not Touch," after all, and I still don't know what it is. I'm not going to clean up some unidentified murky liquid. That's beyond the scope. Besides, there's no way for anyone to know it was me.

On my way to the elevator, I stop at Coaster Woman's desk to see if it smells. I've been avoiding really cleaning it, just emptying her trash, and doing a quick swipe across her desk, using as little cleaning spray as possible. It's not awful, but I can detect a hint of mayo, a lingering sour smell, and I wonder if she's even noticed.

I almost think I can smell the mayo in the elevator, and I'm worried that the odor has permeated my hair or clothing, so I do what I usually do: spritz my shoes and the bottoms of my khakis with a little cleaning solution. The strong smell overpowers everything else, and no one was ever hurt by a little soap and enzyme.

When I let M. into the lobby, they immediately ask, "Where's L.?" and I want to ask, "For what?" but I'm very composed about it.

"You can wait right here for her," I say, nodding at the stool and turning to leave.

"No," they say, shaking their head emphatically. "It's just nice to see you more often. That's what I'm saying."

They hadn't said that. I hate this sort of roundabout puzzle talk where people don't say what they mean, and you have to guess at it. You have to use your imagination. But M.'s looking at me so earnestly and with so much eye contact that it's hard to be irritated.

"It's just—" I shrug and gesture at the lobby. "L., you know?"

M. laughs. "There's a guy like that in my office," they say. "Vanishes for a half hour at a time and then pops back up. I think no one's asked where he's going because they don't want to hear it, you know?"

I nod. It could be gross or personal or just uncomfortable. I don't blame them.

"But also," M. says, "it's nice to imagine it's something weird or interesting. He's found a secret room in the building or something."

"L.'s secret room is probably our breakroom," I say. "She's in there taking a nap or eating someone else's food."

We both laugh and stand there for a few seconds.

"Thanks for letting me in," M. says. "For looking out for me."

My phone buzzes and I ignore it. It's almost like *whoever's* calling is intruding on my time at work on purpose. No one ever takes my work seriously. I'm only cleaning an empty building, after all. Nothing I'm doing could be pressing. Nothing could have a real sense of urgency. I know my mother feels that way. My job isn't a real thing to her. It doesn't take up any space. But more likely it's A. calling. She does this, even though I never answer anymore. She at least knows me well enough to know I'm awake at night. She'd never call me during the day, when I was sleeping. But this isn't enough to make answering a call from her feel worth it.

"I wouldn't want to stand outside," I say, letting my voice warm.

M. touches my arm, briefly, and even after their fingers are gone, I feel a bit of warm shock travel along my skin.

They turn and we both look out the window. It should be cold outside, but it hasn't been that bad. A little brisk in the coldest part of the night, but otherwise fairly bearable. But there's something unsettling about standing outside in the dark alone. You're not part of anything. And it must be frustrating to have all this work ahead of you, and to have to stand and wait. It only makes their shift longer, slower. I've always resented having my work dependent on someone else's whim. I wouldn't tolerate that kind of work environment, not again, and never here, in what I've carefully carved out as my own domain.

But M. never seems irritated. Maybe they think it's part of their job. They've calculated it into what they have to do. Sort of how I clean the gray floors, but they don't really count. Probably everyone's work is like this. There's their job, and then the part of it that they really care about. The part that consumes them. Of course, I don't do a bad job on the gray floors. I'm just not doing anything more than cleaning there. I don't really know them.

After they leave, I wonder if this is the part of M.'s job that they care about. Or maybe there are people all along this street, in every building, that they know and talk to. Maybe that's just the kind of person M. is.

OUR BUILDING IS gray-colored in the night air. You'd walk right by it without giving it a second glance. It looks like all the other buildings on the street—maybe smaller, but not shockingly so. In the daytime, you might think it looks slightly dingier than the other buildings, or older, but at night you'd never notice. You'd look through the windows and see L. sitting on her stool, sometimes in her security uniform, and you'd have an extended feeling of safety.

You shouldn't feel that way, of course.

Last year, L. watched someone get mugged and didn't do anything about it. She told me she'd felt safe, locked inside our building, and she wasn't going to give that up. It wasn't a violent mugging, she said. She couldn't tell if the mugger had any kind of weapon, but the lady being mugged only yelled twice before the mugger presumably told her to be quiet. There was no hitting, no evident assault. The lady just handed over her bag and what looked like a necklace. The mugger lightly jogged away, not really at a run, just very casual and loose-footed. The lady who was mugged turned and looked at L., but L. got up and went to the breakroom. I guess you can't make someone care about other people.

L.'s made herself scarce lately—she doesn't follow me around whenever the intern is in the office. I think she's worried about someone else seeing her slack off. She stays on her stool or aimlessly patrols, carrying her Maglite, which she must think lends her an air of authority or importance. Hopefully she kills the new roaches I saw in the bathroom last week. I didn't report them, because I'm sure someone would look at the bathroom in the middle of the day, before I've had a chance to clean it, and blame me. "If the bathroom was cleaner, this wouldn't be a problem," they'd say.

If the people who worked here were cleaner, it wouldn't be a problem, either. They could all use a refresher on sanitation and basic hygiene. Or if the building would pay for decent and consistent pest control, we'd be all good. I don't think there's anything in the current guy's chemicals. Maybe just sugar water. Last year, the guy said he wasn't even going to spray. "I'm just going to leave a few sticky traps," he said. And then he never came back to check them. So yeah, we have roaches, but not many of them make it up to the top floor.

I roll my cart onto the elevator, hit the button for the fourth floor, and hum to myself. No roaches and no L. yet, either.

As usual, I can tell the intern's here before I see her. She likes to work in a well-lit room. That hasn't changed. But she looks even more frazzled tonight, hunched over her computer, goblin-style. Her hair is slicked back and oily. I'm not sure she's even hitting the dry shampoo. Her face is still made up, though. Maybe she believes this masks it. Like she believes her perfume covers her sweat.

"How's your night?" I ask, running the dry mop along the floor, keeping my voice light and easy.

She grunts without looking at me.

I bend over to pick up a stray pen and then try again. It's only a dry mop, after all. It's not like it's loud or disgusting. "How's the gala?" I ask.

She finally looks at me. "It's hard," she says.

I think again of the walkathon, but just nod.

"I think I have a new account, though," she adds.

"Oh?" I say, keeping my face neutral, but relaxing my grip on the mop a little.

"I just had to put my head down and make some calls," she says, sitting up a little straighter. "I've always had a good work ethic. I'm used to juggling a lot at once."

The mop clatters to the floor. She looks a bit startled, but I scoop it up and give it a little spin. People drop things. No big deal. It's fine.

"Who'd you call?" I ask.

"I just did some client research," she says. She waves her hands like it's too boring to even discuss. "But I think I'm on a good track there. I just need to get everyone on board with this gala. They should all care about it anyway. It'll boost morale, promote company engagement, increase overall productivity. Everyone here should want to contribute."

"Contribute how?" I ask. "Are you asking the people who work here to donate actual money?" If she was, she hasn't asked me.

"In a soft way," she says. "But mostly it's time or connections I'm looking for. And, of course, I was going to branch out."

I push the mop right up against the baseboard to get the line of dirt that's accumulated there.

"How much have you raised?" I ask.

"Not enough to get started," she says. "It's going to take so much longer than I thought."

"You have to be patient," I say.

She shakes her head. "It's frustrating to pour all of my energy into this one thing that won't budge. At some point, it's like, why bother? I think I'm going to start working on my résumé."

"Don't do that," I say, nearly dropping the mop again, but juggling it into my other hand. "You can do this."

She looks at me.

"You can," I say. "And then you'll be important. People will know who you are. You should talk to someone else about it, someone who can help you figure it all out."

"I've been talking directly to the CEO," she says. "I don't know who could be better than that."

I look around, trying to think of who to point her to. Yarn Guy? Mr. Buff? One of the Cheery Guys?

"It's late," she says. She gathers her things and smiles at me, kind of sadly, then heads for the elevator.

After she's gone, I look over her desk and find that, for once, she's left her notepad. The last few pages are clearly notes for her résumé, qualities she feels she has, jobs she's done, years in school. I wonder what makes her think she's organized or a people person. I've seen her desk. I've talked to her. But I suppose for most people, these sorts of job documents function more as speculative fiction.

I was fairly straightforward in my application to work here—because I had cleaned another building, I knew I could clean this one. I didn't mention why I left that job, how things had crumbled around me. That didn't seem important to this job. And I was a different person here. I understood that my real work would go beyond the sort of surface-level cleaning the position advertised. I knew keeping a company afloat was a team-wide effort. If you left it to the people who *seemed* to be in charge, things could easily become muddled. Those people see workers as interchangeable, like parts of a machine that need to be swapped out every so often. But if you do that enough, the whole thing becomes compromised, and eventually the machine breaks down. Years of raising and caring for myself had put me in the position to do it for others. It's the work I was truly meant for—I hadn't understood that when I was younger.

It is, of course, difficult to distill what you're capable of into the space allotted on an application. No matter what you say, you've left something out. Or maybe you've overdone it—where's your sense of modesty?

The intern has two jobs listed right now: this one and some sort of freelancing gig. No wonder she's tired. No wonder she needs so much help. I rip these pages from her notes, ball them up, and put them into my pocket, where they bulge uncomfortably. She doesn't need them, shouldn't be looking for a way out, but I don't want to throw them away here and risk forgetting to empty the trash. How awkward if she were to see them there, or how terrible if someone else did?

I slide open her top drawer and see she has laxatives again, but one of my flaxseed cookies is still there, uneaten. She literally cannot get her shit together. Maybe granola will be more palatable than the cookie, even though I think the cookies are pretty good. You'd never know they were good for you, and I've never been so regular. I decide to keep her notepad because I'm worried that she'll see the missing pages ripped out and connect them to me. A missing notepad won't register, though. If she notices at all, she'll just replace it. There was nothing that important inside.

Down in our breakroom, L. and I talk over a bag of cookies I intended to leave at Yarn Guy's desk. Cookies seemed substantial enough that he wouldn't just assume Coaster Woman had left them. He'd ask and she'd have to decline, and then he'd see that he has options. He's desirable. He'd think of her more critically, because for a few moments he believed she did something nice for him, and then the reversal of that action will feel like such an unkindness. I don't know why I didn't think of this sooner.

But after talking to the intern and poring through her notepad, I wanted the cookies, needed the sugar boost. It's easy to find yourself dragged down by another person's attitude. You have to put your own oxygen mask on first, before you can adequately consider theirs—and whether they deserve it at all.

So, L. and I eat the cookies, even though she doesn't appreciate that they're homemade with sunflower butter and organic everything. She doesn't even look at them—just mindlessly puts them in her mouth and hulk-swallows after chewing with her mouth open. She's drinking orange juice with them, and my throat starts to close up imagining the flavor combo. Add a dollop of toothpaste and her feast would be complete.

While we eat, I talk to her about the gala and the intern's job search.

"She's just an intern," L. says. "How much can she be making? If she's having a hard time, she's probably better off leaving anyway."

I roll my eyes. L. has no work ethic, no drive. She's not as invested as I am, doesn't care about the company or the people who work here.

But there has to be a way to make the intern's gala more exciting, the kind of event that other people want to get behind. She needs to talk to someone besides the CEO about it. A partner, a team, a committee. If it's big enough, maybe it'll be the kind of thing that can right a sinking ship.

"And it's weird that she can't start spending," I say. "Book a venue, entertainment, think about food. We've already raised some of the money. Why not get things underway, build some momentum?"

L. nods, but she's looking at her phone, staring at the screen with her mouth open. I sigh and wipe crumbs off the front of my shirt. After I put the cookies in my bag, L. goes to sit on her stool some more. She's got to book some important time hunching and staring into the distance.

I lay my head on the table to watch the plant die. It isn't doing anything, but I know it's dying, and I like to watch it. When I roll my cart back to the lobby, L.'s vanished on one of her endless breakroom scavenges, probably taking a break on every floor, settling into these spaces that don't belong to her. Her breaks stretch across such huge swaths of time that

they often overlap. She could take almost the entire night off
and it'd be pretty much the same as her being here.

When I go up to the fourth floor, I'm half expecting to find
her there, maybe in the breakroom, lying on the sofa, but the
floor is empty. I take a piece of mail from Cheery #1's desk
and leave it on the intern's. She'll need to return it to him, and
maybe they'll start talking, find things they have in common.
They could both use a friend. He could use the distraction.

While I empty trash cans, I also collect all the scissors. It's
important to create moments of levity for yourself. Scissors
Guy is fun to rile up, and I enjoy watching this kind of thing
play out. I take every pair I can find. I look in desks and pen-
holders and go slowly through the copier room to make sure
I've found them all. Then I put them in the breakroom cup-
board, next to the cleaning supplies that no one ever touches.
The expectation is that during the day, people will clean up
after themselves: spill something and wipe it up, scrub out the
microwave, throw away their own rotting food. But no one
ever does any of this, so the cleaning supplies under the sink
are untouched. It's a great place to keep the scissors. If anyone
decides to clean up, they'll be rewarded. And Scissors Guy will
finally have proof that there's some kind of scissors bandit running around the office. I wonder if people will think he did it,
that he finally lost it, and took all the scissors home with him.
If I thought I could get away with it, I'd break into his apartment and leave them there. Imagine, he pulls back his covers
and there are thirty-two pairs of scissors in his bed. Perfection.

When I go back to the lobby, I find M. standing outside,
patiently waiting for L. to do her job, so I let them in.

"I think you were right," I tell them. "The deliveries are getting smaller. We're doing less."

M. doesn't have an I-told-you-so face and just tilts the dolly, setting it down level, and waits for me to say more.

"I'm worried some of the employees might be thinking of leaving," I say, though I'm only thinking of the intern. "Their work isn't being appreciated. You can only do so much without a little positive affirmation."

M. nods. "What will you do?" they ask, but not like, what would YOU do, you insignificant little peon. Instead, it just sounds like they want to hear my plan, like they believe I have one and can execute it and make a difference. It's nice to be taken seriously. We stand in the lobby talking for a long time, and I don't even mind when M. tells me that they got a new rat, and how they're keeping it separate but in a wire cage that the other rats can sniff, so they'll get used to him. "I don't want the other rats to attack him," M. says. "I want them to be friends."

And it's nice, someone caring about the happiness and friendships of others. You don't find a lot of people who go all-in for facilitating that kind of thing, because it's a lot of work to watch over someone.

A WEEK LATER, there are some empty desks, including Mr. Buff's and Scissors Guy's. It's unsettling to see their things gone, drawers emptied, surfaces cleared of paperwork. There's still a desktop computer on Mr. Buff's desk but not on Scissors Guy's. Maybe it's been relocated elsewhere, but I can imagine him lugging it home. If someone was going to steal an entire computer, it'd be him. He got so used to looking at it and using it that he truly thought it was his. After putting in all that time, he felt entitled to it.

I wonder if he blew up once he found all the scissors gone and his public tantrum got him fired. And how did Mr. Buff come into play? Did they fight? Mr. Buff could take him, no problem. It'd be nothing. Maybe he seriously injured Scissors Guy and it's circuitously my fault that he's gone. But then there are other empty desks strung throughout the room, so it's probably unrelated.

A familiar uneasiness creeps over me—like I'm coming down with a cold. That pre-sick weakness, the soreness in my muscles and back, the beginning tickle of a cough. But instead of in my body, I feel these things in the office, in the literal and concrete space of the building. There's an invisible wheezing.

Toilet Woman is gone too, but both Yarn Guy and Coaster Woman are still here. The intern is too. Not physically, in this moment, like she sometimes is, but her desk is still clearly in use. She's the bottom rung of the ladder, pay-wise, so cutting her wouldn't make much sense. If anything, they can saddle her with more labor to make up for their losses. But I feel bad for pushing Mr. Buff on her, because now what? She's developed these feelings for him, and he's gone forever? She's become used to seeing him, used to thinking about him and all the things they have in common, and now all she's got is this empty space where he used to sit, a reminder of him.

I tilt her desk to angle her line of vision away from Mr. Buff's empty seat, but I know it won't be enough. Cheery #1 is all the way across the room, and there's no good vantage point of his desk. She'll enter another wilting season, and I'll have to find ways to perk her up. Maybe she can try a dating app. The CEO might have had the right idea there if he hadn't gone to such excess. A few dates, a few bits of positive affirmation. But he wants it all. Wasn't happy to have a wife and a dog and be the head of the company. He had to go and ruin things. Men like him always do.

And now it's not just his personal life, but the company too. What will all those missing people do? Find new jobs? Move back home to live with their families? He's certainly not thinking about them.

It's strange to see Porn Guy and both Cheery #1 and #2 are still here. Why keep them but get rid of someone valuable, like Mr. Buff, or harmless, like Toilet Woman?

On one of the conference room doors, I see a flyer for "Snack Hour Wednesdays," and I feel sick. Will everyone still happily gather to eat cream cakes and talk about their weeks? The cutesy font is in such bad taste amid our losses. The CEO ought to be the one cut. He ought to be the one who's gone.

I pace the room, nervous for Yarn Guy. These things sometimes happen in rounds, and he could be next. I sit at his desk, but it all looks like business as usual. His bottom drawer is still stocked with yarn and crafts. There's not much progress on his latest hunter green throw, but maybe he's been extra busy. It doesn't mean anything. Now that Mr. Buff is gone, I need another ally for the intern, someone she can talk to, a daytime friend, and if Cheery #1 doesn't work, I wonder if Yarn Guy would.

She's still working on her résumé and looking at jobs online. She doesn't try to hide it. The proof is right there on her computer and in her browser history. I tried to tell her that those are all fake jobs too. Her current job isn't worse than any other job. Things are like this everywhere: fake. I do a few quick searches and find an article about economic turmoil, joblessness even though the unemployment rate is way down. The article says that companies aren't truly hiring—they only *appear* to be hiring. Another tactic to get as much as they can for as little as possible. I leave the tab open but erase my history. People forget what they've opened all the time. It's the kind of clutter that just accumulates.

The intern's been staying late almost every night, so I'm

surprised she's not here tonight, but maybe it's a boon. While she's getting some rest, I don't have to feel anxious or impeded by her company. I don't have to waste time coaxing her along, thinking about how what I'm doing is affecting what she's doing. No one wants a perpetual houseguest. And maybe after all the layoffs, she wanted to escape, distance herself from that negativity as soon as possible, lest she be caught in the riptide.

On her desk, buried beneath a stack of papers, I find the list of potential clients I left her. She's crossed out all but two names. One of the two is circled. I wonder if she's still working on the other one. I leave the list on the top of her desk beside a blank piece of paper and a pen. A blank slate, so she can start her own research. I don't mind helping her, but I want her to learn to help herself. It's important to stay motivated.

What I'd really like to do is draw the CEO's wife into the office, get her on his computer or in his desk, and forcefully collapse his personal life into his work. I might not know how to read financials and figure out why we're downsizing, but I know how to hurt a man. I know how to make him track through his own shit.

"What do you think?" I ask L. in the lobby. "How do we get to his wife?"

"Maybe you could email her," she says.

"What if she doesn't believe me? What if she turns around and tells him my name, asks who I am, and why I'm emailing her?"

"You could use his account," she says. "On his computer. That'd prove it was valid and she wouldn't know who you were."

"An email in the middle of the night from his work computer? He'd figure out in no time that it was me. Or you. We'd be out of a job. Maybe worse." Because sometimes people can't appreciate being saved. Sometimes they fall into the water and swat your hand away if you reach for them. I shake my head. If something happened to me, what would this place do? Who would save them?

We use my phone to set up a fake email account, so I can email her in the daytime, using one of the computers in an internet café near the office. That way, it could be anyone. There'd be no way to track it back to me.

"What will you say?" she asks.

"If I say too much, he'll know exactly where all the information is coming from, and then he'll change his password to cover his tracks. If I don't say enough, she won't care, or she'll think it's fake."

"Just tell her about some of the women," she says. "Ones we know he's met, which hotels he uses. Someone could have seen him. The girls could have outed him. The hotel could have. It won't even occur to him that it was you."

"Us," I say.

She nods.

We draft an email with all that information and take turns proofreading it.

"I don't think you have to apologize," L. says, pointing to that part of the email.

"Why not?" I say. "What's wrong with a little kindness?"

"It's not a kind email," she says.

"You don't think the person emailing her would feel bad about it?"

"You're the person emailing," L. says, as though I don't know that.

"And I feel bad," I say.

L. shakes her head. "I don't know," she says. "Seems inconsistent."

In the end, I leave the apology but make it briefer and sandwich it between the list of nights and hotels, and brief descriptions of the women. I don't get overly crude about it, and keep my language formal, hoping this will make her take me more seriously and help temper the vulgar content.

"What if she emails back?" I say.

"Answer her," L. says.

"From my apartment?" I ask. "Or from the office? If I do that, what's the point of going to the café?"

"Then go back to the café," she says.

This is starting to sound like a lot of work. If I interrupt my sleep every day and go to this café to respond to emails, I've basically taken another job, unpaid.

"What if he tracks me there?" I ask. "And he's lying in wait?"

"Go to a different café," she says. "Or don't respond. Who cares? It's done."

But I don't want to leave his wife hanging. After all she's been through, she doesn't deserve that. I wish I could meet up with her in person to tell her everything. I wish I didn't have to include so many graphic details in the email, but I don't want her to doubt the veracity of what we're saying. No use half-hurting someone and letting them limp on toward the thing that's hurting them. Best to take them all the way out.

I spend the rest of my shift feeling guilty, like I'm the one who's done something wrong. Part of me feels like I'm making it up, so I go to the top floor three times to look at his phone, his messages, and remind myself that it's real. He's done these things and ought to be held accountable for his actions. All I'm doing is helping. Seeing his dick and then the empty desks is a reminder of the people he's hurting. If I let him keep going, no one will be safe. The company deserves better than him. They deserve me.

I make a note to buy my own roach spray because the roaches have found their way into our breakroom. Between the dankness and L.'s carefully cultivated mess, it'll be hard to get rid of them. And if I complain about them, my supervisor will find a concrete way to trace them back to me. "I don't know what you do at home," she'll write, "but you have to be tidier here."

As I'm heading through the lobby, I see M. walking up, so I double back to the breakroom to get my latest batch of cookies. I had imagined myself knitting M. a little sweater for their rats, basically as practice for what I could show Yarn Guy, but knitting is much harder than I'd thought. What I intended to be a small sweater is only a knot of yarn. No urging could make it a sweater. And because I know I intended to give M. the sweater, to not give them anything now feels like theft.

"Cold out," M. says, wheeling in the dolly.

I wince, thinking of the nonexistent sweater, and then the nonexistent scarf and hat I want to make for Yarn Guy. But M. takes the cookies and eats one on the spot, not knowing anything about the sweater I didn't make. They eat slower and more thoughtfully than L. ate my last batch, like they're really appreciating the cookie, and like I matter.

"Sunflower butter?" M. asks, and I nod.

They sweep their hair out of their face with one hand, and I wonder how different they look from Yarn Guy. I try to picture the two of them standing side by side. Yarn Guy is dressed more neatly, in a collared shirt and dark pants with a crease. He's probably less buff than M., because unlike them, Yarn Guy is tethered to a desk all day. I also imagine Yarn Guy's hair is cropped shorter, so he looks neater. His apartment is just as neat as his desk, but with an entire corner devoted to crafts, all sorted into clear bins on neat shelving. Instead of rats, he has knitting. M. could never have all that yarn—the rats would get into it, maybe eat it and hurt themselves.

Yarn Guy's place is probably larger and nicer than M.'s. After all, he works full-time on the fourth floor, is respected by his colleagues, and is running his own team. It makes sense that he has more money, more things. But even with all these responsibilities, he's still just as relaxed as M. I picture them holding themselves the same, looking at me the same way. There's something gentle about them, both people who really listen to me when I talk, people who really care.

M. leaves the dolly in the lobby to go and put the cookies in their truck, "To make sure they're okay," they say. "Imagine if I accidentally crushed them." They laugh, but still pat the cookies, seriously.

When they come back, they're eating a second one.

"What's your favorite kind?" I ask, without meaning to. I thought it and said it before I fully computed the question.

"Maybe these," they say.

It's nice to interact with a real person, to see someone enjoying my labor. All the people on the fourth floor—I don't get to see them persevering or even appreciating my efforts. And L. would never. She isn't wired for it.

I stay in the lobby, waiting for M. to come back down, but L. shows up first and I've already maxed out on L. for the night, so I head out to do a quick loop around the parking garage before I go home. I pick up a few cans and some food wrappers, but there are no major spills tonight. Sometimes people will dump an entire meal onto the concrete. I think they feel hidden out here. No one can see them make the mess, so they haven't made one. They're only socially acceptable human beings when someone's looking at them. Otherwise, they're basically feral.

The office isn't just a family—the space itself is an extension of everyone's homes. They all, for at least eight or nine hours during the day, live here. They pretend they can't see one another. They pretend they aren't doing all the things they're doing. No one calls anyone out for leaving paper towels on the bathroom floor or not wiping their feet on the front mat before they track in the muck of the street. Everyone is invisible while they do these things, because for a few seconds, they're at home and not at work. They go into the office bathrooms and they're at home. Their food explodes in the microwave and they're at home. They're here but they're not. They've projected entirely out of the building. Then later, when the workday's over and they go home, they're still here. They can't seem to keep themselves in one place.

IT'S STRANGE TO be heading toward work in the daytime. I've grabbed prework breakfast near the building before my shift or had dinner afterward, but it's been years since I've gone to the office, or even near it, in broad daylight. Today, though, I cut my sleep short, shower, and head toward work before noon. The trek, which I normally make mindlessly, as though my body knows the way on its own, feels unfamiliar and harsh in the daylight. I'm worried I might turn the wrong way or miss my street. There's more traffic and people than I'm used to. Even the polite people who probably believe they're very quiet make a lot of noise: their footsteps, the rustle of their clothes, their exhalations and coughs and hums. It fills the air around me.

Ahead of me, a man loudly talks to himself, getting more and more heated, and I'm worried he might react to someone around him. He's large enough to be menacing, and he's carrying a thermos that he could easily use as a weapon. I'm slowing my pace to create a buffer between us when I realize he's on the phone and isn't some unpredictable man yelling at himself on his lunch break. No one else is looking, though. They're all accustomed to this kind of scene and this kind of man. I'm trying to figure out who he's yelling at or why, but he turns down a side street and he's gone. I'll never see him again, but I'll see lots of people just like him. They might not be as boisterous, but that's because they're in their resting state.

Everyone, no matter how calm or friendly, could shift gears and ruin everything if you let them.

The café is over half full and I walk by it twice without going in, then stand outside pretending to be looking at my phone for nearly ten minutes before finally ducking inside. I'm worried about people seeing me, really looking at me, but no one even glances up, so I relax and set my stuff down next to one of three workstations. I had imagined there would be more, but most people have their own laptops, not worried about anyone tracking them down. They're here for the change of scenery and the idea that they'll be more productive in public than at home. But who would say anything if they online-shopped or even watched a movie with their headphones on? They don't notice anyone around them, but they each think they're very important and interesting, so other people must be watching them, criticizing them.

I go to the counter for a coffee and then log in to the email account that L. and I made. The email's sitting there, ready to send. Even now, I'm anxious that there might be some way of knowing when and where the email was written. L. had promised there wouldn't be, but technology is always sur-

prising me, and it's not like she has any kind of formal training or experience with computers. It'd be different if I asked
her a question about spending hours hunched over a stool. I
would totally trust her expertise on that.

Even though the café isn't crowded, people bustle in and
out, grabbing coffees or occasionally settling down at one of
the empty tables or side booths. It takes a while to get used to
it, like any new space. My first few weeks at the office were
the same. Even though there weren't actually people coming
and going, it felt like there were. They left evidence of where
they'd been, what they'd done, and what they were planning
to do. It was disquieting, and I had the sensation I might run
smack into one of them if I wasn't careful. I worried I'd move
something or overlook some small task and ruin their whole
routine. I was very worried that someone might think I was
bad at my job. But I've learned to move carefully around them,
sidestepping any potential collisions, righting their course if
they lean the wrong way.

I'm settling in, lifting my coffee to smell it, and trying to
will myself to take a sip, when a man plops down beside me,
taking the last available computer. He does it so quickly that
I slosh some of my drink onto my face, but he doesn't even
notice. He's older than me, wearing dark pants and a red knit
shirt, tucked in but starting to come out at the back. His hair
is parted neatly on one side, and he either has a professional
manicure or takes very good care of himself. This man could
easily be from the office. I don't think he's from my floor—I
would recognize that energy—but he could be from one of
the gray floors. I look around, trying to suss out any other
potential people from the office.

There's a muscular man across the room who could have been Mr. Buff, if Mr. Buff still worked at the office. Maybe it *is* Mr. Buff, and he's just using the café to look for jobs. But if I was downsized, I would pick somewhere farther away to do my searching. I wouldn't want to risk the embarrassment of running into a former coworker or boss. I couldn't muster the awkward small talk that kind of encounter would require. But L. pointed out that it'd be impossible to downsize me, and she's right. This office couldn't go on without me. How would anyone manage to do anything? But maybe Mr. Buff's not worried about it, since it seemed to be a group layoff, affecting several people. I'm trying to work up the courage to go and talk to him when a woman taps me on the shoulder.

"Are you almost finished?" she asks.

"Oh, sorry, give me two minutes," I say in a loud whisper.

"Thanks," she says at a regular volume, ignoring my politely muted response.

This makes me want to take my time and let her wait on me. But I don't want her to come back and draw more attention to me with her full-volume voice, so I send the email, log out, turn the computer off for good measure, and head toward the door. I think about stopping in front of her to give a little half bow, but I don't want someone to pinpoint me as having been in the café at this time on this day.

I'll be rehearsing things I could have said to this woman for the next month. I'll think of her before I fall asleep every morning, after work. Her face will mutate over time, become meaner, uglier. In a month, she'll be an utter villain.

I stand outside, trying to decide which way to walk. It wouldn't be strange if I went ahead to the office now. "I'm only a few hours early," I could explain. "Just needed to catch up on some things." They haven't seen me, but they all know me. We know each other. "How's your mother?" I'd ask Yarn Guy, because she was sick a few weeks ago. I saw the note to buy flowers, and then the email about it from his sister. And "Is your knee doing okay?" I'd ask Tea Woman. It's nice that her desk is right by the breakroom, so she doesn't have to hobble as far for tea or snacks. She's a big tea drinker. I often clean rings off her desk, and there are tea bags in her trash every night.

But I'm too tired to present myself at the office. I want them to see me at my best, both emotionally and physically, after we've worked together to save the company. I want us to have something to celebrate.

IT FEELS DISINGENUOUS to not mention all the empty desks scattered across the floor, but when I ask the intern how she's doing, she smiles and says she's great. There's no edge to her voice and she doesn't even glance toward one of the vacant desks, so I don't press it. I wouldn't want to bring her down.

"How's the planning?" I ask. I position my cart alongside a desk, so it blends right in. I'm here, but not taking up space in a discordant way. Everything about me aligns with the room.

"I've pivoted to some other projects," she says, smoothing her hair back. "So it's on the back burner," she adds. "There's just a lot to do."

"What about all the money you raised?" I ask.

"It's there," she says. "It'll wait."

She's still clicking away, staring at her computer screen, and not looking up at me, so I spray the desk beside her, which is actually pretty clean, but a little extra scrubbing never hurt anything. I move the keyboard and a plastic tray of papers onto the desk chair to clean underneath.

"What are you working on?" I ask, resettling the keyboard and tray.

"Just some mock-ups," she says.

"For your new client?" I ask.

She looks at me like my words have come out garbled. "I don't have any clients," she says. "Just because I brought in new business doesn't mean they're mine."

No wonder she isn't motivated. She wants acknowledgment for her work, but you don't always get credit for every little thing you do. Sometimes you have to think of the greater good, the team. If she doesn't see it that way, it'll be hard to reason with her. I need to make sure she feels valued, appreciated. That kind of thing can go a long way.

After she leaves, I use her computer to order her some flowers and schedule them to be delivered this week. I wish I'd thought of this sooner, but sometimes you have to play the slow game. I buy the medium-priced bouquet, even though it'll seriously cut into my grocery budget. But *I* appreciate being part of a team. On the card, I just have them write, "Thank you for all your hard work." I wish I could be here to see her face when they're delivered. What will the people around her think? Maybe they'll be extra nice to her. Or maybe everyone will double down when they see that hard work does not go unappreciated.

I remember to clear my browser history on the intern's computer, and then I go and sit in the CEO's office. His wife still hasn't responded to me, but these things can take some time to digest. I don't hold it against her because it's better to be calculated, purposeful. I admire her restraint.

His cactus is growing a little crooked, leaning toward the window, and I think about straightening it but decide to let it reach toward whatever it wants. It's probably the kind of plant that needs lots of sun. He should have put it directly in front of the window but didn't. Instead, it's tucked against a wall, underappreciated.

There are no new emails in his secret account, though there are a few texts on his phone that he's read but not responded to. He sees himself as someone who's very busy even if he doesn't do anything. He's just a busy man, that's his nature. Look at him. Besides, he wants the women on his time, not theirs. Maybe there was a meeting or an unavoidable project that drew him away from the secret phone in his office drawer. This is, to him, a small thing. He doesn't yet see the ruin in it. I know there's no use in trying to warn him or point him toward the truth of his actions. He would only grow defensive. If anything, his behavior would become worse. He'd want to prove, maybe just to himself, that everything he does is fine. If anything, I would be the obscene one because here I am, pointing out obscene actions. Only an obscene person would do such a thing.

So, I put his phone away, close the drawer, and clean the rest of the building, like I always do. I leave everything a little wetter, a little more astringent than usual. I don't sop anything up. I leave it to air-dry. The harshness of the chemicals feels reassuring, proof of my existence.

"THE WIFE HASN'T responded," I tell L. the next night.

We're in the hall outside our breakroom. I have gloves on, and I'm smushing the tiny roaches while L. stands a couple of yards away and sprays the crack between the wall and the baseboard. She's standing too close to the wall with no mask on, so she's probably inhaling the fumes, but I don't bother telling her this. She is, after all, an expert on most things.

"Give her some time," L. says, like it isn't a big deal.

"But what if she never emails back?"

"You only sent it a couple of days ago," she says. "Maybe she hasn't even seen it yet."

Of course she's seen it.

But I wad the dead roaches in a paper towel, throw them away, and head upstairs. While I'm cleaning the copier room, I see that someone's found the scissors. They're all in one big cup next to the paper cutter now. I wish I knew who it was and what mess they were cleaning when they finally found them.

I do see that the two jars of no-touch gray water are both full and upright again. They were missing last night, and I imagined the person sitting there had given them up, but no. Next to them is an index-sized piece of paper with instructions for "Assignment B on sediment" in a big, friendly font. Maybe they're doing their child's science project. Here's a person who had to metaphorically drag their child with them to work. No wonder the office is suffering. They might as well have left their child running around the building all day, all night. I can almost feel their handprints along filing cabinets, doors, and windows. Everything feels dirtier now. Children are so hard to keep clean. It's a form of work that people treat as just a lifestyle choice and not an additional job. J., the man I shared an apartment with before I got this job, has children now, and I wonder if he thinks the work his partner does is valuable. It's hard to imagine him appreciating someone.

I consider knocking over one of the jars again, maybe both jars, but I leave them alone for now.

Across the room, someone's propped open a conference room door. Maybe they wanted to listen in on a meeting. It's someone that wasn't included but wanted to be. It could have been the intern, or someone else very junior. There's a fairly nondescript man's desk nearby. There's nothing at his desk to signal a personality, no snacks or books or interesting notes. It's as though he just works here and nothing else. Imagine waking up, going to work, doing nothing but your job for eight or nine hours, and then leaving, like all this isn't even part of your life. He's the kind of guy who would have to take shortcuts to get ahead, might listen in on a meeting he's not invited to.

I find what smells like some kind of seafood stew poured sloppily into the conference room trash. If I really try, I can smell fennel and saffron underneath the day-old fish odor. They're just airing out the room. It would have been more helpful if they'd gotten rid of the stew, but I guess that was too difficult a chore. Instead, they've made the entire floor smell like fish. I hadn't noticed it before because I'm always encased in the scent of disinfectant and soap. But now I can smell fish, and I carefully dribble the stew on every rug across the entire floor. Then I rub it in with the sole of my shoe— really get it in there. They don't deserve a fresh scent if they can't even be bothered to take the stew out. They left it there all day and it's leaked through the trash bag, so I have to wipe stew out of the trash can as well. I wish I knew who was responsible for the mess, but everyone must have smelled it, so they're all guilty by association. At any point during the day, someone could have done something.

The rest of the office feels almost orderly, except for the CEO's little nook. On his desk, one pile of papers slants into another, threatening to slide onto the floor. His keyboard is half-covered, and I don't even see his mouse. I don't know how this happened so quickly. It was clean yesterday. His wife must have finally read my email. Things have changed for him at home, and now they're going to change here too.

I think about trying to sort his clutter, but instead, I push one of the piles off his desk and then stir the papers around so they're out of order. I clean the rest of the fourth floor as usual. I just think it's strange that his wife would react but not email me back. I keep refreshing my email, expecting her response to pop up, but by the end of my shift, she still hasn't replied. L. thinks that there's nothing to worry about, because why would she email me in the middle of the night anyway?

But if I were her, I don't know if I could sleep. I'm extra tired from waking up all throughout my day to see if she emailed me back. All day, I turned my phone off and on, dragged my finger down to refresh the browser, but nothing. I just kept waking up and hitting refresh, refresh, refresh. I even got out of bed to restart my router and modem. Why wouldn't I expect the same dedication from her?

I want to picture her as the mad wife, harried, wide-eyed and pacing her house, dragging her fingernails along the walls while he sleeps. But I know in reality she looks like she always does: blandly attractive and pulled together. People are never as interesting as you want them to be. The truth is that they're basic, tending toward shitty. The really shitty people seem interesting only in their flaws. Porn Guy wouldn't be interesting if he wasn't a little repulsive. Tea Woman is probably hard to pay attention to. She tells a story, and people start to sideways rock away from her, smiling to be polite, pretending something important has caught their eye across the room. The Vomiter just seems anxious. No one thinks anxiety is interesting. No one sees a depressed person and goes, "Oh wow, tell me more!" But everyone thinks their own quirks and problems make them fascinating. Cheery #1 probably goes home and talks for hours about Cheery #2. His partner is fed up, because in turn he wants to complain about someone from his own workplace, but Cheery #1 won't stop talking.

It's better to be alone, to have no one to ignore you and

talk over you, because they think everything about their day is more important than yours. I like to go home each morning, knowing that all I'm dragging with me is my day, my work, my responsibilities. No one will overshadow me.

But when I pull open the CEO's drawer, his secret flip phone is missing.

I look through all the other drawers, pull out papers and folders and junk to be sure I'm not overlooking it, but it's nowhere. Did he take it with him? Discard it? Maybe he's starting fresh.

I log in to his email and he hasn't slowed his dedication to extracurriculars at all. If anything, he's more fully throwing himself into it. If he tried this hard at work, things might be different. His office would certainly be cleaner and the company would run more efficiently. We wouldn't be in danger of sinking.

But the entire tone of his emails has shifted. Instead of sounding childishly sexual, he almost sounds romantic. He's starting to use longer fragments, more fully formed thoughts. He compliments a few of the women and uses their first names instead of "babygirl." Some of these women are becoming people for him, and they're wearing it well. They match his tone, declare their love and affection too. They're used to shifting gears and don't find one mode any harder than the other. This is just their job. He's not a person to them, either. Maybe these women have phones full of men who say "babygirl," and all the dick pics look the same, blur into one single dick, another knob in an endless collection of knobs.

A couple of the women do stop responding, but that's not an anomaly. He's had ghosters before. I figured the women moved on, found someone or something better, or became so overwhelmed by him personally that he didn't seem worth the effort. Who could blame them?

When L. makes her rounds, I try to tell her how poorly he's doing and how strange the fourth floor seems, but she says, "Well yeah, what did you think would happen after you emailed his wife?"

But it's something more. He's lost his footing, sure, but I think everyone in the office can see there's something wrong with the company. Why else would they be working so hard? No one even had time to take the fish stew out to the dumpster, even though it clearly bothered them. Otherwise, why would they leave the conference room door open?

But across the rest of the floor, everything else remains rigid, perfect. It's all team-building exercises, learning lunches, happy-hour meetups. They must all feel happy, because here are all the things that make people happy. Like Karaoke Thursdays! Outside their frivolity, it seems like they spend most of their time sorting and stacking, building their anxiety into something beautiful.

And I'm glad to see that the CEO's tone in professional emails has changed too. He seems more formal, complimentary. But three times now he's gone onto job sites and looked for positions at similar companies. Maybe the problems are compounded by his issues with his wife. It's clear she's never going to email me back, and emailing her again feels desperate. It turns out that infidelity isn't actually noteworthy. Or maybe their relationship is open. Who am I to judge? "Who isn't cheating on their wife?" he would say if pressed. "Who isn't dicking around?"

Before I leave, I spend around twenty minutes comparing financial statements to examples I found online. Some of the formatting is different, as though I'm looking at the wrong version of the program, but I finally figure out it's one of the settings I've selected. The tools all resettle into their proper places, and I feel pleased to have sorted it out. This would be easier if I could watch someone else do it, if I could ask questions. Imagine if any of the people who worked here had to learn this way, just thrown unsupervised into the deep end. They could never do it.

THE INTERN NEVER mentions her flowers, and I don't see them anywhere in the office. I check online and the tracker shows them as delivered. Did someone else get them? Is the florist lying? Did the intern throw them away? I check all the trash cans on the fourth floor—in the breakroom and bathroom too. I've looked multiple times in the dumpster. Maybe she took them home. I can't think of a way to ask without her figuring out how I know about them. But her mood seems slightly lifted, and there aren't any new empty desks.

Things are mostly stable, except for inside the CEO's office. There are additional folders and papers on the floor beside his desk now, footprints already visible on the whites of the pages. Without thinking, I bend to pick them up—but what am I doing? Let him deal with his own wreckage. Leave him stranded at sea, sail away with everyone else safely aboard.

I take some notes from his desk and feed them through

the shredder. It feels so gratifying that I go back for more, and empty out nearly half the contents of a folder left tucked under his keyboard.

Then I work extra hard to clean everything outside of his office, so maybe he'll be shamed into picking up his own slack. To get to his office, he'll have to walk through the pristine fourth floor, desks shining, floor polished to a high sheen. It doesn't even smell like fish anymore. The smell of clean has fully overtaken any lingering odors. I take care to wipe down his door frame and the handle on the outside of his door, to clearly delineate the border between his office and everyone else's workspace. He's so eager to set himself apart from everyone else, so why not let him? Why not let everyone enjoy his deleterious flop?

If anything, the rest of the floor works more diligently than usual. His frantic energy must be evident to everyone. There's a desperation to their work, as though they want to keep his stink off them. Who responds to emails within ten minutes? Who would ever sort all their paperwork into such neat piles? But now they all do it. They're like a perfectly run but semi-frantic machine. *We're so productive*, they all think. *And so important. Nothing could ever happen to us.* They double down, several of them reaching out to older contacts to drum up new business. They go home at night and tell their partners and friends, "I killed it at work today." Their friends and family smile politely, but they've worn their desperation home. Everyone can see it. But then, everyone showed up in the same pathetic outfit, so it doesn't really matter.

On a second pass, I notice that the CEO's fountain has run out of water. I carry it to the bathroom for a refill and put it back in his office, but it won't run. The motor is fried. Everything has a limit. Everyone has a point where they dry up and won't keep running. Cars get left on the side of the road. Old electronics are recycled or thrown away. Food spoils. People, as commodities, aren't any different. They get used up, burn out, and have to be replaced. No one complains when it's someone else, but they think of themselves as different. The pain and unhappiness they're experiencing is singular.

His computer screen is dirtier than usual, too, visible fingerprints and grease streaked across it. I imagine he's doing something like dissolving, bits of him sagging and falling off, all of this happening while the office keeps running without him. I leave the rest of his mess, but clean his computer screen, hoping he can see himself reflected in it. *I am a good man*, he thinks, looking at his shadowy reflection. *I am a hard worker. Things are going to turn out okay for me because they have to.*

No one ever believes themselves fallible. Your car won't go over the cliff, you won't drop what you're carrying, your card won't decline. Someone will catch you, help you, split the meal so you can afford it. Because you're special, aren't you? The CEO thinks, *I'm special, aren't I?* and tries to smile at himself in the glare of his computer screen. His style of management encourages everyone to think this way—they're all in it for themselves. This is the career track of any industrious employee. Work, work, work, and if you get the chance, stand on the bodies of everyone around you in order to stay above water. But if everyone clambers that way, no one can make it.

All night, I keep thinking of him and going to stand in his office so I can enjoy the ruin. I wonder if his cactus needs water. I can't imagine him taking care of it. But cacti are sturdy plants that you can let go for a while before they really start to need you. I'll keep an eye on it.

I worry that I'm distracted, not paying enough attention to the rest of the office. I don't intend to let everyone run around with no supervision, so I decide to start coming in earlier and staying later. Maybe they'll notice the difference in their day-to-day lives and want to pay me more, invite me to discuss benefit options, the works.

It'd be nice to come in during the day shift, sign some new paperwork, see how everyone's doing. It's just nice to be acknowledged as part of their lives.

WITH MY RECENTLY extended hours, my shifts begin to overlap with the intern's more steadily, and I think we're getting used to one another. She never talks about the gala anymore, but she's also stopped mentioning her job search. Maybe she's settled in. She smiles at me when she sees me, tells me hello, asks how I'm doing. She'll even talk to me while I'm working, not so put off by the idea of me anymore. It's not just work stuff, being involved in more projects, or her day-to-day tasks. She talks about what she's making for dinner and who she's dating.

"He's so much hotter than me," she says, showing me a picture of a young man who probably doesn't have body hair yet. He's not hideous, but he's well below average. And she is, objectively, a conventionally attractive woman, but she's been conditioned to believe that extremely mediocre men are out of her league.

Men are always overselling themselves, so that you don't really know what you've got until you're stuck with it. I've learned that it's best to avoid the grift altogether. It doesn't even seem like this man has a good personality, though. She tells me that he talks about how he's cheated on other women, and he sometimes disappears for days at a time. "He's just so busy," she says. "He's studying medicine." I hadn't believed he was old enough for this, but perhaps he's older than he looks. "He's so tall," she says, as though height makes up for his shortcomings.

It's hard to take her seriously, and I wonder if I've ever felt this way about a man. It's difficult to picture even my most recent relationship with J., from four years ago. He'd criticized the way I cleaned our apartment, pointing out little problem areas he thought I should work on, like I was his cleaner and not an equal partner. But the whole thing had mostly been playacting at house. I was never going to be with him forever. But at the time, had I imagined, like the intern, that he was the one? That we'd be married and build a life together?

The only relationship that really seems important is the one I have with this building. I worked at another building before this one, but I never felt attached to it. In the months leading up to that company's collapse, management had lashed out, criticizing me and everyone else, trying to hold us accountable for any issue they had. I'd been written up, lectured, condescended to. I'd quit as much as I'd been fired.

This building is entirely different. We're in sync. I step in and rectify issues before they become overwhelming. The building's small enough that I can focus on the individuals who work here—at least on the fourth floor. All these relationships are more than enough to satisfy any urges I get.

While I'm cleaning, I hear the intern talking to her young potato on the phone, and she laughs more than she speaks. Maybe he leeches all her positive energy so that she has to maintain a kind of aloof sourness the rest of her day and night. It's not her fault. She only has so much to give.

"You should move desks," I tell her, once she's off the phone.

"Why would I do that?" she asks, but not harshly.

"If you were in the middle of things instead of off in a corner by yourself, you'd have a better idea of what's going on. You'd be more involved. Something comes up, and you can jump in. People start to think of you as a person who can juggle things, a person they want to work with. People know you and feel like you're their friend. You aren't just the intern."

"Maybe," she says, but the next night I see that she's moved a few desks over, finally farther away from the CEO and near a block of very active desks. These are people who could really use her help. I can tell by the piles of papers on their desks, but also by the kinds of snacks they eat, all grab and go, lots of granola bars, crackers, things like that. Energy drinks and coffee—not just tea, which almost everyone in the office drinks to some degree.

Now that we're comfortably colleagues and friends, I ease into more questions about the online systems the company uses. I try to keep it light and nonreactive if she doesn't answer my questions in as much detail as I'd like. It's important to continually reiterate our friendship. It's a lot like coaxing a feral animal, edging gently forward but staying ready to spring away if they turn vicious.

"You got a tattoo," I say, and she rotates her wrist so I can see it better. "An acorn," I add. Beneath the acorn is the word "sweet."

"It's a strawberry," she says. Her eyes go a little sad. "Men keep telling me how sweet I am."

I'm stuck then, listening to how some tall man broke up with her, and I wonder about him. No one could really find this woman "sweet." She patently isn't. But they use this word to get away from her. It's a kind word, and she enjoys believing she's kind. In the depths of a breakup, she latches on to this idea of her kindness. It is, she believes, the reason for the split. It's not how off-putting she is, how desperate, how bad at communication. No, it's that these men find her abstractly sweet, and for some reason her innate goodness is driving them away.

It's also kind of tragic that anyone would tattoo themselves with the thing that hurt them. It would have been less pathetic if she'd just gotten his name inked onto her. But I make sympathetic noises until she empties herself of all these feelings, and we edge back toward the company. In the wake of her descriptions of heartache, she's excited to demonstrate that she knows things, has worth.

"Oh, we don't always use email," she says, and she shows me their online forum, where I can scroll through threads and comments going back well before my start date. I'm shocked that I didn't see it on anyone else's computer, but she tells me she normally looks at it on her phone. I could never read it all, even if I sat here and read full-time every night.

The CEO uses the same kind of childish lingo he uses in his texts, omitting "babygirl" or anything overtly sexual. I try to imagine how this would impact his speaking voice. Does he sound overly cutesy? Or is it that he just can't be bothered to write out full sentences? His time is simply worth too much money.

There's a man across the office who refuses to go to the grocery store and has all his food delivered to his apartment. He left his texts open in a tab on his browser, talking to some woman he was seeing. He told her his time was worth too much money to spend it grocery shopping. He had calculated it, to be sure. He must have thought this would make him more appealing, but I felt disgusted for her. When she stopped texting him back, he texted her that he "didn't deserve to be treated this way." Men have such funny ideas about what they deserve.

I clean around the intern while she reads through old threads. I don't think she meant to become this absorbed, but while she was showing me how it all worked, she trailed off and began reading some old conversation, and she never returned to me. It's like she got lost in the woods.

"It's late," I tell her when I'm getting ready to go downstairs, and she grunts at me. She'll be exhausted tomorrow, will have trouble focusing or getting anything done. I consider pulling the fire alarm to prompt her exit, but this would disrupt my work as well. I don't want to stand out on the sidewalk with L., waiting for someone to confirm there's no fire while L. pitches theories about unsafe wiring and how if I'd been observant like her, I would have noticed it too.

Near the end of my night, I go to wait in the lobby, and when M. comes in, they're already smiling.

"What?" I say, and they hand me a container of neatly packaged lime tahini cookies they've made.

"It's my go-to," they say. "What do you think?"

I don't actually like them, can't stand this much tahini, but I tell them they're good.

M. looks disappointed, like they can hear my thoughts, and I eat another. "So good," I say. "It's just been a long night."

They brighten and I tell them about the intern's tattoo.

"Do you have any?" M. asks.

"No," I say. "Do you?"

They pull up their khakis to show me a drawing on the side of their calf. It's a rat holding a smaller rat-shaped balloon.

"What's it mean?" I ask.

"Just seemed nice," they say. And it is kind of nice. To do what you like because you want to.

THE NEXT NIGHT, I sit at the intern's desk, scrolling through the online forum she showed me. She hasn't stayed late tonight—probably exhausted from last night. I wonder how her workday went. Nothing new has accumulated on her desk, but sometimes her days are like that. She comes in and believes she works, but doesn't produce anything tangible.

The forum seems innocuous enough—some work-related stuff interspersed with idle chat. TV shows and concerts and new restaurants. Someone's having a baby. Someone got a new dog. I look for the forum on several other computers and finally find it on one across the room. This woman has a few private chat sessions, and one of them piques my interest.

"Where would we get the money to consider intern's proposal?"

"No kidding, like, we can't even get new breakroom furniture. Have you seen the couch? The spring is almost coming through."

"What's an intern even doing on the fourth floor? Shouldn't she be down on two or three?"

"C. knows her father."

"Oh, of course."

"Wish C. knew *my* father."

"We have two parties a year already. Why would we need another? And why would C. agree to it?"

"Maybe she's bored. Just needs something to do."

"Let her help me, then."

"Are you sure? You'd probably end up having to redo it. Have you seen anything she's written?"

"She has some sort of communications degree."

"What even is that?"

"Is that like typing school?"

"Ha ha."

"What did you want for lunch?"

"Oh, let's put it in that channel and have her to run and get it."

Then they pick it up again.

"Did you see intern's handout?"

"Who does she think she is?"

"Ridiculous."

"How long has she even been here?"

"She basically started yesterday."

Then it's work stuff again, for pages and pages. I give up reading before I find anything else, but I still wonder what was so captivating to the intern last night. Did they talk about her on a public channel where she could see? These messages are older, so maybe things have improved. Maybe now they feel like she's one of them. The fact that her dad got her the job probably didn't help.

I don't really know the woman who sits at this desk. Before now she was quiet, unobtrusive. I click her profile and it doesn't give me any real information about her. She likes hiking and travel, has a sunglasses and lipstick emoji next to her name. It's always strange to see how people conceive of themselves. I click the intern's profile, and she's more fully filled it out. There's her full name, job, college, and a list of interests that seem mostly true. I'm not sure I can picture her doing any rock climbing, but maybe it's an aspirational interest. She typed it and thought, *One day.*

I clear my history and survey this Bitter Woman's desk. I take a stack of her papers to the copier room and feed them, a few at a time, into the shredder. Afterward, I empty the shredded paper into the trash bags on my cart so there won't be any evidence left behind. This doesn't feel like enough, so I also go through her desk drawers and throw away a ring of keys, along with a few high-end chocolate bars. Too greedy to leave them in the breakroom, she's been hoarding them in her desk. And for what? Certainly, they haven't made her a nicer person. As I'm getting up, I tear a few pages off her one-a-day inspirational calendar and make a mental note to do this again in a few days. Ruin her conception of time. Drain the little bit of joy she has.

Feeling bolstered, I go to the intern's desk and give her some extra attention. I move everything off her desk and take the time to wipe the undersides of her penholder and mouse pad. I even get between the keys on her keyboard. She deserves a fresh start to cleanse any residual bitterness she's absorbed. I try to think of something else nice to do for her, and when I can't, I go back to the Bitter Woman's desk and rip a whole week off of her inspirational propaganda. Because honestly, I'm not sure if this woman needs anything to tell her that her dreams matter.

Then, while I clean the windows, I stare out at the sidewalk below, nothing but a silver glint from up here. There's a courtyard next to the building across the street, and over it I can see down the block, rows of buildings and streetlights. It used to feel strange to see the typically bustling streets completely abandoned at night, but now I feel the opposite. This emptiness is normal. Any stir of activity is an aberration, something to draw attention or unsettle. I actually feel incredibly safe at this time of night, or later, when I head home. It feels so unlikely that anyone would disrupt the peace here.

I stand for a long time at the window after I finish cleaning it, appreciating how clear the glass is and how far I can see. No one from the day shift would be able to stand here like this. They need to appear busy, even if they aren't. They watch videos and chat and shop online, but they can't stand here, stare outside, and think about how lovely it all is.

Later, when I tell M. about the forum and the Bitter Woman's comments about the intern, they look truly hurt. It's nice to have someone else care about the intern. L. always shrugs it off, but M. understands what it means to care about someone. I feel not exactly romantic, but like we could parent the intern together. I could picture us building things, being helpful.

"Do you think they've said anything like that to her face?" M. asks.

"She has to know," I say. "At least to some degree."

"The way they look at her. The way they treat her," M. says.

"It's terrible," I say.

M. nods. "To know what people really think of you."

But even if they played nice and she didn't know, they'd still be talking about her. They'd still think all these things.

"I think I'd want to know," I say.

"What people think of you?" M. asks.

I nod.

They start to say something, but L. comes in, watching a video on her phone at an incredible volume. I don't think my phone even gets that loud. When M. leaves, she turns it down.

"What were you talking about?" L. says. "You both looked so serious."

"I looked how I always look," I say. "What are you watching?"

She tilts her phone screen toward me. "K-drama," she says. "Weather forecasters fall in love."

The couple, of course, do not look anything like real weather forecasters. They're too beautiful. It's their job: to play a part, to look a certain way, to have those faces, those bodies. It's like any other job. I'm paid to have calluses and strong knees and ankles, but also a kind of deftness and adaptability. How else would I keep things running so smoothly? It's raining there, in the show, but here, it's clear and dry. Completely cloudless. You can almost see the stars.

L. FINALLY COMPLAINS that her plant is dying, which is funny because it's been dead for weeks, no sign of green left on it. It was exciting to watch the last leaf turn yellow and die, waiting to see if L. would notice or try to save it. It's still there, shriveled and lifeless. The whole thing is shades of yellow and brown, no possibility of resurrection.

"My grandmother gave it to me," she says. "To take care of because she was sick. She worried that she'd have a couple of rough days, forget to water it, and it'd die." L. caresses the plant while she talks, like she can bring it back to life or comfort it with her touch. Then she picks it up, carries it over to the sink, and waters it. This drowning only makes it deader, and I feel a twinge, but there's nothing I can do. I can't dig the already dissolved salt out of the soil. I can't tell her what's wrong with the plant without explaining that I'm culpable. It's a plant. She'll move on.

"How's she doing now?" I ask instead.

"About the same," L. says. "At least she's still living on her own. It'll be hard when she can't anymore."

"Maybe a bigger pot," I say, gesturing toward the plant.

She doesn't respond, and I head upstairs, but I hope she listens, for once. It'd be nice to see this small thing I did undone.

At least the intern hasn't seemed so sad lately. I think she's starting to really turn things around and feel like part of the office and not such an outsider. The more the CEO falls apart, the more pulled together she seems. He's her Dorian Gray, getting uglier in the attic, becoming his truest self, while she unfurls and thrives.

All but two of her self-help books are gone. Her supplements are still here but unused, only present as a reminder of who she used to be. I don't even bother to throw any more of them away. They don't seem so threatening now. Her desk is piled with more work than usual, too, like they're letting her take on more, but it's all well-ordered. Nothing is in disarray, and she's in the office at night less frequently, even with all the extra work. It's one or two nights a week now. She's starting to find some balance, maybe not pitting her life against her work, and just living.

All the office people seem to need this balance. Without breaks, they grow sluggish and unhappy. It's how toddlers throw tantrums when they need a nap. Only the office workers' tantrums are quieter, more harmful, and sometimes malicious. As adults, they've learned to weaponize their unhappiness. Who can they get fired? Whose life can they make more difficult? If it wasn't Scissors Guy, it was Cheery #1 and #2. Even Toilet Woman told the story of her ex in hopes that it would spread among people he knew. Who would want to socialize with a man who touched the inside of toilet bowls?

"How's it going?" I ask the intern and she smiles at me, makes direct eye contact.

"Really well," she says. "I'm working on four different projects. Normally, someone only works on two or three at a time, but they're letting me do four because they know I can handle it."

"What kind of projects?" I ask, and she lays them all out, shows me files on her computer and documents on her desk. She reminds me of a kid at show-and-tell, or coming home from school to tell their mother what they worked on that day. I try to pay attention, but most of what she says is too boring to grab hold of—it's the kind of busywork that people are trained to be really proud of, but sounds fake to anyone outside of it. Moving things from column A to column B, trying to get everything to column C. But I smile and make encouraging faces and lean gently over her desk. When she's finished and I've asked the right amount of questions to clearly demonstrate my interest and enthusiasm, I ask about the gala.

"What happened to the money from your fundraising?" I ask.

She shrugs and I can see her hackles start to rise, but I make myself smaller, slouching and curling my shoulders inward. I soften my face and smile at her.

"You worked so hard," I say. "That money ought to go toward something."

"I guess it was just absorbed," she says. "I don't have that system on my computer. It's okay, because I'm really focused on these now. I just wanted something that felt like mine."

"You think he's using it for something else?" I ask, nodding toward the CEO's office, but I can see this question pushes her too far and she's turtle-style withdrawing from me. "You could look on his computer," I say. "You'd figure it out, I bet." I hope the compliment puts her at ease.

She doesn't say anything, and I go to his office, shake his mouse, and softly type his password so she won't hear it.

"His computer's on," I call out to her. "You could just look around."

She comes and stands in the doorway for a long time, looking at me behind the CEO's desk. I sit here all the time, feel perfectly at ease, but I can see from her face that she thinks me being behind the CEO's desk is strange. I'm not wearing the right clothes for it. I don't have the right posture or makeup. So, I stand up and take a few sideways steps from the desk, holding my hands up like, *Who, me?* And I smile at her because I want her to remember that we're friends, colleagues. This is no big deal.

She doesn't say anything, and I worry I've taken things too far, that she's going to tell someone or even begin to reprimand me, like she's that far above me, but she comes around the desk and plops into his chair. It's irresistible, I know. She rocks back and forth, scooting the chair forward and trying to make herself more comfortable. I watch her scan the room. Even if she's been in here before, she's never sat behind his desk and looked out. She's never thought about what he sees. I back into the doorway to help her imagine what people look like to him.

"Just a peek," she says, and she looks at me, waiting.

I take another step back, not in the doorway anymore but

still looking in, and she nods for me to leave. Like I'm a dog. Imagine this woman believing that other people think she's sweet.

Down in the lobby, I reiterate most of it for L., leaving out how the intern looked at me behind the CEO's desk, and how she waved me away like I wasn't a person.

"It was easy," I say. "I'm not sure what I was even worried about."

"Finally, someone on the inside," L. says, even though we're both people on the inside. I know what she means, though.

We watch a man and a woman standing outside on the sidewalk, talking, lit up by a nearby streetlight. At this hour, we don't normally see people idling. If someone's out, they're in a hurry to get somewhere. Everything that happens at this hour is transitory, wedged between concrete pieces of life, folded so small that no one would ever notice. But after a while, they see us. The woman scowls and they hurry away. No one thinks about the people who live reverse days, working while they sleep or play. It must be unsettling to see us, to be reminded that people like us exist.

I go upstairs to finish the gray floors, and when M. arrives, L. and I tell them about setting up the intern at the CEO's computer. For once, we all stand in the lobby, easily chatting. It feels so normal. This could be my every day. The intern might get a promotion, and if she does, she's going to remember how she got there. "I couldn't have done it without her," she'll tell people. I'll be modest about it and encourage her to take as much credit as possible, because this is all I wanted: for her and the company to be okay. Maybe they can hire back some of the people they let go. They'll be so grateful to be working here again. Scissors Guy will be nicer. Résumé Woman will regret thinking she could do better than a place like this. With the boosted morale, everything will run more efficiently, more productively. All because of me.

"WHAT'D YOU FIND?" I ask the intern the next night.

She shakes her head. "Nothing," she says. "I just logged off. I don't think you should be looking at his computer."

"I would never," I tell her. "I just thought it might help you."

"I'm fine," she says. "Probably be careful when you're in there. I know he's very particular about his things."

"Did he say something?" I ask.

She shakes her head and turns back to her work. I stand there for a few moments, but she doesn't look back up at me. Just keeps typing and staring at her computer. I can't think of what to say, so I head back toward the elevator. I look over my shoulder, but she's not looking at me. She's intently staring at her computer screen, hand poised over her mouse. It's frustrating to try to help someone only for them to refuse. People will stay comfortably miserable if they don't have to change anything about their lives.

I take my time doing all the gray floors, and when I come back, she's long gone. Her desk is neat and she's pushed her trash can to the side, as though she's offering it to me.

When I sit down at the CEO's computer, I'm nervous that his password will have been changed, but she hasn't ruined that for me. Everything seems as usual. But in his alternate email account, I see that he's mostly been emailing one particular woman instead of his usual barrage. I wouldn't have guessed that this woman was one of his favorites. They've texted and emailed, she sent pictures of her breasts, and told him she wanted him—the usual. She hadn't stood out to me. But now they're sending full emails back and forth. A lot of it is sentimental, describing some extremely heightened feelings and a desire for their relationship's longevity.

But then he begins to talk about money. She softly encourages him. I can see how careful she's being not to say too much or come across as desperate. He tells her he just needs more time to get the money and then they'll go. He's so stereotypical, it's difficult to believe he's real. But she professes love and belief in him. Each of them pretends they believe his plans will coalesce. They'll run away together, they'll be happy. "Almost," he keeps telling her. And "soon." There's no mention of any concrete plan but if he's going to luck into a large sum of cash, I have some suspicions about where it'll come from. I print two copies of the email and close his account.

His wife's picture is still on his desk. Maybe he doesn't want anyone at the office to guess what's going on. A separation or a divorce would be an embarrassment. Or maybe she's fully forgiven him and won't see this latest betrayal coming at all. He's not only going to abandon the company—he's going to abandon her and their dog too.

I think of emailing her again. I could forward her copies of his emails. I could give her tangible proof. Maybe it was all too murky before. Had she thought I was only some woman trying to steal her husband? Or some bot trying to swindle her? I hadn't known how to strike the right tone, to sound dependable and open.

It's been a long time since I had a close female friend. After I lost both J. and my last job all in one blow, I'd reached out to A. She had always been the person I talked to, and even though we hadn't seen each other much, my first thought was of her. She was *with* him, though—if not the reason for the breakup, certainly its encourager. I didn't piece things together immediately but eventually the story fell into place. I guess I hadn't paid very good attention to them, how they spoke to one another, the way they looked at each other first whenever something funny happened. I saw it in hindsight, of course. It was one long string of obvious events. I'm more observant now and would never miss these kinds of clues.

I tilt the wife's picture away from me and then look up the four accounts the intern is working on, first in the financial system and then in the CEO's email. Maybe I am getting better at this. I didn't know how to use the financial system a few weeks ago, and now I navigate it easily, though I don't always understand what I'm looking for.

I find an email referencing one of the accounts, no problem. It's from the company in question, and they've told the CEO to close the whole thing out. Just scrap it. He's hav-

ing her work on a worthless project, one that's already dead.
He's trying to keep her happy, quiet. Or he wants to see her
fail, to watch her log worthless time and energy into something she's convinced might be the thing to leapfrog her out
of being an intern and into being a full-time employee. Is he
trying to make her one of his women, dangling the prize of
his approval so he can get her to do whatever it takes?

I print copies of this email too. I'm not sure what to do with
them, or the others, not sure the intern would listen to me
if I showed them to her. If I leave them on her desk without
context, will they be enough? It's hard to lure a stagnant person out of an unhappy situation. They can only imagine more
unhappiness. They won't undertake any additional labor because they don't believe it could lead to anything different or
better. Nothing could ever be better. And if she were to take
the emails to the CEO, he'd know that someone has access
to his alternate email account. With a little detective work,
he'd find me. But if I don't do anything because I'm afraid of
being caught, I'll be partially to blame.

And then when the company crumbles, I'll know I could
have done something. I could have stopped him. In the end,
I tuck the copies into my cart where no one will find them.
Give myself time to mull it over and build my case.

Before I go downstairs, I do a thorough excavation of the
intern's drawers, but other than an odd collection of hard
candy for someone her age, I uncover nothing new, nothing to tell me anything more about her unpleasant attitude. I
douse her keyboard and mouse in cleaning solution, though.
After a few seconds, I dry them off. Fifty-fifty chance they
still work okay.

Once I get downstairs, I find a note on the glass about a missed delivery.

L.'s in the breakroom, not even eating, just sitting at the table, looking at her grandmother's dead plant. When she doesn't look up, I shake the note at her.

"I called," she says. "M. says they'll bring it tomorrow."

"And you just left the note on the glass?"

"Wasn't hurting anything."

"What were you even doing?" I ask.

"Bathroom," she says.

She primarily uses the one right off the lobby. It's the one I never use because even though I cleaned it, I don't like the idea of using a bathroom that any number of strangers have used. I only use the ones upstairs, for the people who work here. During the day, you could walk in off the street and use the lobby bathroom, do whatever you like. The building is only locked at night. No one is worried about what people might do in the light of day. But L. has no problem using this public space. She probably thinks of it as hers, since it's so near her stool in the lobby.

"M. comes at the same time every night," I say. "It wouldn't be hard to meet them, let them do their job."

"I can't help that I had to go to the bathroom," she says. "I'm not a machine."

I shake my head.

"Why don't *you* let them in?" L. asks.

"It's your job."

"It's not my job to let M. into the building. No one's paying me to be the door person."

And yet L. sits at the door almost all night. I guess we all do work we aren't paid to do.

"Besides," she says, "isn't M. kind of *your* thing?"

"I have no idea what you're talking about."

"I just meant, I thought you were friends and all."

I shrug. "CEO's down to one woman," I say. "I mean, other than his wife."

"Good for him," she says, completely unsympathetic to the wife he's hurt, the same wife who's sat bravely and namelessly on his desk for the last several years. That's all she is to him and to L. A photo on a desk. But I look at the picture and see an actual person, conceive of her beyond a piece of desk ornamentation. Everyone deserves that recognition.

But not everyone's willing to give it.

I resent the way his personal life bleeds into my work. All I want is for the company to run smoothly, but I've had to deal with not just his mismanagement but his burgeoning personal life. I wouldn't have to do any of this if he weren't hurting the company, trying to sever me from these people who clearly need me. I haven't invested all this time and work for nothing.

And I feel a twinge that no one knows about me. My picture isn't sitting on anyone's desk. Surely they know someone cleans the offices, but they probably don't have a collective idea of everything I've done, the scope of it. It'd be nice to be recognized. Even if just the CEO's wife emailed me back, that might be enough.

"What's wrong?" L. asks, but I can tell she doesn't care. She's already on her phone, endlessly scrolling, thinking about people she doesn't even know, in television shows or movies, or maybe just herself. My phone buzzes, but I don't look at it. Nothing could be so important that I would let it infringe upon my time in the office. A few seconds later, it buzzes again—a voice mail I'll never listen to.

I shake my head and we sit quietly until it's time to leave. We both clock out, and L. goes to do who knows what, while I go home to sleep in my self-made mini office, a tiny replica of what matters to me. When L. leaves, she doesn't think about this job at all, but I go home and think about all my employees, everyone still left on the fourth floor, and how I can protect them. When I'm at home, I'm waiting to be at work. I want to fall asleep so the next night will come sooner. While I lie in bed, I can still smell the office: not just cleaning supplies but warm paper and ink, old coffee, and a stale odor from the storage closets and the stairwell, unused meeting rooms, and any untouched nook that no one else ever thinks about. It's a smell that other people wouldn't notice, but I do.

THE INTERN ISN'T in when I start my shift, and her absence feels particularly frustrating because I'm eager to finally talk about the CEO. But it's also a sign of renewed normality. No one should be staying late, and her absence is a sign that things are running as smoothly as they can. While I'm cleaning, the only noteworthy observation I make is that the Rogue Shitter has hit twice tonight. He's feeling sloppier—or maybe more productive than usual.

I still have no idea who he is, other than a man who uses the bathroom on any floor he likes and doesn't clean up after himself. Maybe the CEO's the culprit. It would make sense: the way he inhabits space, how he doesn't think of anyone else. Any floor, anytime, he's good to go. I cringe thinking of his wife cleaning shit streaks off their toilet. We're a lot alike. She's his cleaner at home. I think of the calluses between her thumb and pointer finger from holding the mop. We have,

I am certain, the same hands. She just sleeps in a more comfortable place, has a more comfortable life. But she has her own difficulties. I think of her walking his dog—she never wanted a dog, but she's the one taking care of it. She's structured her life around this dog that she doesn't even like, and the CEO only admires him, thinking, *I have such a nice dog.*

It's upsetting that she hasn't emailed me back, not only because I wanted her insight, but because I think I'd be a suitable friend. We're so much alike.

I sit at the CEO's desk but use my phone to compose potential follow-up emails to her. I just need to find the right words. In one, I tell her all about me, who I am, what I know and why. I think she would understand the nature of my work, how important it is, and how ingrained in the company I've become. Some of my work, like emailing her this unpleasant information, is just a burden I carry. She, too, has undertaken a series of tasks she doesn't enjoy. I picture the CEO lumbering over her, his vacant eyes and stale cologne. It would be easy for me and her to become friends.

But then what? I try to imagine her taking the company from him, but this idea is too unrealistic to hold on to. All my daydreams go slippery and gray. In another draft, I pretend to be the night manager of the hotel he frequents. I'm much more forthcoming about how often he's been there and the number of women he's seen. I let myself drip with judgment. He's crass, I tell her. Not even polite to management or the people who clean his rooms. Always leaves an unseemly mess. I think she would appreciate knowing this. It would assure her that I was talking about the right man, because she knows what kind of mess he leaves behind. When I reread the email, though, it sounds cruel, like I crafted it to intentionally inflict the most harm. But she isn't the one I want to hurt so I delete this one too.

Finally, I dash off a quick message: "Checking in to see if you're okay. Let me know if you need anything or if I can provide you with more information."

And then, before I can overthink it, I hit "send." I'm still worried about the hour, my IP address and location, but if I had waited, I'm not sure I could have brought myself to actually do it.

I've been imagining seeing her near my neighborhood, out walking alone, happily dog-free, finally untethered from the responsibilities of being his wife. We'd strike up a friendship, she'd see how alike we are, and she'd tell me everything. But maybe this more direct route is better. Why bother hiding from the woman I've saved? I know what it's like to remake your life, to reimagine the kind of person you are. At the very least, I could be a mentor for her.

I finish cleaning the top floor, stopping to check my phone every few minutes, then head down to a gray floor. I leave my phone on my cart. There's no reason to look at it. Constantly checking it is desperate, and I'm the furthest thing from desperate. Thirty seconds without checking. Two minutes. Three minutes. Five minutes. It's easy. I don't even need her response. It's just that I know she needs me. I wish I could find the right way to explain this.

I'm completely lost in thought when L. trudges in, scuffing the floors as usual. She somehow manages to do it with both feet. I don't think I could do that if I tried.

"Well," she says. "I guess you noticed."

I look at her, but she looks the same as she always looks. No new haircut or clothes, no noteworthy scar or blemish.

"I just got here," she says.

I generally have no way of knowing whether L.'s here or not. I often don't see her for several hours when I first come in—she dips in and out with ease. But she shakes her head and says, "My hours got cut."

I drop the trash bag I'm holding, and the contents spill out. I have to kneel on the floor to gather everything back into the bag. L. doesn't offer to help, and I try not to feel irritated, because maybe this is one of those instances where I can cut her a little slack, but it would have been nice to at least gesture toward an offer. I would have waved her away.

"I won't be able to pay rent," she says. "Not even if I cut corners. I just won't have the money."

I pick up some wadded-up paper towels that are very near her feet and look at her.

"I'll have to move," she says.

"Moving's expensive," I say.

"I just don't know how I'll do anything," she says.

Maybe if she had worked harder and been more valuable. Considering her work ethic, it makes sense that when the time came to cut away unnecessary expenses, she was trimmed. But she's received no reprimand or further instruction, so how could she have really known? It feels unreasonable to cut her down without any warning.

"The whole floor under us is cleared out," she tells me.

"I haven't been down there yet," I say, trying to imagine the space empty. "The desks and everything?"

She nods.

I should have seen that coming. I should have noticed the

preparation. You don't clear out an entire floor of office furniture in one day on a whim. It takes planning. I try to remember if there were any signs, and I can picture boxes half full of stuff, desks stripped down to nothing, their breakroom almost entirely empty. But I don't know if I really saw all that, or if I'm just imagining it now. I would have noticed this on the fourth floor, but I've been moving through the gray floors in a haze, thinking of the intern, the CEO, his wife, my people.

"They're probably going to rent it to someone," she says. "I hear about that kind of thing all the time."

"Well, at least that'll be some income," I say.

"That's the beginning of the end," she says. "It's an image thing. It's not just that we're having money problems, but that we'll *look* like we're having money problems."

It's clear to me that the CEO is the anchor dragging us down. Everyone else has to see it too. We'll drown along with him if we don't cut him loose. But sometimes when things go askew, everyone keeps their heads down, because they don't want to draw attention to themselves. They're afraid they'll be tossed overboard.

Hearing about the cuts to the gray floor makes me want to rush upstairs and check on my people again, see how they're all doing, comfort them. But I was just there, and I know nothing has changed. So I still myself and finish picking up the trash I spilled. I make nice with L. and hurry through the floor. If it's not cleaned perfectly, no one on this floor is going to complain or draw attention to themselves, not now. They're lucky to still have a job.

When I circle back to the fourth floor, it's the same as before. But even if no one else has been downsized, I think I can feel a frantic energy. There's a nervousness to the way papers are stacked. The stapler, pushed right to the edge of the copier room counter, seems ominous, knowing. I reclean surfaces and desks to try to get the gleam to settle in so things feel normal, but it doesn't really help. I spend extra time cleaning the CEO's office, and leave everything on his desk perfectly straight, all beautiful angles. The room screams, "Get it together!" in a way that has to be impossible to ignore. But the floors, even though I've mopped them twice, seem streaked, almost greasy, and the overhead lighting isn't bright enough. Just the feel of the room makes me nauseated.

In the bathroom, I wash my hands several times, counting. One, one-two, one-two-three, one-two-three-four. I get up to seven and then hold my hands over the sink and let them drip dry.

When I head downstairs, I can feel an extra grittiness to my teeth. Even the lights in the elevator are dimmer, and I think it moves slower, creaking between each floor. I'm grateful when the door finally opens and I'm in the lobby.

M.'s already waiting outside, next to the front door, and I let them in. They have a new haircut. It's buzzed on the sides and back, and only a couple inches on top. It sticks up awkwardly and seems vegetative in nature—a shrub that's been poorly trimmed.

"You got a haircut," I say.

They smile and offer me the clipboard. I sign for the delivery and try to do something like smiling too. Their hair isn't as short as Yarn Guy's, but is notably shorter than it was. M.'s long hair was their strongest feature. Now that I can see more of their face, it feels like they're a stranger. With their hair cropped this way, I can make out the shape of their skull, but it means nothing to me. I've always been this way: slow to adjust to changes in appearance. I read once that however someone looks when you first meet them, that's who you see for the rest of your life. But that isn't the case with me. When someone changes their appearance, I can't help but see who's there, as startling and unfamiliar as they might be.

"What made you do it?" I ask.

"Just needed a change," they say. "I cut it off every few years and then grow it again. It's hair. It grows."

"But why like this?" I press. "Why now?"

"Do you not like it?" M. asks.

Then L. comes in. "Your hair! It looks great."

"Thanks," M. says, rubbing a hand over the top of their head, unsettling the shrubbery.

"It's such a good fade," L. adds, and she smiles at me, like she's fucking with me.

"How're you doing?" M. asks. "With everything."

L. tells them all about her diminished hours. She goes on and on about some extra weekend work she's picking up, how she's helping her grandmother, and how much she's dipping into her savings.

"I know some people who are looking for a house cleaner," M. says.

"I couldn't do that," L. says.

"I think you could pick it up," they say, like what L. is worried about is having the necessary skills to do the work. But I've seen her grimace at me cleaning.

"My grandmother's doing a little worse too," L. says. "I don't want to leave her when she needs me. She's asleep right now, but during the day? She needs someone who can drop everything and be there."

I try not to think of her grandmother's dead plant. Instead, I focus on the way they're talking to one another, like I'm not even here. They have this easy back and forth, like they're picking up an ongoing conversation. Neither of them even looks at me, so I start backing toward the breakroom, thinking of laying my head down on the table there, because I'm feeling uncharacteristically tired.

"Getting a snack?" L. says, finally looking at me. "Want to take a break with us?" she asks M. But, of course, M. demurs because, unlike L., they have work to do. As M. leaves, they look at me several times like they're waiting for me to say something, but I just go to the breakroom.

L. follows me and watches while I take an aloe drink from the fridge. I started drinking them because I found one in the intern's desk, and then got kind of hooked. I like the vegetal, almost bitter taste of them. I've always liked bitter things, felt like it said something about me and what I was capable of doing. I never even see them in her desk anymore, but I still buy them. It hadn't occurred to me until this moment that she might have influenced me the same way I've influenced her, and I put the drink down. What else have I picked up from her? How has she changed the way I think about the office or the fourth floor?

"Do you want this?" I ask L., nodding at the drink.

Maybe I'll feel differently once I talk to the intern about the CEO, once things are settled and everything is running smoothly again. But until then, I think I'll keep her hands off my throat.

THE INTERN IS absent again, the night is quiet, and I fall into a well-worn routine of trash cans, surfaces, floors. Sometimes, after I clean one of the gray floors and get on the elevator to go up to the next floor, I'm not entirely sure whether I'm coming or going. I have to get off the elevator and check. Until I see that the floor is damp and the desks shine, it's hard to see through that blanket of sameness. So, my night is fairly monotonous, and I don't see L. until just after I finish lunch.

"I packed mine today," she says, pulling a plastic container from the fridge. It has her name on it, as though she's the one whose food is being taken when it's exactly the opposite. I don't know how many times I've sat in this room and watched her rummage through every last container in the fridge to make sure she didn't want mysterious leftovers or pizza that maintenance didn't finish. "I'm like you," she adds.

"What do you mean?" I ask.

"You always bring your lunch. No one ever brings you anything."

"There's nothing open at this hour that I would eat," I tell her.

She shrugs and keeps eating. She's brought in stuffed cabbage leaves, and it smells lightly pickled and meaty. I've already had lunch and I'm eating an apple now, presliced into thin pieces. I could take it with me, eat while I work, but it's actually nice to see her, since she hasn't spent the night following me around, giving me pointers on my work. So I launch into the CEO's wife.

"She finally emailed me back," I say.

"Who?" L. asks, her mouth full.

I'm not sure whether she's being serious.

"The CEO's wife," I answer. "But I think there's some sort of confusion, because I can't tell what she's saying."

"Let me see," L. says.

I think about pulling my phone out to let her see the email, but I shake my head. "She responded like I was spam or a bot. Like I wasn't a real person."

"That's weird," L. says.

I don't tell L. that what she really said was, "I don't appreciate your emails." I responded asking what she meant, because why wouldn't she appreciate my emails? I'm the only one looking out for her, the only one who even thought of her as a person. But that email bounced back, marked undeliverable.

"At least I told her," I say.

L. nods.

"But he's still here," I say. "He seems almost fine, like

nothing happened. And have you seen the deliveries? Almost nonexistent."

"You miss M.?" she asks, half-smiling.

"This is about the CEO," I say.

"Nothing else you can do about it," L. says. "No use worrying on and on."

"I'm not sure that's true," I say. "There's got to be something I can do. I can't just sit around while the company falls apart."

"You could clean somewhere else," she says, probably thinking of M.'s housecleaning suggestion. But cleaning a house is entirely different than cleaning an office building. To go from a place like this, full of so many different people who I guide and care for, to a single-family household? The demerit in significance would be too much to bear. Even if I did a dozen houses, it wouldn't be the same. Who cares what people do at home? I'm supposed to clean up after kids snacking on the sofa? Scrub people's private bathrooms, where they pick at their faces and remove unwanted hair? But here, I'm important. I already know everyone. I know the building. It's not just a routine or a job—it's an ongoing relationship. I couldn't let all this go. What would the last four years of my life mean if I just got another job?

"I do more than clean," I say.

She stops eating. "What else do you do?" she asks.

I finish my apple and stand up. "I should get back to work."

L. starts to say something else, but I turn and leave before she can get it out.

Upstairs, I find Yarn Guy's yarn is completely gone—not even the tail end of a spool left behind. His drawer is empty.

Even the candle I bought him is gone. All his thread, his embroidery, everything: gone. But the top of his desk is still covered in the usual work stuff, pristine and neatly stacked. He must be nervous about his job, trying to appear very on-task. But if anyone thinks he isn't on-task, they don't understand him at all. He's the most together person here. I dig through his desk again, but I can't find a single needle or bead. It's all gone. I hope, at least, that it was his own choice, that he hauled it all home because he wanted to. I can't help but imagine the CEO stopping by his desk, letting him know that he needs to focus, or sending a curt email that he should "leave his little crafts at home." I don't find an email like that in his inbox, but I can picture that kind of bullying all the same.

I owe it to Yarn Guy, to all of them, to do the CEO in.

His office has gone to shit again. It doesn't matter whether I clean it or not. He erases my efforts without even thinking of me. I tear into his desk with renewed vigor, less careful than usual, because with all the mess, he'll never know the difference. There's a chocolate-smeared wrapper between two pieces of paper, and an excess of crumbs across one side of his desk.

Then, folded and tucked underneath everything, I find a note. It's his handwriting, but slower, more careful than anything else I've seen. I can picture him sitting here, fully upright, very aware of his own posture. I can see the rigid way he's holding his pen, the people walking around outside his office.

"I'm so sorry," he's written. And then he's crossed that out and written, "I'm sorry for everything," and then simply, "I apologize." Then so much scribbling that I can't tell what it says, even when I hold it up to the light and squint. In contrast to his perfect handwriting, the layers of jagged scribbling threaten to tear a hole in the paper. He's a virgin apologist and just can't figure it out. Maybe this is a practice note and he's written a full and detailed apology elsewhere.

I log in to his computer to see if there's a more polished version in one of his email accounts, but there's nothing. He has so much to be sorry for, but who was he writing to? His wife? His mistress? Someone here at work? I read and reread the sparse note, looking for some clue in the curl of his scrawl, but there's nothing more than the words. I go through his desk again, starting from one side and carefully working my way to the other to be sure I haven't missed anything, but there's nothing else.

I shake the crumbs off his letter and add it to my portfolio. If anyone deserves an apology, it's me. Then I sit cross-legged on the floor behind his desk, looking out the window at the blankness below. I recently realized that the financial system they have on all their computers is outdated. That's the reason I've had so much trouble figuring it out. But of course, they're all used to it. He certainly is. Why would he want to install anything that worked properly, that might highlight the kind of *work* he's accomplishing?

When my legs get sore, I stand up and spritz enough cleaning product onto his chair that it'll never evaporate. He'll come into work and sit in a pool of disinfectant. Not enough to clean him up or straighten out all that's wrong with him, but enough to make him uncomfortable. And what's he going to do, complain that there was too much cleaning solution in his office? It's become a pit, trash-strewn, cologne-heavy and stale. He'd draw the wrong kind of attention to himself if he voiced any kind of complaint about cleaning.

It's still dark outside, but later than I usually stay. I'm worried that some go-getter might pop in on me, so I close all the CEO's drawers and leave things mostly how I found them.

His mess behind me, I head downstairs. Of course, it's too late for L. to be in the lobby. Even before she got her hours cut, she would have been gone by this time. She never stayed a minute late, got here a minute early, went anywhere beyond the bare minimum. She could see the bare minimum out on the horizon, rising up against the sky like a mountain range she would never climb.

But if I were her and my hours were cut, I would make myself indispensable. I'd make it so the company could hardly function without me. I'd spend all my free time arranging things very precariously around me so that in my absence, everything crumbled. But L.'s already home, watching television, wondering why people like her aren't more appreciated. "It's pretty messed up," she'll tell her grandmother. "I'm basically keeping the whole thing afloat. You should see how people run rampant without me."

TONIGHT, THE TWO jars of gray water are gone. Whatever the experiment was, it's over. I look for them in the drawers of the desk they're usually at and then in the breakroom, but there's nothing. It seems fair that if Yarn Guy can't have his yarn, this person shouldn't get to keep their unidentified murky water. They shouldn't be able to drag the specter of their child to work for everyone to tolerate.

There are a few more empty desks, but no one I'm attached to. The woman who kept coupons for discount sandwiches at the place down the street is gone. She's taken her coupons with her but left her chewed-on pens. I throw them away. No one will miss her. Porn Guy's also gone. I wonder if his friend is still here, and if they'll keep corresponding daily through lewd gifs. And I wonder if anyone ever saw what he was looking at on his computer. Maybe that's why he's gone. He got caught. I wish I could have seen it, the moment when everyone around him knew, and they watched him packing his things and trudging toward the elevator. I put gloves on to clean his desk: his mouse, his keyboard, each of his pens, his stapler, and hole punch. I don't want to leave any trace of him behind.

Then, on the CEO's computer, I find a longer-than-usual email to his mistress. There haven't been any emails with other women for a while. It's just her now. The *Other Woman*. And he talks to her like she's a real person and not some vague sexual being. He tells her about his day, and it's hard to believe she isn't bored by all this: long paragraphs about what he's thinking, where he's going to eat, what he saw on a walk.

I try to remember conversations or even texts with J., but all I can remember is him pointing out that he never felt bad about any of his clothes or hygiene, because he saw how I left the bathroom sink, caked with makeup that I don't wear anymore. It was a simple fix—after he left, I threw everything away. It made keeping the apartment clean much easier. But had he ever told me about his day? Did I talk about mine? I just have the lingering sensation that he thought I wasn't good enough, that the way I did things was objectively the wrong way. But the closing of the CEO's email is the important part. "I can't get a large enough sum until the end of the quarter. So we just need to tread water for now. But soon!"

I hit "print" so I can add this one to my collection.

The email was sent during his workday. While all the people outside his office were consumed by the drudgery of work, he was fantasizing about escaping with the Other Woman. He was here, but he also traveled across time and space to somewhere better. All these people stopped being real for him—

if they ever were. Had he once considered their livelihoods, their ambitions or needs? Where is this large sum of money going to come from if not from them, their pockets, their imagined earnings and bonuses?

And surely he never thinks of his wife. He probably doesn't really think of this Other Woman, either. She's easily rotated out for any other. It's almost too mundane to bear. Even if he weren't destroying my company, I'd fault him for how boring he is, how predictable. This is all he can imagine: collecting things and people so that he might be happy. He cannot conceive of anything else.

His wife's picture still sits on his desk. I'd love for this Other Woman to know that every time he emails her, he's looking at his wife's face. I consider taking a quick photo of the CEO's desk, focusing on the wife's picture, to send to the Other Woman, but this would fully clue him in to my surveillance.

Instead, I go downstairs to eat, and L.'s already in the breakroom, eating another lunch from home. She sighs and stirs what looks and smells like mapo tofu. I can tell she wants me to ask what's wrong, but I give my full attention to my own lunch, a porridge dish that I overwarm in the microwave so that it goes a little crusty and congealed at the edges.

Finally, she blurts out, "My boyfriend and I broke up."

"I didn't know you had a boyfriend," I say.

"You've seen him," she says, talking with her mouth open. "He used to bring me lunch."

"You said that guy wasn't your boyfriend," I say.

She rolls her eyes. "That means he's exactly my boyfriend."

"Why would you say he isn't, then?"

"How do you not know this?" she asks.

I shake my head. I thought boyfriend was a clear moniker, not something subtle that could creep up on you. We eat, and while I chew burned, solidified porridge, I think about showing L. all my research materials on the CEO, everything I've collected from his computer and emails. But I'm worried she might want to take immediate action. She probably imagines that her diminished hours would be given back if we could only repair the company, but I'm not sure that'll ever be the case. Once they've seen that everything runs fine without her, why pay her more than they have to?

I don't want to argue with her, so I don't bring it up, and instead we talk about her job hunt and her apartment. She's behind on rent, but they're letting her stay while she works something out. There's some money from her grandmother that she's waiting on, and payment for some of the weekend work she's been doing. Even with her hours cut, she's doing basically the same amount of work as before, so it seems a little unfair for her to be making substantially less. But I can see there's no way to pitch this argument without admitting how little she's always done.

After she heads off for a probably hour-long bathroom break, I dawdle in the lobby, because it's around the time M. usually comes by. And of course, M. is reliable. I barely have to wait before I let them in, and find I've already become used to their hair—or maybe it's less springy-looking now, and therefore more tolerable.

"You doing okay?" they ask.

When I say yes, they tell me about the weird bird they saw outside.

"I think its wing was damaged," M. says. "But I couldn't get close enough to help. It kept skittering away. I hate to think of it out there, helpless. But you can't save everyone, I guess."

I nod because I understand. I also have this urge to help, but I realized early on that I couldn't take care of everyone in the building. So I decided not to care about the gray floors. One floor was all I could manage.

Without pulling out my collection of emails, I tell M. about the CEO and the Other Woman and everything else.

"Do you think he's actually stealing money?" M. asks.

"I don't know," I say. "Where else would he be getting it? And it's not like he's displayed a lot of concern for the company."

We talk about the CEO and his office, and M. seems to understand much better than L. how responsible I feel for everyone.

"It's a lot for one person to shoulder," they say.

"It's been good to talk to the intern," I say.

M. sees how important it is for me to have a confidant who's in the deep end with me. This makes me want to understand them better too.

"How'd you become a delivery driver?" I ask.

"I've only been doing it for around a year," they say. "A friend got me in. But work has never really mattered to me. It's not my identity. I'm a dozen things that are more interesting and important than my job."

This is hard to conceive of: to be someone who does something that they don't think matters. Why do it at all?

"Do you like it?" I ask.

"It's fine," they say. "I don't go home hating it or even

thinking about it. Work has little to no effect on my idea of myself, you know?"

Before I knew their name, I only thought of them as the Delivery Person, but I nod to be polite. I've wondered how people think of me. Am I the cleaning woman? The Cleaner? This is reductive, of course. I've guided these people through breakups and deaths, oily skin and mismanaged time. I've seen them through rough periods and promotions, and I'm going to see them through the problems the company's having now.

M.'s looking at me, smiling, and I wonder what they're thinking.

"I've been meaning to ask you," they say. "Would you like to maybe take a walk this weekend?"

"A walk? Where?"

"Just a walk," they say. "Give us some more time to talk when we're not both working. A chance to get away from all this."

I don't say anything and look over their shoulder, out at the street. What difference would it make? But I think of the way the elevator hums and a certain acrid smell in the parking garage. Even when you truly, fully love someone, their flaws can start to dig at you if you don't take some time to recalibrate, spend time with other people, do other things. Maybe the building could stand a little time away from me, too, in order to fully appreciate my work.

"You can think about it," M. says. But they gesture for my phone, I hand it over, and they put their number in it, still smiling at me.

Then L. comes back from her staycation in the bathroom, and M. goes upstairs with their delivery, but I keep thinking about what they said, that work has no effect on their idea of themselves. I'm the opposite. I think my home life probably has little to no effect on how I exist in the office. In fact, my apartment has become a mini office that I can practice managing. I have a spool of yarn on my kitchen counter, where I imagine Yarn Guy would drink his morning coffee. In the bathroom I have a ream of paper under the sink. It just creates a feeling, not like I'm going to use it for anything in there. It helps me remember who I am, even when I'm not physically at the office.

I also use all the same products to clean at home as I do at work. It's been easy to bring home the dregs of my supplies: the last of my cleaning spray, gloves worn almost too thin to use, and even a mop with a broken handle. Sometimes I leave tools on my cart for a while, and then if no one misses them, I take them home too. I've acquired a lot of nice things this way, so that I can easily make my own repairs and I never need anyone to come and fix anything for me. Between the internet and my industrious nature, I keep things under control. Everything about my apartment is well-ordered and gleams in the light. If it didn't, I would polish it until it did.

TONIGHT, THE INTERN'S finally in, and I consider presenting her with my collection of emails from the CEO, but I'm still not fully convinced she would act on them. Everything he's said could be read in different ways—and she's only the intern, after all. But read together, it's at least a little damning. No one can actually doubt what he intends to do. It's not just unethical—like his dalliances with other women—it's blatantly criminal. But I worry that she'll shrug me off, throw up more walls, and then what? So, I smile and make nice, bide my time.

"He's really good-looking," the intern tells me, showing me a picture of a man who doesn't look any different than the last guy she dated. Just another generic potato of a man. She has a type, I suppose, and it's potato. "He's getting a business degree," she adds. "But he's very creative."

"You don't often see that from someone in business," I say.

I know which people on the floor have business degrees, including the CEO. I've gone through all their files. They're the most boring people imaginable, but they're convinced that they're incredibly important and that others find them fascinating.

"I know," she says. "And he's planning to study law."

He's the perfect potato for it.

"How many dates have you been on?" I ask.

"Just two," she says. "But I think we really get along." She smiles like she's embarrassed to have told me something personal about herself. As though I don't already know every little thing about her.

"I was asked out recently," I say.

"By who?" she asks, putting her phone down and pivoting toward me. She looks me up and down. It must be like hearing about your mother's dating life.

"A friend I've known for a while," I say, because I don't know how else to describe M.

"Handsome?" she asks.

I shrug.

"What kind of date?" she asks.

"A walk," I say.

"Is a walk a date?"

"We'll have a chance to talk," I say.

"If you already know them, haven't you talked already?"

"The exercise would be nice too," I say.

"Is walking exercise?"

"I think so," I say.

"I don't think any of my friends would call walking exercise," she says.

I have no clue why her friends' thoughts on exercise are important in this moment. She must feel inadequate, like she can't stand on her own, so she needs this fabricated expertise. People do this all the time. They make up anecdotes and statistics or readily believe anything they hear that confirms what they already believe.

"And do you really need exercise?" she asks. "Isn't your entire job manual labor?"

"I wouldn't say that," I say. If I explained how I guide and care for everyone, she might begin to imagine all the interventions I've made on her behalf.

We just don't have the same set of givens. And is it her fault that her view is so narrow, privileged? This really might be all she's capable of doing, the most she can possibly manage. Supplements and self-help books and pimple patches and dates with men who are notably tall. Maybe I shouldn't expect someone like her to help deal with the CEO's transgressions. I could paper the entire office with his emails, and then the elevators, the lobby. Let everyone see. But that feels too impersonal, too scattershot. I care about these people. I just need to find the right time, the right way in, so that I can present it to the intern in a way she really understands. Leave her no room to back away from it or pretend she doesn't see. This is something that she and I can handle together, the kind of thing that bonds two people.

I try to think of ways to broach it while she packs her things and smiles at me. I wish my own mother thought this much about me, cared about my well-being, really paid attention to what I needed. But this is the least I can do. I pull things from one caddy on my cart and put them into another, but she finishes before I work my way up to it.

When she's almost all the way to the elevator, she calls back, "Good luck on your *date*," letting her voice drop when she says the word "date."

But it's not like I've fully committed to going out with M. I like to relax over the weekends anyway. Give myself time to reboot. Where would we even go for a walk? Does M. expect me to meet them at the office? Somewhere else in town? My own apartment? I haven't had anyone over in years, and I don't like to imagine anyone in my personal space. How would I explain all the office décor?

I go through the intern's desk and find that everything around the gala and the fundraiser is now in her bottom drawer. She had been so enthusiastic about them, so consumed. How painful must it be to sit here with this body of work burning a hole through her desk, day after day? But she doesn't even seem sad anymore.

It's hard to justify these two versions of her—one committed and desperate to do a good job, and then another nonchalant, ignoring the imminent collapse around her. Which version is true? It's like there's no substance at the core of her. She's still here late, sure, but she's not frantic about it. She's just putting in the time, and then leaving in order to go out and live her real life. She's stopped thinking of this place as something that actually matters.

I use the old screwdriver I keep on my cart to loosen the screws on the CEO's door hinges. Not enough to take the door off—but enough to make it wobbly. Enough to make the whole thing fall over if anyone handles it too roughly or slams it. I picture him trying to shut himself in his office to email the Other Woman, and watching the whole door tip and crack off the door frame. It would be glorious. Everyone would see. I stand there for a while, just picturing it, lamenting that I won't see it happen.

Then I move to Yarn Guy's desk. His crafts are still gone, and I wonder if he's been working on them at home. I can't find any mention of them in his emails, but it's probably a strange thing to interject: "Here's that project we discussed, and also several pictures of my newest blanket," or "Sure, 2 pm works great for me, and, I've been wanting to ask you, which kind of glitter do you think is best?" He's still the same person he's always been, but if I hadn't seen all the crafts in his desk before, I'd never really know him. It makes me wonder what else I don't know about him and the others who work here.

I scroll through his browsing history again. There are a few more sports inquiries, and even a few video recaps he's watched. It's not an overwhelming amount of athleticism, so I still think he might be looking into this for someone else's benefit. It's not like he does it every day. Maybe someone at a nearby desk is very into sports and he's trying to appease them. It's the sort of kindness I'd expect from him.

I wonder how he feels about his job, whether he goes home thinking about it, or thinking about his coworkers and all their ongoing projects. Does he fall asleep at night rehashing presentations or composing new emails in his mind? Does he wish he'd spoken up in that meeting when they weren't hearing him? Does he go home thinking, *Why did I let them talk to me that way, like I'm not even a person, like I'm so much lower than them?*

But we aren't lower than anybody, and we don't have to accept being treated that way.

I lay my head beside his keyboard, where I imagine him laying his head too. It's like we're resting together, thinking the same thoughts, feeling the same things. Does he see how clean his desk is, and wonder about me here at night? Every day he looks at all the work I've done, and he reconstructs me the same way I reconstruct him. Am I different than he thinks? He knows my work, my reliable nature. He must picture my toned arms and calves. Maybe he thinks my hair is shorter or lighter, but that's such a small thing. Without picking my head up, I draw a trail of hearts going up one side of his desk calendar. I keep them very neat, and I don't get near anything he's already written. I would never mess up any of his work. But he'll see them later and this will help him conceive of me as a concrete person, someone he could know.

After I've rested a few beats, I give the floor a once-over, wiping down desks and chairs, reordering piles of papers and sorting folders. I stop near the elevator to give Cheery #2's desk some extra attention. Cheery #1 was let go, and I think it's getting to him. His former adversary's desk is bare, drawers empty and pulled open. I don't know if Cheery #2 is reacting this way because he's worried he'll be fired too, or if he misses having a nemesis, someone to focus on. It's nice to be able to gather all your problems and anxieties together and pin them to a single person. It's easier to focus that way.

ON MY WALK to work, I think about how sad it was for the two Cheeries to be split up. Each of them seemed to be driven by spite and hate for the other. What do either of them have to work for now? What do they even talk about without one another? I can't imagine not working here. I'd miss the people but also the building. The shape and size of it, the sounds of it settling, the smell of the parking garage. I think of all the empty desks scattered throughout the building. It happened gradually, so we all got used to it and just kept going. But as things worsen, the upbeat flyers only multiply, to make sure everyone knows about all the incentives to work harder, be happier. Bring in a new account and get a gift card! Trust exercise at lunch! Pastries for Monday morning early birds! The walls are always exclaiming something. How could anyone not be excited to work here?

But underneath all the colorful paper and exclamations,

things are getting worse—and if I don't act, who will? How many people will be cut before they don't even need this kind of office space? Would they merge the floors? Move to another building?

Spurred on, I walk faster, get to work earlier. When I ride the elevator up to the fourth floor with my cart, I see that the intern is here. I knew she would be. She had to be. I leave my cart next to the elevator, no immediate plan to clean, and close the distance between us. I thought I would feel nervous, but I feel energized, ready.

"How's it going?" I ask her, already unfolding my collection of evidence. Together, the emails articulate a clear narrative—a desperate man stealing from the company he thinks of as *his company* so he can escape and leave it to collapse behind him.

"Really great," she says. "I got a promotion."

"You're not the intern anymore?" I say, the papers half-unfolded in my hands.

"Not anymore!" she says.

"Amazing," I say, and I'm rereading the emails in my head. "Just a few loose ends," he said in his latest. "Nothing to worry about. We're all set." I look down at the paper and then back at her.

"I knew it was going to happen," she says. "But I didn't expect it so soon. I think they're just really excited about me. I'm quite the get." She talks about what college she went to, and how impressed they are with all her connections. "It means something to people in this industry," she says, talking about her school. "And it was so expensive." She tells me exactly how much it cost her parents, and then how much similar schools cost. She's simply more valuable and more qualified than other people.

"I've been wanting to talk to you," I say.

"I know, it's really exciting," she says. "My mother was excited, but my dad said it was expected. He's always like that, but I think he was happy for me too."

"I mean," I start. "I have these emails." I hold them out to her, wishing that I hadn't folded them, or that I'd put them in a folder to make them look more professional. I turn the papers to face her.

"It's the late nights," she says. "They could see what a go-getter I am. That's their phrase, not mine: a go-getter. And that event I planned. Even though they didn't have the money to host it, they saw what I was capable of. I'm glad I put in all that work. I almost didn't, but I'm the kind of person who can't sit still."

She smiles at me, probably grateful for all my input and guidance over the past several weeks. Otherwise, she wouldn't be here.

I'm still holding the papers, and I wonder if I should put them on her desk.

She clicks her mouse a few times and then looks back up at me. "This new project is really going to build out my résumé. Very splashy. I'm looking for a new apartment, one with better light. It's important to have the right light."

I have dark curtains on all my windows to block out any light and simulate the night. Very little of my day is committed to brightness.

She tilts her computer to show me the apartment she's

thinking of. It's actually in a pretty bad part of town and would be a terrible commute here.

"A little far away," I say.

"I can bike," she says. "It'll be nice to get some exercise."

Walking isn't exercise, but biking is. Okay.

"I think I'd see about replacing these sink fixtures," she says, pointing out the perfectly normal sink fixtures. "And then I'd replace the ceiling fan with an overhead light."

"Why would you replace a ceiling fan?" I ask. "I wouldn't want to live somewhere without a ceiling fan."

"They look tacky," she says, and makes a face like I'm gross for keeping a thing like that in my home. I'm gross for putting my comfort above her lofty sense of aesthetics.

I put the emails on her desk and pull at the edges to smooth out any creases. "This explains everything," I say.

"What is it?" she says, reaching for the papers but stopping short of touching them. She scrunches her face like they smell, even though it's just a stack of paper.

"The CEO," I say. "It explains why things have been rough. Why there's been so much downsizing."

"What downsizing?" she says.

I gesture toward the rest of the office, nodding at the scattering of empty desks, which seem to have increased since just last night.

"There's no downsizing," she says. "You mean the people who were fired because they were doing a bad job? And how do you have all this? Was it in the trash? You shouldn't mess with this stuff. If anything, put it through the shredder."

I take the papers off her desk, crumpling them in my hands. "It's nothing," I say.

"Do you know how to work the paper shredder?"

I nod. "Sorry for bothering you," I say.

She laughs. "Just don't look through the trash," she says. "Did you wash your hands?"

"I'll let you get on with it," I say, and head back toward my cart.

"Can you do this floor after I leave?" she asks. "Sometimes you're so loud."

I get on the elevator without answering her. If Scissors Guy still worked here, I'd take every pair of scissors and leave them in a cup on her desk. The elevator moves slower than usual, and I think I detect a new clicking noise under its usual hum. I wonder how long someone could be trapped inside an elevator before it became dire. Would the intern find me? L.? M.? Maybe some early-morning go-getter.

But the door releases with a gasp. On the gray floor right above the lobby, everyone has moved desks so they can all sit together, leaving the empty desks from layoffs all on one side of the room. They haven't done anything like this on the top floor. All their empty desks are scattered across the room, each person their own island. No one was willing to give up their original space. I wonder what made all these people move. Did they do it naturally, or was it someone's idea? Did a supervisor make them? Are they so friendly that they wanted to be closer together? It is easier to talk and collaborate that way.

After I finish all the gray floors, I go back to the top floor. It's quiet and empty now. The CEO's door hinges have already been tightened, and I wonder if the door completely fell off or if it just swung there, unevenly. I don't feel the joy

I expected to, though. I pace the floor, looking over everyone's desks, thinking about how the intern recoiled from me, tried to chastise me. After everything I've done to help her, she acted like I was nothing but the woman who cleans the building. We both know I'm so much more than that.

There's a desk halfway across the room that belongs to a woman I think is some sort of supervisor. She at least has seniority, and her projects seem concrete and ongoing. This is where the real work of the office happens. I take one of the folders from her desk and leave it on the intern's, cocked at an angle and highly visible to passersby. I double back and take both of the supervisor's nice pens, along with a little heating pad, shaped to fit a coffee cup. I leave it all on the intern's desk. If she thinks she's big-time, let her be big-time. Let her be so big. The biggest.

For the rest of the week, I avoid the intern while she's here. I do the top floor last, after she's gone for the day, and I take a folder from someone's desk every night and leave it on hers. Sometimes, I take their pens and snacks too. Everyone will see her stocking up. Let them think she's stealing work or clients, or just trying to mess with them. After how unliked she'd been initially, this won't be difficult for everyone to believe.

Then, on Friday, I leave one of these folders on the supervisor's desk, with some of the intern's notes paper clipped to it. She's worked out some figures and has her name and two other names written out with some numbers beside them, so there won't be much of a question about whose handwriting it is. If she hasn't been caught so far, this will do it. *Enjoy your promotion now,* I think.

I'M TRYING TO kill the roaches in our breakroom again, sprinkling poison behind the fridge and under the sink. The harder I work to get rid of them, the more agitated and active they seem. Week after week, I kill them, but they're always here.

L. crinkles her nose, as though she can smell this scentless white powder. Everyone pretends to be so sensitive to smell, but no one thinks about their own scent.

"Are you avoiding M.?" she asks.

"What do you mean?"

"You're never here when they deliver anymore. For a while, you were hovering around the lobby like you were waiting for them."

"I have no idea what you're talking about," I say. "I've just been working, the same as always. I guess I just have more to do than you."

"How are things upstairs?" she asks. It used to irritate me how quickly L. bounced back from anything I said or did, but it's kind of nice, really.

"I think I have proof he's stealing," I say. I haven't quite untangled the financials, but it's all there—I can tell.

"What kind of proof?"

"Something he wrote."

"You should tell someone," she says.

I can see she's getting excited. She's picturing having all her hours back, and then maybe some kind of promotion too.

"I will," I say. "I just want to do it right. The intern—"

"She's not the intern anymore, right?" L. interrupts.

"You know what I mean. The intern should be the one who reports him. Then there's no reason for anyone to know I was in his office, at his desk, on his computer."

L. nods. "She'll be grateful we helped her."

"I helped her," I correct. "And she'll remember."

The intern just needs guidance, a reprimand, something to get her back on track. Upstairs, I find her crying again, and I think of the first night I met her, when she was at her desk, loudly weeping, unaware that anyone might hear her. She sounds remarkably similar tonight, and I feel a gentle wave of nostalgia. It's comfortable to be needed. Her hair's unkempt and she holds her face in her hands like before, but this time she looks up at me when I approach. We aren't strangers anymore.

"What happened?" I ask.

She wipes at her face and says something unintelligible, but I shake my head and wait for her to calm down enough to talk. "My project," she finally says, and I nod for her to go on. "This one guy, he basically redid the whole thing."

She points across the room to where Vinyl Guy sits. Over the course of the last several weeks, he's been learning how to make his own vinyl records. I've seen him reading about it online, buying the materials, and emailing some woman about it. "It's the most artistic thing you can do," he told her. I wished I could log in to the woman's email account so I could see her forwarding his email to friends. Was she making fun of him or was she entirely duped, utterly besotted?

"It wasn't any better his way," she says. "Just different. But everyone was thanking him like he really saved the day. Like I had messed things up. But he didn't do anything! Everything would have been perfect without him. They didn't even get a chance to see my work before he ruined it. And he was so smug. You should have seen him."

I can see him perfectly without seeing him. Vinyl Guy is one of the people whose folders she stole. At least, that's what he believes, because why else would it have been on her desk, where I left it? No wonder he wants to ruin her work. He thinks she's trying to close in on him, take credit for things he's already done.

I give her a sympathetic smile. She's softer now, more malleable. I think about reaching out to touch her arm, to reassure her, but I don't want to go too far, so I just incline my head toward her.

"I don't know what to do," she says.

I won't get Vinyl Guy tonight, because it's too soon. Anything I do would be tracked back to her. But I will get him, because that's why I'm here—to take care of people.

"You're good at your job," I say. "And you deserve to be here. You just have to show them."

"I tried to," she says.

"That wasn't your one and only shot," I say. "And don't worry about that guy. People like that get what's coming to them."

She keeps crying for a while, stopping long enough to tell me more about her project, what he did, how he smiled while he made *her* presentation to the room. How he softened his voice when he spoke to her, like she was being hysterical when she was just sitting there calmly, no expression on her face. I assure her several times that it's okay, and then once her tears dry up, she asks, "How was your date?"

"I've been putting it off," I say.

"I'm sorry if I didn't seem enthusiastic," she says. "I was so distracted. A walk really is a cute idea."

"It's just, I'm kind of into someone else," I say.

"Oh, who?" she asks, brightening, the promise of any kind of gossip bringing her back to life.

"He works in a place like this," I say. "We're both really into crafts. You should see the stuff he makes."

"I love an artistic man," she says, and I think of her artistic business potato. I consider asking her about Yarn Guy, what she thinks of him or what he looks like, but I can't think of a natural enough transition. I'll save it for another night. She tells me more about the potato she's dating—things are getting pretty serious—and then she says she has to go. He's expecting her.

After she leaves, I survey Vinyl Guy's desk to see what else is going on with him, but beyond his extremely artistic hobby, he's pretty boring. He might as well work on a gray floor. I'll get him in a few days when he's comfortable and she's already moved on. Even if she hears about what happened, it won't occur to her that it was me or that anyone might think it was her. She'll think he probably had it coming. The way he treated her is how he treats everyone. Anyone who behaves that way is eventually going to stumble into some bad karma.

The CEO's office is still in disarray but hasn't become any worse. He seems to have plateaued, finally. The room smells of body odor and cologne—he's gone extra heavy to try to cover his own scent. I've always found colognes and perfumes repulsive—strange artificial odors that burn my nose. A person spritzed with perfume is little more than a scented trash bag, the chemical smell meant to cover up the harshness of what's inside. But he probably imagines this odor is his signature scent. He thinks it's attractive, alluring. If someone asks what the smell is, he would never notice them cringing, and he'd recommend his cologne, thinking that they too want to smell of perfumed trash.

His poor cactus is starting to look notably shriveled, so I pick it up to go water it. But on the back of the cactus are a couple of little baggies of white powder. They're just tucked into the spines. I stare for a few seconds, trying to imagine some easily explained phenomenon that would require this—but no, it can only be one thing. Not only is he doing a shitty job, but he can't even properly hide his illicit habit. I think of throwing the drugs out or leaving them prominently atop his desk. I could sprinkle the white powder all over his keyboard, his paperwork, make it snow. But instead, I put the dying cactus back where it was, and I drop one of the little white baggies onto the floor beside it, as though it just fell off. Anyone could see it.

Then I write the name of the hotel he's been using with
the Other Woman, the same hotel he took so many of his
women to, on a sticky note, and leave it right beside his keyboard, in pretty much the only clean space left on his desk.
I underline it a few times and then trace over the words to
make them more noticeable. He'll feel caught, but this isn't
the kind of thing that he can confront anyone about. Imagine him bursting out of his office and shouting, "Who wrote
down the name of the hotel I've been taking my mistress to?"
He'd be shaking the sticky note, pinched between two fingers. "Who did this?" he'd shout, raising his voice even more,
shaking the colorful square of paper with increasing vigor.

But no, he'll only see it and feel anxious and watched.
Maybe he'll tell the Other Woman about it, but he won't
mention it to anyone else. He might not even tell her, because why unsettle things more than necessary?

I'm flying high, picturing the CEO scrambling. It's a nice
way to end the night. For good measure, I loosen his door
hinges again. He'll just think it's the nature of his door—
slippery thing.

THE NEXT NIGHT, the CEO's desk is notably cleaner and his cactus is without illicit ornamentation. If I'd known that leaving a note with his preferred hotel's name on it was all it would take for him to straighten up, I would have done it sooner. It's not perfect—there are still smears of coffee and crumbs stuck in his keyboard—but it's better than it was. His stacks of paper are neater and somewhat diminished. Visible patches of desk have been wiped down. Maybe he felt anxious enough to do a bit of his job.

In response, I buy a small bottle of lube at the store down the street. I squeeze half the bottle into the trash can, because the idea of a half-used bottle of lube strikes a better note. It's more realistic. He'll wonder whose lube it is, how they were using it, how it got into his office. I leave the bottle, curling slightly from where I squeezed it, on his desk. It's like a smile.

And enough time has passed that I can begin to deal with

Vinyl Guy too. I settle in at his computer and after some digging, I print an email where he disparages three of his coworkers to a supervisor. The email is verbose and largely unstructured, but the heart of it seems to be that he finds these three people unlikable and wants to make them someone else's problem.

I make a few copies of his email to leave around the office for someone to stumble upon. Once they see what he has to say about them, none of these people will want to work with him. And once a few people don't want to work with you, no one will. A little shunning goes a long way. They'll talk about how you can't trust a guy like this, who bad-mouths you one second and smiles at you the next. The nicer he is in response to their treatment, the worse things will get. "So fake," they'll murmur. "Did you hear what he did to the intern?" She can tell them the whole story, like she told me. They'll all be on her side. If he's not fired, he'll be miserable enough to quit. I think of how happy she'll be, and I wish someone had ever watched over me this way. How nice, to feel so cared about.

Afterward, I feel extra energetic and take the stairs so I can pick up any stray trash or catch anything in need of a spot clean, but it all looks pretty clear. Other than the phantom door-propper, who still crops up once or twice a week, most people use the elevator, even if they're only going up or down one floor. They're used to it and do it without even thinking about it. It's a dissociative space. Even when the elevator is full, no one is ever really in the elevator. They're still at home, trying to remember if they left the oven on, or they're already at their desk and they're writing a brisk email back to the person who's been passive-aggressively checking in all week. Some of them are days ahead, already well into their weekends—though later, when you ask them what they did over the weekend, they'll say nothing. It's all nothing.

I'm used to working at night, but I have to admit, even I find the stairwell dim and cold. The rugged concrete steps are sloppily painted gray, and the walls are uneven, crumbling in places. It gives the impression that they aren't solid—if you pressed hard enough, you might sink into them. I like the idea of the building absorbing stray employees, punishing people for leaving early or getting in late. I like the grainy echo if I talk to myself as I walk down. I try whispering, and it's like the walls scratch back at me and make a little rustling noise. The whole stairwell is sharply different from the rest of the building, which is all lit up and given a fresh coat of paint in an attempt to make it look new when it obviously isn't. I can see why someone might not use the stairs when they aren't accustomed to them. If someone sanded down the walls, painted them, and then installed better lighting, I wonder if people would begin to use the stairs. Or would their earlier impression stick? No matter how nice it looks, maybe taking the stairs is always going to be beneath them.

As I'm coming out of the stairwell, I see M., and I duck back inside. It's a reflex. I saw them, and my body jerked me back. They had to have seen me, but maybe they think I simply forgot something upstairs and am heading back to get it. They probably don't think that I'm hiding or plainly running away when I see them. They only asked me on a walk, after all. They didn't even use the word "date." Maybe they think because I'm cooped up indoors all night, I could use the fresh air. Maybe we're friends and this is the nature of friendship. Who hasn't gone on a walk with a friend? But it's awkward to transition from colleagues to friends who see each other outside of work. I don't know how anyone does it, or why they would.

I'm standing in the stairwell now between the second and third floors, listening for the sound of a door opening above or below me, but there's nothing. I can't bring myself to go back, too embarrassed to have been seen fleeing. Something about running away makes me feel small, childlike. I sit on the steps and feel the beginning of a headache—a tightness around my temples, a heat pulsing along the back of my skull. I close my eyes and try to think calming thoughts—glossy floors, perfectly clear windows, chairs tucked under desks.

After enough time passes that M. is surely gone, I head back upstairs and sit at Yarn Guy's desk. I still miss his crafts and all the colorful ornamentations he kept. His yarn drawer remains empty, a memorial to what was. In his top drawer, there's a card for two free meals at a fancy place down the street.

I think of the two of us, sitting across from one another in a softly lit room. Ambient music plays, and he says, "Oh, I know this song," and tells me the artist. This is the kind of thing he's always surprising me with: some small fact or piece of information that can be easily integrated into conversation. He'll reach forward and hold my hand under the table. That, too, will be a shock—that he could easily reach so far without slumping over, and that he would. His hands would be much warmer than mine, and the roughness of his knitting calluses would be reassuring. Here's someone who won't let go.

I take his card for two free meals and leave it on Vinyl Guy's desk, clearly visible. What kind of man digs through another man's desk and takes something like this? Vinyl Guy won't see it here and go around the office asking "Whose is this?" so he can return it. Instead, he'll tuck it away and begin imagining his dinner. Could he split these two free meals into two separate visits, or is the expectation that he brings someone? He'll call and ask. Maybe someone will notice the card on his desk and remember it later when Yarn Guy laments the loss. Maybe someone will see him eating Yarn Guy's dinner. An additional perk is that Yarn Guy won't take someone to dinner who isn't me. I'd hate to think of him eating with someone else, reaching under the table for their hand, looking into their eyes.

To twist the knife, I log Vinyl Guy's name in for the conference room every afternoon this week. It's not like he's taking the entire day—it's not excessive enough that he would need to be directly confronted. But it's enough for other people to notice and be annoyed. They have meetings too. They're important too. Is he just reserving it all week to make sure he has it the one day he might need it? So inconsiderate.

I MANAGE TO avoid M. all week, but I keep wanting to talk to them about the intern or the CEO. And then I found three pairs of scissors in one guy's desk, and it was like Scissors Guy was being reborn. I tried to tell L. about it—Son of Scissors Guy, Scissors Guy Strikes Back—but she wasn't listening, didn't appreciate it the way I knew M. would. Maybe I could tell M. that I'm busy the next few weekends, put off our walk for a while, and we could go back to how things were: me letting them into the lobby, us talking about our nights, and generally knowing each other. It had been easy. So, I resolve not to avoid them tonight.

On the fourth floor, the intern is still upset. "No one's taking me seriously," she says. "No matter what I do, they're still treating me like I'm just the intern."

"Who?" I ask.

She points out two desks not far away from her. One is Leftovers, who once or twice a week leaves an unwrapped half-eaten sandwich in her desk drawer, and the other is a person who I suspect is Sticky Doorknob, based on the grease smeared across his desk and computer. That either of these people believe they're in a position to treat anyone like an inferior is amazing. I've tried leaving a small plastic container and a few brand-new paper bags on the desk for Leftovers, but she doesn't care. Her desk drawer is container enough. I can't think of her without picturing the infestation of her desk, the small roaches that crawl over and in her sandwich. Maybe she's even eaten one of these roaches without knowing. Certainly, she's prompted the spread of vermin to other desks, other floors. Without her, the building might not have fruit flies.

Sticky Doorknob is not much cleaner. I'm always wiping down his desk, his computer, his keyboard, and then chasing him around the office, wiping off doors and walls, the copier, the fax machine, the edges of other people's desks. It makes sense that these two are a duo.

"What happened?" I ask.

"They took one of my projects," she says. "They said I wasn't fast enough, but I only got the project a few days ago. And they didn't even ask for an update. They wouldn't listen to anything I said. I could have been almost done for all they knew. But because I'm newer than them, they decided I must be slow."

"You're not slow," I say.

"I know!" she says. "I had it all mapped out in my head. I knew exactly what I was going to do. But because I couldn't show them some sort of handwritten or typed-out notes, they said I hadn't done anything. Just because they work that way doesn't mean I have to. There's no rule about it. And it's not like either of them is my supervisor. We have the same job. We're the same!"

"If anything, you're better," I say. "You'll show them up. They'll see the kind of work you can do."

"I shouldn't have to, though," she says. "I've been here long enough that I don't need to prove myself."

I nod at her, give her the soft smile, the gentle eyes. If she'd really been here long enough, she'd just do her work. But she's still desperate for everyone to think she's doing a good job. She still wants to be seen as productive, valuable. Appearances are more important to her than the actual work. It's hard, sometimes, to do the kind of work I do, so unnoticed, behind the scenes. But I know I'm pulling the strings, and that's nearly enough.

She talks for long enough that eventually she feels okay again. She circles back around to how much she deserves this job, how lucky they are to have her, and her sniffling subsides. Her face is dry. "What do you think of these shorts?" she asks, showing me a pair of wide-legged knee shorts on her computer.

"Nice green," I say.

"They're kind of silly," she says.

"I don't see how," I say.

She laughs like I'm joking, and I give her another smile. She shows me several more pairs of shorts, a jacket, and some shoes, talking about the prices of each, what those prices mean, and what people will think about her based on how much each item costs. "Everyone can tell these shoes are expensive," she says, even though I would've had no clue if she hadn't told me. In her world, the price of each item is all that matters. It's the lens through which she sees and is seen. She goes on to tell me about her new credit card, how anyone who sees it will be impressed. She takes it out and puts it on the desk, as though she's practicing paying for dinners, drinks. She smiles but looks earnest about it. All these status symbols convey something specific about her, and she believes everyone else knows and cares about this special language. I suppose most of them probably do.

After she leaves, I go through Leftovers' and Sticky Doorknob's desks. Neither had been very interesting to me before, and if they hadn't been complete assholes, I wouldn't have had any reason to pay them much notice now. The first thing I do is flip over each of their chairs and loosen enough screws to make the chairs not only squeaky but almost imperceptibly shaky. It's not bad enough that either of them will actually fix their chair, but they'll either complain about it to everyone around them or be quietly miserable. I sit in each of the chairs to make sure I've nailed it, looking across the room to the intern's desk, which I think is far enough away that the noise won't aggravate her. I sit there for a few minutes, rocking from side to side, enjoying the sound of it and then the quiet of the office.

Then I write Leftovers' actual name on a few sticky notes and stick them on the oldest items in the breakroom fridge. Let everyone think she's the reason the fridge is disgusting. If I keep this up, she could be tasked with cleaning the fridge out for everyone, a chore I can attest is pretty sickening. It's hard to get anyone to take responsibility for the murky, unidentifiable leftovers in the fridge. No one wants to admit that the container growing pink and orange molds is theirs. Better to let it go, buy new containers, or quit eating altogether. "I don't even eat lunch," they might say.

Then, with significant effort, I pry the shift key off Sticky Doorknob's computer. A real tough one to work without. They'll eventually get a new keyboard, but in the meantime, everything they do will look sloppy and childish. Or they'll have to copy and paste existing capital letters. This is going to slow them way down.

The CEO's office still looks fairly well-ordered. When I check his email, there's another email to and from the Other Woman. It's more of the same, and I print it off. I almost need some kind of folder to keep all the emails together.

I do the rest of the floor and find the coffee machine in the breakroom has leaked all over the cabinet for the third night in a row. The stain is nearly dry now, and I'm annoyed no one wiped it up or repaired the leak. I could fix it, but I feel like they deserve the broken machine for not doing anything about it.

By the time I finish cleaning and get downstairs, I've missed M. and L. is gone for the day. I do a few quiet loops of the parking garage and spend the remainder of my night resting in our breakroom. L. has finally taken her dead plant home. She's left a scattering of soil and a few dead leaves on our table, and I leave them as a memorial.

THE NIGHT AIR is cool and there's a small stretch of my walk where I can almost see the stars, even with all the lights of the city. I'm running even earlier than usual, so I stop and watch some long-billed birds hopping around a fenced-in patch of overgrown grass. It almost looks like they're playing some game I don't understand the rules to, hopping in one direction and then the other, staying mostly clustered together, and then circling around a couple of empty glass bottles. One of them has a mouse dangling from its mouth. The mouse's legs twitch, and part of me would like to save it, but I recognize that it's probably mortally injured. The mouse is too damaged to run away now.

For the rest of my walk to work, I'm filled with a kind of wonder. I've made this walk more than a thousand times and never seen anything like this. No matter how accustomed to something you are, you can still be surprised. Your night can still be fresh and new. I catch myself nearly bouncing as I approach the office, so energized by the sight of that bird with a mouse gripped in its beak.

Maybe this is how M. feels about their pet rats—they don't see them as gruesome at all.

I bound up the few quick steps to the building, swipe my card, and go inside. It's nice to know that L. won't be in yet. I have some time to myself in our breakroom, the lobby, and all these spaces that she thinks of as hers. Strange that she would claim for herself the most public, oft-used spaces. Even our breakroom is accessible to people we'd never see or interact with: the pest control guy, if he ever came, a plumber or electrician called out in an emergency, the guy who repainted all the lines in the parking garage. There are probably people we couldn't imagine who sit at our table, rifle through our fridge, and think they know us. Regardless, L. seems to believe she owns this room, though she doesn't feel she's responsible for cleaning it. It's hard to enjoy anything left in such disarray, and I'm tempted to begin straightening it, but I don't want to establish that pattern. I let myself sit for a few moments before I head up to the fourth floor.

The intern isn't in tears tonight. Her hair is pulled back into a neat, low bun, and her eye makeup is intact and shimmery.

"How's it going?" I ask, and she tells me how much better things are now.

"I think I had it all wrong before," she says. "People wanted to work with me, not take projects from me." She points at Sticky Doorknob's desk. "You actually just missed him," she says. "We've been working on this all day." She tilts her computer so I can see some spread that she's created. It's all brightly colored text and pictures of a room from overhead. "It's going to be interactive," she says, whatever that means.

Even from where I'm standing, I can see he doesn't have a replacement keyboard yet. It's still missing the key I pried off.

"He was perfectly nice when he asked if I wanted to collaborate," she says. "I feel stupid for getting all upset."

She seems so relaxed that I almost bring up the CEO again, but decide to wait. Why ruin a good thing? There has to be a way to guide her more naturally toward the truth. Several months ago, one of the wheels on my cart got twisted and stuck. I tried to roll the thing and it wouldn't go. I could only drag it along, scraping and clicking like it might break. I emptied it out, flipped it over, and kept trying to twist the wheel back around. I knew it would go back to how it was eventually. I just had to keep working at it. I could feel its need to right itself. L. saw me doing it, and said I should put in a request for a new cart, but then I'd still be out at least one entire night of work, or I'd be stuck carrying supplies, making multiple trips, the whole thing. So, I ignored her and kept fiddling with it until it popped back into place and the cart rolled again, no problem. I couldn't explain how I'd done it. I just kept working at it until it was right. That's how things go sometimes.

I clean around the intern while she works. It feels so normal, like we're relaxing back into who we usually are. She stops me to ask if I like the blue background or the green one, tilting her monitor for me to see.

"The green," I say, and she nods and goes back to clicking and typing, working to get things how she wants them, knowing eventually it'll all fall into place. Our work is not so different.

After she leaves, I sit down at the CEO's desk like I always do and watch a new online tutorial. I find that tonight, it finally all makes sense. I've got a handle on the financial system. It's like learning any new thing—it seems impossible until everything clicks. After weeks of trying, it feels astounding that I ever had trouble reading any of this. And the CEO's just as bad as I thought—possibly worse.

Later, I'm standing in the lobby with L., watching some man walk up and down the sidewalk.

"Do you think he's lost?" she asks.

"He doesn't look distressed," I say. He's dressed in dark colors, kind of formally, with a collar, and something that looks like a suit jacket. Maybe he's coming from an event, walking off the booze, or he's headed somewhere, trying to work through his nerves. His hands are in his pockets in a way that makes him look jittery. Anxious people never know what to do with their hands, their arms. They're upset that they have bodies at all.

Finally, he walks off in one direction and doesn't come back. He either worked up the nerve to go wherever he was going, or he got tired and went home.

"Happens all the time," L. tells me. "And it's always a man."

"Women know where they're going," I say. "They have a plan."

"Probably unsafe for a woman to walk up and down the same street all night."

"And they know how strange it looks," I say. "They wouldn't want to make anyone else feel uncomfortable."

We talk about what people are doing out at this time of night. It's either recreational or extremely necessary. There's no in-between. Then I tell her about the people messing with the intern, and how I put them in their place.

"Why do you care so much how anyone treats her?" L. says.

"It's not a crime to care about other people."

"It very nearly is," she says. "The way you do it."

"People should have more empathy," I say.

She cocks her head. "You don't even work there," she says. "You can't really know what's happening."

"What do you mean, I don't work there? I literally work in the same place."

"It's not the same," she says.

"It's exactly the same."

"I know you're bored," she says. "So you like to dig through people's stuff, mess with them, see what happens. I get it. This is a boring job to have, sometimes."

"You don't know anything about my job," I say. "Our jobs aren't the same."

"We do pretty much the same thing," she says, gesturing at the lobby, like I'm supposed to see something here that's indicative of us both. She smiles, but there's nothing good-natured about her expression.

"Our jobs are very different," I say. "And I do more than clean."

She just looks at me.

"I watch over everyone," I say. "Sometimes they make the wrong decisions, and I help them see their mistakes. They just need someone to force them to do the right thing." L. takes a step back, like I'm threatening her in some way, but I was only gesturing, trying to illustrate my point. I hold my hands at my sides and speak carefully, keeping my voice low and even. "They need someone who makes the wrong thing so uncomfortable that they have no choice but to stay away from it."

"Do you even know what the company does?" she asks. "Do you even know what kind of company it is?"

"Of course I know," I tell her. "How could I not? I see their computers, their desks. I'm here night after night."

"And?" she says.

I look at her. I'm not going to play some guessing game where if I don't say exactly what she's expecting to hear, I'm somehow ridiculous, only the cleaning woman, playacting at something more.

"You've been here how many years?" she asks.

It's almost four, but I don't tell her that. "What matters is people, and I know the people here. All of them."

She shakes her head.

"The CEO—" I start.

"If the CEO is doing something wrong, all you have to do is tell someone. Why haven't you told someone?"

"The intern—" I say.

"Why are you fixated on her?"

Of course L. doesn't understand. She watched through the window as a woman got mugged on the street and didn't do anything about it. She didn't even let the woman in afterward. She told me about it later as though it was an amusing anecdote.

"I've got to get to work," I say, and I leave her to finish her partial shift, hunching over a stool and not caring about anyone but herself.

I try not to hold it against her, because her job is very different than mine. She's just not as involved in everyone's lives. She's not fundamental to the company like I am. It's hard to explain to someone else how important I am to the company, because part of what makes me so essential is that I don't need constant praise for every little thing I do. I have a clear vision of how things will best work, and I set about ordering them that way.

At this rate, L.'s hours will be cut to nothing by the end of the year. If I thought she cared more, I might try to save her too. But she'll go and work somewhere else and won't give another thought to our office or the people in it. Whatever her new job is, she'll do that for a year or two as well, never caring about that work either, or the people around her, and then she'll move on again. She'll see all these moves as progress, not caring at all about what she leaves behind. She'll live an entire life not caring about anyone or anything around her, and anytime she sees someone who does, she'll think, *Oh, how strange.*

I manage to catch M. while L.'s wandering the halls or maybe she's already gone home.

"It's been a while," I say.

"Everything okay?" M. asks.

"I've just been swamped," I say. "All that downsizing has left some wreckage."

"Makes sense," they say. "You've been so busy. They should give you some time off."

That's the last thing I need. But they didn't say it judgmentally. There's no malice in their face.

"Light night?" I ask, pointing at the two packages.

They give the packages a jostle and nod.

"I can take them for you," I say.

"It's no problem," M. says.

Their hair looks much better, and I can already see how it's going to grow out and look exactly how it did before. I think if I'd had some warning that they were going to cut it before I saw them, it wouldn't have bothered me as much. I just like to be prepared before I'm confronted with so much change.

"I realize I've never asked," I say. "But is this the beginning of your shift or the end of it?"

"Closer to the beginning." They look down at their watch, a slim, sporty-looking thing. "I've been on about an hour."

"I don't mind working at night," I say. "But I think I'd hate waking up early if I was at home, just sleeping."

"You get used to it," they say. "Like most things. If anything, I wish I started earlier. Traffic gets worse the later it gets. Things are so easy right now."

"I'll ride up with you," I say, and I stand very close to them in the elevator but look straight ahead. I can feel heat emanating from their skin, and I can smell their soap, clean and straightforward. Nothing strange or perfumed.

We drop things off at the top floor and then a notably emptied gray floor.

"Does it make anything easier, some of them being gone?" M. asks.

The elevator doors close and I can smell M.'s clean scent again.

"Not at all," I say. "The people who are still here make the same amount of mess, even manage to spill things on the empty desks. People will spread out to fill whatever space you give them, I guess. Even if it doesn't look like it," I add, thinking of the gray floor where the occupied desks are all clustered together. "They act like they're at home and all the new space is a luxury or some kind of reward."

"That's hard," M. says, and they're right. It is.

When we're back in the lobby, I tell them that I'm busy for the next few weekends, but maybe we could do that walk near the end of the month.

"That'd be great," they say. "And feel free to text anytime before then. I know things have been stressful lately."

It's nice to be seen. I watch them walking back to their truck, and before they get in, they look over their shoulder and catch me watching. When they smile at me, I don't look away, and at the last second, I smile back.

L. AND I avoid each other all week, and while it's relaxing to clean without an audience or a pseudo-supervisor, her interruptions do help break up my time. Without her, the nights feel a bit shapeless. I clean one thing and another and another. Even if I change up the order, there are only so many variations to my night. And I feel a little sorry for her. If I don't miss her, no one will. She's entirely unnecessary to the company. She could basically clock in and go home, then come back to clock out, and it'd be the same as her being here all night.

I wonder at what point someone decided this building even needed a security guard. Did something happen? Did someone break in or vandalize the place, and they wanted to take steps to prevent that from happening again? More likely it's an insurance thing. On some paperwork somewhere, there's a line explaining that the building must employ a security guard, and thus L. exists. No one has ever cared what she actually does.

Other than missing the variety L. brings to my night, it's been smooth sailing without her. The intern is generally happy, and the CEO hasn't gotten any worse. I'm starting to think I can adjust to all these cutbacks and even the general downsizing. It's not as disastrous as I thought. Then, of course, I find the intern sitting sullenly at her desk. If she hasn't recently cried, she's come very close. Her eyes are glassy and her face is notably red and puffy.

"What happened?" I ask, looking out over the other desks for clues.

She looks toward the CEO's office and then quickly back at me. She hadn't intended to implicate him. I try not to look at his office, because I don't want to bear down on her, as skittish as she already is.

Instead, I turn my body toward her and make steady eye contact. What did he do? Did he say something inappropriate? Make a pass at her? Touch her in some way? I know how he talks to women, but it's just been the one woman lately, so this is a little surprising. I'll believe whatever she says, though. I've been tolerating him, tolerating the state of the office, but I'm just as happy to destroy him. Happier, even.

"It's just, he still treats me like the intern," she says.

"He what?"

"I know," she says, nodding emphatically. "He wants me to make copies and take lunch orders, and today he asked me to fix the coffee machine. I don't know how the coffee machine works. I don't even drink coffee. Why couldn't he at least ask someone who uses the thing? But I'm new and should do any old thing he says."

Who does she think should repair it? It's not part of my

job to repair appliances. It's not my coffee machine. Not my breakroom. I shake my head at her. I would have thought she'd be used to this. She could have found someone else to fix it. She could have called someone, put in a request for a new one. He probably wasn't suggesting she personally get some kind of toolbox and disassemble the thing.

"Then I heard him telling someone, 'That girl is going to fix it.' Like I'm a child. He knows my name. I'm a person."

"What'd you do?" I ask, because I can imagine her throwing a fit, pitching her voice higher, the way people do when they're upset and they want to be able to say, "I wasn't yelling! I didn't raise my voice!" but they were so shrill that it would have been more comfortable if they had just yelled.

"I looked at it," she says. "But it looked normal to me."

It has been visibly leaking for days. This seems hard to miss, but I don't say anything.

"Then he asked me if I got it fixed and I said no, I had no idea how to fix it, and he acted shocked. Like I was dropping the ball or something."

"So what happened?" I ask.

"Someone else fixed it."

"Oh good," I say.

"They said it was easy, that anyone could have figured it out. There was a part inside that needed to be cleaned. But do I look like I clean stuff?"

I have doubts that she's even showered this week. I shake my head.

"I don't deserve to be treated like there's something wrong with me because I'm not an appliance mechanic," she says.

It's like that moment when the wheel on my cart finally

clicked into place and I could roll it again. I have been very patiently waiting, and she's finally finagled herself into the right position.

"You're good at your job," I tell her. "That's just not your job."

"It's not!" she says. "I could go do the same thing for someone else and probably make more money."

I nod. "You're obviously not the problem. *He* is."

"He's barely even here," she says. "And when he is, he doesn't really do anything. He outsources work to other people and then complains about it."

"The company would probably be much better off without him," I say. "And with someone newer, more energetic. You're just starting out. How he runs the company and the public perception of it reflects on you."

"I know!" she says. "I was telling my dad that I should probably be at a larger place with more name recognition."

"I hear you," I say. "But I guess the good thing about a company like this is that you have more opportunities to do things. You were saying how they assigned you so many projects. How you're collaborating with different people. The problem is really him."

"People get so comfortable and lazy," she says. "He used to be someone people admired. People say he was out on the floor, working with them."

I suspect it's been quite some time since he did that, if he ever did.

"I shouldn't say anything," I say. "But I think there's a good chance he's stealing from the company."

She narrows her eyes.

"I know you wouldn't want to stir up trouble," I rush ahead, making my voice as gentle as possible. "But the company deserves better than that. And what happens to everyone else if he takes enough to really hurt this place? Are they all out of work? And for what? So some entitled guy can take a few trips?"

"Didn't you have some email about that?" she says. "I remember you mentioning it before."

"Oh, maybe," I say, pretending to dig through my pockets and then my cart. "Oh, here," I say, and I hand her the emails.

She looks excited to take them this time, holding the stack with both hands, reading each email, shaking her head and smiling. "Fuck this guy," she says.

"Fuck this guy," I repeat.

This time, when I log in to his computer, I stay seated at his desk. I pull open his financial system, navigating it so easily that I can almost feel how impressed she is. I don't look at her to see. I wouldn't want to slow my momentum.

I show her account after account. He's taken payments that were due to vendors or employees and paid them into an account that he has access to. Then he moved the money into his offshore account, the same one that holds all her fundraising money. He's been doing it for years, actually. It was very small amounts at first, but in the last few months, his efforts have ramped way up. Clearly, he was planning to skip town with it soon. Everyone's been doing trust falls and happy hours and competing for gift cards, and he's rolled up his sleeves so he could pick their pockets. Any special attention he's paid anyone has only been so he could get a better look at their wallet.

I lean back and let her absorb it all. It's nice to feel so appreciated, so necessary. When she says, "What else?" I log in to his secret email account too. Let her see all of it.

"I can't believe this," she says, even though I've been gently bringing it up for a while. But I don't say that. I'm just glad things got repaired before too much damage was done. I'm glad it was the two of us who busted him.

"Tomorrow," she says, printing out copies for herself. Her posture is better than usual and I can feel that I've fixed more than the company—I've fixed her too.

After she leaves, I find that Yarn Guy's desk calendar is entirely gone, and I think of the hearts I drew. They hadn't hurt anything, hadn't infringed upon his work or overall productivity, but he hadn't been allowed to keep them. Was it the CEO who made him throw out the calendar, or some other overbearing supervisor? It's hard to tell sometimes who's in charge of who, because often the people in charge do the poorest work, accustomed to some assistant picking up their slack. Maybe once the CEO is gone, people will be able to relax. Maybe Yarn Guy will bring his crafts back in. I've made some real progress on my knitting at home. I think I have most of a passable sock done. It's too small for me but would work great for someone with very small feet or maybe a child. Next, I want to try my hand at a little free-form coaster that I could gift him.

I wonder if it's too late to rehire some of the staff they had to downsize: people like Mr. Buff. But we can do without Scissors Guy. Things run smoother without him or the kind of energy he brought to the office. And besides, his position as scissors hoarder has been filled.

A FEW NIGHTS LATER, I run into L. I'm getting on the elevator as she's getting off.

"Hey," she says. "I heard." Then she apologizes for her overstep, tells me she was just frustrated about her job and my slowness to act. It all spills out of her in one long rush of words. She says now that things are settled so neatly, with so little fuss, she understands. She tells me she's sorry but adds, "I mean, I don't know what else I could have done. You should have told me what your plan was. Then I would have felt better."

It's the way a child apologizes, distancing themselves from any blame. I smile and tell her I understand, and she smiles back. Even though I haven't made any apology, she's heard one. It exists in her head. I think she missed me at least as much as I missed her. She follows me around for a couple of hours, talking about the building, the CEO, what will happen next, and how ready she is to stop her weekend work.

And I think she's being careful to not scuff the floors. She keeps looking at her feet and then at me in a knowing way.

When I get upstairs, the CEO's office has been fully cleared out and then scrubbed down. The desk and bookshelves shine, and it smells fresh. I don't think I ever appreciated how shiny this furniture was or noticed its slight red tint. I wonder who did all this—and during the day too. I'm surprised that they didn't simply ask me to do it at night. Maybe they didn't want to pile any extra responsibility on me. I've been working longer hours for a while now, and I'm not being paid any extra for it. I didn't put it on my time card, but I think the difference in my work is clear. Messes don't clean themselves. Problems don't just go away.

I feel a pang for the CEO's wife. She's been carted away in some box. It's hard not to think of that two-dimensional rendering as her. But she's out there, somewhere. I hope she left him. I hope him losing his job was a nonissue for her, something she wouldn't notice at all, because to her, he's basically dead. Maybe she even grew to like his dog. Maybe he curled up in bed beside her. She didn't even notice when the CEO stayed out late or all night. She preferred it that way. Now she has his dog and the house too. The Other Woman has his money. They're both happy.

There's a fresh notepad in the top desk drawer, and an assortment of office supplies: new pens, sticky notes, paper clips, staples, the works. I wonder if he took home all the odds and ends that were on his shelves. They probably tossed his Kleenex box, but did he want to keep his lizard statue? His vase? That poor neglected cactus? Probably all of those things are out in the dumpster or in a trash can somewhere in the building. If I wanted to, I could find them. But it's best to let these things go.

I shake the mouse and the log-in screen pops up. I glance at the new sticky note affixed to the monitor, type "admin," and I'm in. The desktop and browser have been wiped clean: no icons, documents, or messy folders. It's a clean office and a clean computer. It makes sense to have a fresh start.

I make a new email account and type a short note: *I hope you're happier now. You can probably appreciate how hard it is to do the kind of work that goes unseen. And I want you to know that I see you, truly. I understand how difficult things have been. If you ever want to talk, let me know.* I send it without worrying a bit about the time or my location. There's no harm now.

On my lunch break, L. and I sit in our breakroom, me eating and her watching.

"How are things with M.?" she asks.

"What do you mean?" I say, trying not to let myself blush.

"Am I misreading it?" she asks. "It seems like there's something there."

I shrug. "I'm into someone else," I say.

"Who?"

I shake my head and L. stares at me for long enough that I grow self-conscious about the way I'm chewing, the sound I make swallowing.

"Is it someone who works on the fourth floor?" she finally asks.

"He's into crafts," I say. "Makes stuff with his hands. We both work with our hands."

"You don't even know him," she says, biting off one of

her nails and spitting it onto the floor. I'll have to clean it up later, unless I want to look at it there for the rest of my life.

"He works here," I say. "I know him. M. only delivers here. How would I really know them? I've never seen their apartment or the inside of their work truck."

"You talk to them all the time," L. says.

"I talk to you," I say.

"You know me," she says.

"And I would never date you."

Neither of us says anything until I'm nearly finished eating, and then we start talking about who the new CEO might be.

"A woman," L. says. "At least, that's what I heard."

"I wonder what her office will look like," I say.

L. crinkles her eyebrows but doesn't say anything.

How else would we come to know anyone who works in the daytime, though? It's not like L. is going to meet her, shake her hand, and become her close personal friend. But maybe in L.'s head, this feels possible.

"I heard she'll start really soon," L. says.

No wonder they cleaned out the office so fast.

"I wonder if they'll hire back any of the people they let go," I say.

"Maybe they'll hire new people," she says.

Sometimes I forget how differently L. experiences the office. She walks through the building, and it's truly empty. Empty desks, empty breakrooms, no one's ghost to trip over. So of course she isn't worried about the people who were let go. But maybe a clean break will be nice. Once you leave an ex and start to move on, it's never a good idea to go back. You reunite and it's not the same. You remember everything they said, everything they did. The relationship is an anemic shadow of what it was.

The next night, the new CEO has fully moved into her office. On her bookshelf, instead of a broken fountain, she has a red betta fish living beneath a plant. The roots are submerged in the water while the fish swims back and forth between them. I wonder if the plant gets something from the fish, if it's a mutually beneficial situation. They both look healthy, the fish a vibrant red and the plant comprised of big green leaves.

Her office is neat and less sparse than the old CEO kept it. The walls are covered in abstract paintings, there's a rug half under her desk, and a few different lamps, one of them tall and in the corner. I turn it on, and its warm glow helps diffuse the harsh overhead lighting. There are a few sculptures on the bookshelves, abstract like her wall art, pieces of wadded-up clay or metal, messy and showing their work. One of them looks like half a baby emerging from a hole in the ground, as though the earth is birthing it. The baby's head looks warped from the pressure and difficulty of being born. I don't dislike it—and after months of stagnation, maybe this rebirth is what everyone needs.

The rest of the floor is immaculate. Each person's desk appears to have been cleaned and detailed. There are no piles of unsorted papers, no crumbs or spills. Even the insides of the desks appear purposefully ordered and sorted. No accidental junk mail or half-eaten snacks. Leftovers' space is remarkably clean: no sandwich at all. Not even an old wrapper or some crackers. And the breakroom fridge has been cleared out and meticulously wiped down. I wonder if the new CEO directed everything to be cleaned, or if everyone banded together and did it before her arrival. Maybe they wanted to make a good impression. Unidentifiable molding meat just doesn't do the trick. But how long will it take for their mess to seep back in? I've seen the way this works. No one but me can really keep it all at bay.

The intern's supplements and books are fully gone, though. Was she simply embarrassed by them, or did she want to do away with them and have a fresh start? Now her desk is all work. You would think she was the most driven person here, until you looked in everyone else's desks and saw they were all like this. What a floor. What a team of go-getters. I try to soak it in, because I know it won't look like this for long. There'll be soup in someone's drawer and a used tampon in the breakroom trash can by the middle of next week.

There's not much cleaning to do, but I empty all the trash cans and do the floors. Everyone's cleaned their own space, and even banded together to do the breakroom, but no one thought to clean the floor. No one wanted to be seen as connected to the dirty floor. They thought it was too lowly a task. And, of course, the bathrooms are untouched. At least there aren't balled-up paper towels on the floor or wads of suspiciously yellow toilet paper in the sink.

L. finds me a few hours later on a gray floor.

"I'm wondering if they're going to give my hours back without me having to remind them," she says.

"Why?" I ask.

"Why?" she repeats. "Everything looks normal. We're doing well again. Why wouldn't they?"

"Why would they?" I ask. "After they saw things were fine, why bother? They're saving money."

"But were things fine?" she asks. "The building probably needs full-time security, night and day. And in this part of the city? It just makes sense."

"No one can get in at night without a card," I say.

"People do all kinds of things," she says.

The only people in the building at night are me and M. What does she think we might do? Maybe she imagines I'll let in women who have been mugged. Maybe I'll make a mistake and let the mugger in too. I'll open the door to a criminal team. The entire building will be ransacked. They'll steal all the staplers, the three-hole punches, the breakroom snacks. What will L. do without all those snacks? How will she get through the night without cured meat sticks and dried apricots?

"Remember all those propped-open doors?" she asks. "The stairwell?"

"You were here when all that was going on, and you didn't stop it then."

"I wasn't here in the daytime."

I look down. If someone wanted to rob the place in broad daylight, with dozens and dozens of people around, L. quietly sitting on a stool is not going to dissuade them. But what's she supposed to do? The building hired L. Someone picked her from a pool of applicants. It's not her fault she doesn't look intimidating.

"Maybe I'll ask them directly about my hours," she says. "I already quit my weekend gig."

"Wasn't that just helping your grandmother?"

"It was pretty involved," she says. "And I think instead of covering my back rent, I'm going to move somewhere better."

"They let you get behind on your rent and you're just going to skip out?" I ask.

"The apartment is small and shitty," she says. "They're lucky I stayed as long as I did."

Then she talks about other apartments in the area that she's interested in, one up the street and then one several miles away. I worry about her living so far from work. Now she's right up the street, so it's an easy commute. But if it was miles away, how long before she doesn't think the commute is worth it, especially if they cut her hours? It took me this long to adjust to L., and I hate the idea of breaking in a new security guard.

"Sometimes it's just about reorganizing," I say. "Move your furniture around, get a new rug. So much easier than moving."

Then she's looking up rugs and interior design on her phone, easily distracted by the idea of putting her money into something tangible. And it's less work than moving anyway. More her style.

THE FOURTH FLOOR remains immaculately clean all week, and I'm startled to come in at the end of the week and find the intern sitting at her desk after such an extended absence. Her clothes seem a bit more formal, a jacket and a man's button-up. She looks uncomfortable, and I can picture her tugging at her sleeves and collar, even though she isn't doing either of these things.

"How's it going?" I ask.

"A ton of catching up," she says. "We were way behind on paperwork. It seems like he really let things go."

"How's the new one?" I ask, nodding at her office.

"Very efficient," she says.

"Her fish is nice," I say, thinking of it swimming back and forth between those dangling roots while the water gently glides over its fins.

"It's cruel to keep a betta in a plant that way," she says.

"People will tell you that the betta will eat the roots and the plant will absorb nutrients from the fish water, but it's not true. Bettas are actually carnivores and need a filtration system like every other kind of fish. If you make them swim in their own filth, in the cold office, with nothing to eat, they'll die in a few weeks."

"I can change the water," I say.

"Don't bother," she says. "Let her fish die. She'll get a new one. She doesn't care."

"It looked okay last time I was in there," I say.

"It's starving," she says.

I hadn't realized she was some sort of fish expert.

I go and watch the fish drift back and forth, and then settle at the bottom of the dish. It must be exhausting, swimming back and forth all the time, purposeless. Everyone deserves something to work for. Everyone needs a goal. I'll buy it some fish food over the weekend. No one will care or even notice if I start feeding it. And I can replace its water. It's not much, to care for a small fish. Not when I've been caring for a floor full of people.

It must be hard to grow accustomed to your boss being so lax and then have someone come in and want to do things extremely by the book. I can understand why the intern is in her feelings about it. She'll adjust, though, and be all the better for it. The company will thrive. She'll thrive. She just has to get used to things. After she leaves, I give her desk extra attention. She'll have the cleanest one. No one will be able to fault her for anything, and she'll start tomorrow fresh and organized.

"I'M NOT SO sure about this place anymore," L. says.

I'm cleaning the lobby windows, and I tilt my head to let her know I'm listening.

"I asked about my hours and they said, 'We'll see.' Like I'm a child. Who tells an adult 'We'll see'?"

"Do you want to quit?" I ask, looking at her reflection in the window.

"Maybe," she says.

"What'd you do before you did this?" I ask.

"Besides helping my grandmother?"

I nod.

"I worked overnight at a car factory," she says. "There was a machine I helped run that cut plastic."

"For how long?" I ask.

"Nearly six months," she says, "and then my knee acted up. I asked for a different job, one where I didn't have to stand all day, but they wouldn't accommodate me. That's messed up, because it's all that standing that made my injury flare up. I was totally fine for years before that. They should have compensated me, but there was a whole big thing."

"Then what?" I ask.

"I moved around," she says. "I worked at a hookah place, putting tobacco in little canisters for online orders. I hated the smell, though. Every night I would go home smelling like fake fruit and tobacco. It was impossible to date. I couldn't even hang out with friends, really. I could see it on everyone's faces. I still get weirded out by artificial sweet-smelling things." She shudders.

"Then you came here?" I ask.

"I was security at another building," she says. "It was smaller, and they didn't need me as much. This is a better fit."

"What will you do next?" I ask.

"I like nights," she says. "So I'll stick to that for sure. I think I could get a bigger security job, something at a bank or a museum, something where the stakes are higher. I mean, I always saw this as a stepping stone."

"I didn't know that," I say, but I guess I did, based on how she's treated the job. She never invested herself in the office or cared about it as a whole. She saw no reason to pick up after herself, no reason to keep our breakroom neat, and couldn't possibly care about all the other people who work here. But I've been thinking of the building as my forever place. I've cared about and maintained it, because I knew I would always be here. It would always be mine.

All these times L. and I chatted and stood together, we were never really in the same room. While L. saw everything as flimsy and disposable, I pictured myself here year after year, so I saw the building as sturdy, permanent. But for L., the walls were nearly see-through. She was looking through them to something better, something far away. Everything here was something that could be crumpled and thrown out. I looked past her and saw it all as something I would keep. Each person was a person I would know, forever.

Maybe L. is right that I can't fully know everyone by seeing their desks, their computers, their habits. But I think we've developed a kind of chemistry over the years. I get along with everyone, and we all work together.

I go upstairs and sit at Yarn Guy's desk. I'm not sure anyone but me recognizes that he's Yarn Guy. Even Coaster Woman thinks his crafting is an unimportant hobby. She calls him by his name, thinks of him as his job or face. That's how most of these people know each other. It's all very surface level: faces and names. Not much else. It must be an empty way to live, to be so vapid and forever unknown.

But of course, I know them all. I understand them, for better or worse. I've seen the grossest things about them, their half-eaten and molding snacks, their vaguely sexual doodles, a woman's list of things she hates about herself, and then later, a list of all her positive qualities, including "ankles" and "integrity," even though I'm pretty sure she hasn't told everyone that she's been leaving bad reviews for the company online under the username "squirrelygurly," which in itself is a whole thing.

I know about everyone's disagreements and subsequent flirtations, and then the judgments they levy across the room, often for things they're guilty of themselves. Sticky Doorknob is mad that people don't dry their hands after they wash them, which means they drip water everywhere. Leftovers thinks people eat too loudly at their desks. There's one man who even chews with his mouth open, taking phone calls and working while he smacks and crunches, bits of his lunch sprinkled across his desk and the floor around him. Leftovers has complained to HR about this man three times now, but it seems like nothing can be done.

I know the best and worst things about all these people, and I still care about them. I think it's time to meet them, face-to-face. It's time for *them* to meet *me*.

I LEAVE EARLY—not before my shift is over, though. I just don't stay late like I've been doing. I clock out on time. At home, I take a nap and wake up invigorated. I keep the shower as cold as I can bear, so I can be at my most alert. Afterward, I put on my only set of nonwork clothes. They're a little loose, but I think I look like the other people in the office, just a bit more casual. It's jeans and a sleeveless sweater with a high neck. The sweater makes the jeans seem more dressed up and office-appropriate. If anything, the high neck of the sweater might be too formal, giving me an almost regal air.

My walk to the office feels shockingly natural after the disconcerting walk I had to the café months ago. I pass a woman on the sidewalk and she smiles at me. We both belong here, on this sidewalk, taking up this specific space. She's the kind of person I might come to know. She works near the office. Maybe she manages a grocery store or small restaurant. We could pass each other every day, get used to seeing one another, and become friends. She'll tell me she remembers smiling at me that first day. "I felt like we already knew each other," she'll say. Everyone looks like that: someone who already knows me.

The office looks different in the daytime. I thought the nighttime was hiding its flaws, smoothing out some of its rough edges, but it actually looks much nicer in the sunlight. It's sleek, more silver than gray. The finish glitters, and I have to squint to keep from hurting my eyes. The windows have a darker tint to them than I realized. At night, with the lights on, you can see fully into the building, but in the daytime, everything's muted. People are just murky shapes, the idea of people. I stand out on the sidewalk, admiring the building. It's really something. A person would be proud to tell someone they work here.

A man in a gray suit stops a step ahead of me, standing so close that we're almost touching. If I were to shift a little, we'd nearly be holding hands. "Are you lost?" he asks. "Can I help you?" He reaches out to touch my arm, just above my elbow, as though he wants to guide me away from the building.

I slowly pull my arm back, careful not to noticeably jerk it away, because I don't want to incite any kind of conflict. I can easily picture a back and forth with him reaching, me dodging, and him saying that I don't belong here, not right now. I'm not wearing makeup and my clothes are too cheap. Who do I think I am? His suit is perfectly creased and almost glimmers in the sun. You might as well have neatly broken him off the building—he fits in so perfectly. He's just another facet of the block and general atmosphere. "I'm fine," I tell him.

"You sure?" he asks.

"No problem here."

He looks at me like I might change my mind given the chance, and then he keeps walking, taking long, heavy strides, very confident that whatever he's doing and wherever he's going is right. He would never make a mistake. He would never need assistance.

So I go inside.

The air-conditioning is running harder than it usually does. They must turn it down at night because of the temperature drop. Or maybe with fewer bodies in the building, they think they need it less. We need it less. L.'s empty stool looks strangely out of place in the daytime. People walk back and forth in front of the building, get on and off the elevator, and stand in the lobby, looking at their phones. It's all very active, and the stool seems stationary and sad, certainly less expensive than the rest of the décor, the rest of the people. But no one even notices it. They have no idea how important it is to someone else's life and work, because it isn't important to theirs. They walk by both me and the stool without even a glance. They've all been here long enough to get used to it. Things would be different if there was no stool and suddenly one popped up. Then they'd have questions. "Where'd that ugly stool come from? What's it for?" I wait to see if anyone is going to register me, but they don't. Once I'm inside the building, I'm no different than the stool.

I decide to take the stairs instead of riding the elevator up. It'll give me some time to process and prepare. I don't see anyone on my near-eternal shuffle. Between the second and third floor, someone's written on the wall in blue pen, "The joy is gone." A few steps up, someone else has written in black marker, "Peasants." I make a note to soak and scrub it all away. There's no rush, of course, because no one ever takes the stairs. That's probably why anyone would feel safe expressing themselves this way. When I get to the fourth floor, I stand for a few minutes in the stairwell, catching my breath, because I don't want to burst onto the floor panting after I've climbed all the way up here. As soon as my breath evens out, I open the door and go out onto the floor.

It's loud in a way I wasn't prepared for. People talk to each other and on their phones with no regard for anyone around them. There's a cacophony of typing, clicking, papers rustling, people walking and opening doors. I've never heard anyone open a door so loudly. I cover my ears for a few seconds while I recalibrate, but drop my hands when I see a woman staring at me. The whole thing is dizzying, but no one looks aggravated or even mildly put out. They're used to it.

Once I stand for a moment and let it wash over me, I get used to it too. I adjust the volume of my thoughts to rise above everything else in the room. I like how busy everyone looks, each in their own world, diligently working at whatever they're doing. It's nice to see the fruits of my labor. I've spent so much of my time caring for them, nursing them back to full-fledged, productive members of society whenever one of them starts to droop. Now I feel overwhelmed to see them all in person, fully inhabiting the room.

They're not my children, exactly, but they're people I basically raised. I've been the woman standing behind each of them, holding them up, pushing them, keeping them going.

Cheery #2 looks exactly how I pictured him: clean-shaven, short, dark hair, a button-up shirt, and glasses. It's probably what Cheery #1 looked like too. No wonder they disliked one another. Nobody really likes themselves these days. But

Coaster Woman is unexpected. She's the spitting image of the old CEO's wife, beautiful, tall, and sad-looking, but in a way that draws me in. I had expected to find her repulsive. I thought she'd be visibly unclean or at least messy, wrinkled. But her suit jacket is neatly folded across the back of her chair, and she sits up very straight, as though she doesn't want to lean back and wrinkle it. If I didn't know what she was like, I'd be fooled too. No wonder Yarn Guy couldn't help himself. His computer is on and his desk is empty but crisscrossed with work, like he got up to run some errand or go to the bathroom.

Over at her desk, I see Leftovers. She's disheveled, which I expected. Someone that keeps half an unwrapped sandwich in her desk isn't going to look well put together. If her hair is falling down at this time of day, I'd hate to see her near the end of it. And her shirt's wrinkled and too large for her. Like L., I imagine this isn't her forever job. Otherwise she would invest in workwear that fits. She'd care what people thought of her.

In contrast, Sticky Doorknob is neater than I imagined. His clothes make him seem hip. He wears brighter colors than anyone else in the office, but not in an off-putting or garish way. He's attractive, too, dimples and sparkling eyes. I can see how he gets away with it.

"Hi," I say to the intern, glad to see a friendly face.

"What are you doing here?" she asks, looking me up and down.

"Just visiting," I say.

"Did something happen?" she asks. "Is everything okay?"

A woman comes up beside me, looking at the intern. "You almost ready?" she asks.

The intern and the woman both look at me. "I'll be just a minute," the intern says, her voice dropping.

The woman squints at me like she's trying to figure out who or what I am, and then she nods and walks away.

"Did you need something?" the intern asks. "Are you cleaning something in the daytime?"

"I thought I'd stop by and meet everyone," I say.

"What are you wearing?" she asks.

The woman comes up beside me again. "Ready?" she says, looking at the intern.

The intern nods. "This is the cleaning lady," she says. "She's fine," she adds, as though someone might potentially see me as a threat. As though I appear to need supervision.

"Oh, I didn't know we had a cleaning person," the woman says.

The intern shrugs. "You know how it is."

Then they both head toward the elevator and leave me standing there.

"You're the cleaning lady?" an incredibly tall man says, walking by and stopping a few paces ahead of me. His voice is loud and carries across the room. He towers over me, and I see a few people look up at us. If he wasn't wearing business attire, I'd think he was frightening.

I try not to fold in on myself and I nod.

"There's been a weird smell," he says. "Like cheap pot-pourri or something. All around my desk." He walks over to his desk, Yarn Guy's desk, and motions toward it. "Did you get my note?" he asks.

"Your note?" I say, taking a few small steps toward him, hoping he'll be more likely to control the volume of his voice if I'm closer.

He looks nothing like I thought, not prim, not pulled together. He's rough around the edges, wrinkled shirt, collar
askew, and his stubble has grown out enough that it's not intentional stubble, purposefully fashioned. He just looks un-
groomed and thrown away. Were all the crafts even his? Were
they a gift from someone else? Coaster Woman's attempt to
soften him? Had I targeted her unfairly?

"I left it on your door," he says, still so loudly that people
look up at us.

"I don't have a door," I say. "Do you mean you left it for me
at the front desk in the lobby? That's where messages are left."

"I taped it on your door," he says. "To be sure you'd see it."

He takes a step toward me and seems to grow taller. I can't
picture this man with knitting needles in his hand.

"I don't get messages on a door," I say.

"Well, anyway," he says. "Can you do something about it?
It smells awful. See?" he says, sniffing and waving his hands
under his nose, like I need someone to mime smelling. "Come
smell it," he says. When I don't move or say anything, he motions again. "Come here," he says.

I walk slowly over and bend slightly to sniff.

"See?" he says, reaching like he might press down on the
back of my neck to make me stoop over more. I step aside.

"Smells normal," I say. "But I'll keep an eye out. I have to
be going, though."

"I'll let you know if it doesn't go away," he says, like he's
my supervisor. I worry the CEO will come out of her office
to see what's wrong. What will I say I'm doing here? "Just
look for a message taped on your door," he adds.

I turn and leave without saying goodbye. I can feel everyone staring at me, because his voice is so loud. Nothing about

his yarn or crafts made me think he was a casual shouter. One woman wrinkles her nose as I walk by and another grimaces. I can see a man staring at my jeans. They're nice jeans, though, not something anybody should really notice. They wouldn't be looking at me this way if not for Yarn Guy. The room feels quieter now, and I walk as quickly as I can, without looking like I'm running, toward the stairwell. I wouldn't dream of prolonging things by waiting on the elevator.

"One more thing," Yarn Guy says, catching up to me and putting a hand on my shoulder to stop me. I nearly lose my balance and try to pivot away from him, but he follows. His hand isn't on my shoulder anymore, but I can still feel it: warm, heavy. "Can you do something about the stairwell?" he says. "It smells awful, like something died. We've tried leaving the doors open to air it out, but it doesn't seem to help. Just makes our floor smell worse than it already does!" He laughs like this is a joke.

I nod at him and then take the stairs two at a time, not nervous at all that I'll lose my grip and fall. I don't slow down in the lobby, and I'm outside before I feel things fully well up. The sun's uncomfortably bright, and I can feel sweat starting to soak through my shirt. Even my collar is damp. But I keep moving, not looking up, not thinking about anyone looking at me. Maybe they weren't looking, but I can picture them staring anyway. Maybe no one said anything, but I can hear their murmurs—even now they're becoming louder and more articulate in my mind. "What's she doing here? Is that a stain on her shirt? Should we call somebody? How'd she even get in? Cleaning Lady. Cleaning Woman. Cleaner. Just The Cleaner."

WHEN L. ASKS what's wrong, I tell her I don't feel well.

"You look tired," she says. "Like you need to eat."

"Just my stomach," I say, because I know she won't ask follow-up questions about that, and I can take time away from her in the bathroom. Even L. will stop short of following me there. But I don't feel the same solace in the bathroom that I used to. It's the same gray tiled walls and clean floors as always, but I keep imagining people complaining about the smell, which is actually *their* smell. It's not just the bathroom. It's the stairwell and hallway and lobby and breakroom and their desks and any speck or smell they might encounter. All day, they're creating a list of complaints that they store in their heads, ready to rattle off to anyone who will listen. It's not just the way they communicate—it's their entire mode of thinking, a tally of unhappiness. It's one thing and another and another. They can only see what's wrong. When they look at me, they can only see the things I haven't done.

All week, I leave the gray floors as clean as the fourth, maybe cleaner. I don't give the fourth floor any special attention anymore. They're not grateful for it.

"They don't see me," I tell L. finally.

"How would they?" she asks.

But I see them. I know them better now than ever, and they simply don't deserve my attention. I don't explain this to L. She can't really hear me anyway.

Tonight, while I clean the fourth-floor bathroom, I try to imagine it's the bathroom on any other floor. This isn't an intimate moment between us. I'm an employee completing a required task. The sound of the fluorescent lights starts to grate at me again, and I try humming to drown them out.

I'm shocked to find that even though the CEO is gone, the Rogue Shitter is still here. I hadn't realized until now how fully I believed the CEO was the Rogue Shitter, and that anything bad was his fault. But there are brown streaks across two different toilet seats tonight. Maybe it's Yarn Guy. But more likely, it's a group of men, probably most of them. They collectively do not care about all the work I do or the general condition of the building. They live shamelessly. They don't notice what services they consume, the people they take advantage of. Instead, they stampede through the office, crushing any helping hand underfoot. Then they complain about the mess they've made.

After this, I stop cleaning everyone's desks. I don't open a single drawer. I empty their trash cans, clean the floors, wipe down the breakroom, and do the bathrooms, but nothing more than that. I try not to see them. I try not to remember Yarn Guy motioning me over to his desk, demonstrating how to sniff, cartoonishly flaring his nostrils. And was he talking extra slow, like I couldn't understand him? Is that why he was gesturing so wildly? I shake my head to rid myself of his image, and I take my time scrubbing the elevator. Its walls and floors are blank and there's nothing here to remind me of any particular person. No lingering smells, no ghosts. No one to grimace or cringe at the sight of me, and no one to complain about all the work I do to take care of them. There's no one here but me.

I thought it would be easier to not care about them, but I can't get rid of their faces, the sounds of them working. I hear them when I'm alone. More than a few times, I have to stop working to be sure one of them isn't tucked away in some back office, taking notes, writing emails. But there's no one. Just me and L. And then I hear them in my apartment. I wake to the sound of them typing and talking, and I have to pace my hall to be sure I'm actually alone. Sometimes I have trouble falling asleep, because I'm sure that at any moment, one of them will peek through my window. I'm not even on the bottom floor. It'd be so difficult for them to do. But as soon as I close my eyes, I start to picture them peering in at me. I can smell their coffee, their reheated lunches. Maybe it's my office supplies, providing a kind of echo from the building. You can't carry home reams of paper and not expect to smell corporate.

I start bagging up all the things I've brought home: the coaster and all the crafts, a few pairs of scissors, the intern's self-help book. But once the bag is full, I can't bring myself to lug it to the trash chute. It's like throwing away everything about myself. So I leave it in the corner, all tied up and ready to toss.

But at work, on the fourth floor, I find it shockingly easy
to throw away documents left on their desks. First, from the
desks of Yarn Guy and Coaster Woman. Then Sticky Doorknob, Leftovers, Cheery #2, Vinyl Guy, and everyone else.
Eventually, even the intern. I haven't seen her since that day
in the office and can't help but feel like she's avoiding me. Her
desk looks semicleared, so she's obviously taking home some of
her work. It's not that she isn't working at night. It's just that
she isn't working here. Still, I have to pace myself. It's not like
I can throw away everything that's on her desk, all at once.
She'd know who did it. So, I spread out and randomize my
efforts. Anytime I see a pile of papers on anyone's desk, I pull
one from the middle and throw it away. They won't know it's
me, but they'll be mildly or even seriously inconvenienced.

I do this for a week, two weeks, but it doesn't make me feel
better. So, I ramp things up. I throw away nice pens, a brass
letter opener, cute paperweights, and then, sometimes, two
or three pages from thick piles of documents. But it doesn't
seem to really affect them. Yes, some people start putting
things away inside their desks, like I can't get to them there.
Like I can't pull open a drawer and do whatever I like. But
that's not enough.

I try to work up the will to do something truly unsavory,
spit in a sandwich, piss on someone's rug, but I can't do it. I
can't leave things worse than when I found them. It's not my
nature.

I ride the elevator down to the lobby, still avoiding the
stairwell. I've stood with the door open a few times, breathing it in, but I can't figure out what bad smell anyone could
possibly find there. Maybe it's something Yarn Guy was bring-

ing to work with him, an acrid odor that he couldn't believe was his and so he projected it onto everyone else.

In the breakroom, L. has a new plant. It's bigger than the other one. It has long, thin leaves in a striped pattern, splayed on either side of its pot. "Supposed to be hard to kill," she says. I look at her, but she doesn't look at me or say it with any kind of menace or knowing. I tell myself I'll watch over it. I'll remember to water it if she doesn't. I'll buy it some fertilizer, an expensive kind, something to really perk it up. I'll ask about her grandmother sometime.

"I just don't know why she had to act like she didn't know me," I tell L. We've been talking on and off about my office visit all week, and I feel like I'm not explaining it right, or L.'s not hearing me right, because she never has the right reaction. She's almost completely consumed by her job hunt. I still think she could make this job work if she really tried.

"My second interview's this week," she says, as though I wasn't talking about something else.

"It was like she was embarrassed," I explain. "What about me would be embarrassing?"

"It's similar work," she says. "So I think I'll be a good fit, with all my experience."

"And then Yarn Guy—"

"Yarn Guy?" she asks. "Is that some sort of superhero name?" She laughs and rifles through the fridge, taking one of my water bottles.

"That's mine," I say.

"It's all the way on the other side of town," she says. "So it makes sense to move over there. Everything works out, eventually," she adds. "You should worry less. Just go along, be easier." She drinks nearly half the water in a single gulp.

"I can't imagine not caring," I say.

"I care," she says. "I do my job. I just don't let it become more than my job. I don't make everyone my problem. I come to work. I go home."

"Why'd you bring in a new plant if you're leaving?" I ask.

She shrugs. "Brighten the place up until then."

It's nice to see her care about the building. If only she'd cared sooner.

She puts my water back in the fridge without even screwing the cap on properly. It's just resting on top of the bottle. The jostle of her closing the fridge probably knocked it off. Maybe tipped the whole thing over. I'll have to wipe the mess out later or live with it.

"What's the point of leaving?" I ask.

"It's better money," she says.

"Everything isn't about money," I say.

"What else would it be about? What else is work?"

I shake my head.

"No, really," she says. "I feel like you don't understand what a job is. You sell yourself, your time or your expertise. And you take that money and live. That's how the whole thing works."

"That's how it works for you," I say, though it clearly isn't working. Why else would she leave? But there was a security officer before her, so of course there'll be one after her. As long as the building and company are here, that's how it'll work. But it's not like that with me, because I'm part of things, invested personally. It's my office, my floor, my desks, my people. This isn't just the place where I work. It's my life.

THE OFFICE BECOMES a place of drudgery. Everything about my job that I used to enjoy would be embarrassing to do now. Help them? Why bother? They see me as more machine than person. I'm part of the equipment that cleans the building, and they probably picture me inside a storage closet during the day, ready to pop out and do their bidding as soon as they clock out. But I feel tired all the time. It's like my body wants to revert to a different sleep schedule, one where I'm awake in the daytime and I sleep at night. I think of the intern's missing supplements and my long-gone caffeine pills. I can even picture myself weathering a little Mood Magic.

And per the CEO's wishes, someone has left me a stringent new list of cleaning requirements. It has exact measurements for the mix of cleaning solution and hot water, with step-by-step instructions for the sequence I'm supposed to clean things in. "Top to bottom," it says, and then it lists nearly every possible item I should clean and how to do it. I wonder who wrote this up, printed it out, and brought it down to our breakroom. I cringe picturing Yarn Guy doing it, invading my space to leave it here for me. The worst part is the cutesy clip art on every page: pictures of mops and gloves and a big oversized vacuum, even though we don't have a vacuum like that. There's even a picture of a woman in a maid's outfit. They've done everything possible to render my role here as fully quotidian, banal. Instead of being a distinct person who works at a distinct place, I'm a symbol for a person, not fully sentient or real. I'm cleaning products and somehow also trash. I'm huge bags of disposable cups and food wrappers and scraps of paper. How strange that they believe I'm made up of what they discard.

I consider calling it a day or a week and going home, but this would feel like losing and I'm not ready to give in yet. Not after I was the one who turned the whole company around and saved everyone. If I quit now, what was all that work even for?

So, I clean, following their tedious and ill-conceived directions. I use hot water for everything, even though this sets stains instead of lifting them. I don't bother to disinfect the fridge or microwave in their breakroom, and instead just wipe the mess out, as instructed. Let the bacteria fester. Let them grow whatever malicious disease they want. Then I spray polish directly on all the furniture instead of the cloth, and, for good measure, I let everything soak. It won't take very many times doing this to stain all the furniture unevenly. A real "bringing Dorian Gray out of the attic" moment. Let them see how ugly they are. I spray disinfectant on their computer screens. I scrub painted surfaces. I even bleach the mold spot in the bathroom, which doesn't get rid of it, but makes it less visible—and therefore more insidious. This is what they want.

On my break, I stand in the lobby with M. I tell them how I've been treated, how ungrateful everyone is, how nothing I did meant anything to them. I can feel the volume of my voice rising, my tone reaching a squeaky pitch I don't enjoy, but I can't reel it in. As a kindness, M. doesn't visibly react or look taken aback. They don't suggest I calm down. I can hear L. in my head, telling me I sound crazy, discounting everything I'm saying. She'd tell me that the way I see things doesn't make sense, my recollection of conversations isn't true, and she'd ask why I'm thinking about any of this anyway? But M. listens, and when I finish, they nod their head and don't say anything for a while. I try to think of what else to say or what question to ask, but M. takes my hand, the same hand that probably smells like the new poorly mixed cleaning solution, and they look at me.

"Are you okay?" they ask. "I mean, really?"

They look so gentle about it that I can't muster any kind of comeback. I'm just so tired. I try to remember if I ate my lunch tonight or last night, but I can't. I can only remember the bathroom mirrors, smearing under the new solution I've been instructed to clean them with. I can only remember squinting at myself and wondering if I, too, had grown blurry.

"I don't know," I finally say.

"You should write everything down," they say.

"And tell HR?" I ask.

"Well, maybe," they say. "But you should tell everybody.

What they were all doing, how you saved them, the whole thing."

I sit with the idea after M. leaves. If I don't tell everyone, how will they know? They'll go on thinking I'm nothing. They'll think this is how the world works, and that they weren't ever standing on someone's back, being carried. Maybe they'll even think their own lives are hard. They'll complain about the hours they work or the people they deal with. Like any of that even matters.

But I could tell them everything about each other. The gross truth of them all. If I could save them, save the company, I can ruin them too. Knock the intern off her flimsy pedestal. Show them how they all cut corners and what they truly think of one another. Then they'd know who they really are—but they'd know who I am too. Someone you don't fuck with.

I BARELY SLEEP for the next few weeks. I borrow a laptop from the office, and when I get home from work, I stay up writing. Then I wake up early and write before I go in. I take notes while I'm cleaning. I do my job exactly as instructed. No one complains about how poorly everything has been done. They must be so pleased that I've adhered to their instructions. It's nice to have someone under your thumb. It makes you think you're important and distracts you from the thumb that's holding *you* down. You don't even notice your own sore muscles, your instability or migraines, because you're busy looking down at someone else.

When I finally finish writing it all down, I stay up all day reading it aloud. It's messy, but true. On my way to work, I send my first text to M. "Want to grab a drink this weekend?"

I get to work early enough that L. isn't in yet, so I go floor to floor, gathering all the best snacks from breakrooms and the secret stashes in people's desks. Expensive chocolate, the prawn crackers L. likes, curried nuts, and some fruit leather I've never tried before because you can only get it at a high-end store that's open in the daytime. It's so much that I keep dropping things and having to stoop over and resituate it all in my arms. I leave it on our breakroom table, circling around L.'s new plant, an offering.

Then I go upstairs and sit at the CEO's desk. Her password is still "admin." I sit for a long time with my document pulled up in front of me. Pages and pages of everything that happened, my nights, their days. The betta fish is looking a little haggard. The intern was right about that. I get up, spray down the desk, and wipe it off. Then I lay my head on the cool, clean wood. I should title the document, but I'm not sure what's most accurate. Office Savior? Corporate Hero? Cleaning Woman? Cleaning Lady?

No—just "Cleaner." The way I left their desks and lives, the office and the company. Cleaner than when I started.

I'll use the intern's welcome packet to figure out the copier. I know the instructions are very clear. It's a nice packet, well organized and detailed. Maybe it'll take longer than I imagined, and I'll have to refill the paper trays to make so many copies, but that's okay. I have the time. Then I can leave a fresh, hot copy on everyone's desk. And, as a final hurrah, I can put one in an envelope with stamps from the intern's desk so I can send it to the old CEO's house too. Let him know how I got him. Let him know who I am.

The last time I left a job, it was hard. I went home and told J. what happened, and he seemed to take the whole thing as confirmation that I wasn't worth his time. I wasn't a *quality* woman. M. would never say anything like that, but if they did, I don't think I'd tolerate it now. I don't think I'd let it reshape me and how I lived my life.

Maybe I'll take the fish when I leave. I can put it in a bigger tank, give it a bigger life. Read up on betta fish and what they need to be well. I'll leave my key card in the lobby and I won't look back. The night air will feel different. I hope I'll feel different. Because it's a lot—everything I've done. It's more than anyone else here could do.

★ ★ ★ ★ ★

ACKNOWLEDGMENTS

HUGE THANKS TO Grace Towery and Hanover Square. So much gratitude to Ella Gordon and Areen Ali at Wildfire. My deepest thanks to my incredible agent and friend Kate Johnson and everyone at Wolf Literary. Thank you to Laura Southern and Rach Crawford. Thank you to the department of English at California State University Fullerton. Thank you to the PhD Creative Writing program at the University of Southern California for their years of funding and support. Special thanks to Aimee Bender, Janalynn Bliss, and Dana Johnson. Thank you to the MFA Program at the University of Alabama for creating space for me. Thank you to Michael Martone and Kellie Wells. Thank you to Eli Dunn and the All-But-Collective. Thank you to Susan Bowie Doss and Leia Penina Wilson. And of course, thank you to friends for supporting me and this book in various ways: Gladys Angle,

Diana Arterian, Matt Bell, Elizabeth Cardman, Tasha Coryell, Stephen van Dyck, Dara Ewing, Emily Geminder, Katy Gunn, Simon Jacobs, and Brian Oliu. And finally, thank you to Caliban and Lune for allowing me to exist.